Praise for Dr. Cory Cohen Mysteries

"A genuine page-turner in the best sense. Her years as a psychologist have earned Ceren a look at the darkness of the psyche and human behavior. Psychologist-sleuth—Cory Cohen—is both compassionate and tough. A strong, heartfelt work from a writer we will be hearing a lot."

T.Jefferson Parker,
Edgar-winning author

"A haunting tale of ambition and betrayal that tests the strength and ethical convictions of an engaging heroine. At every treacherous turn a cunning and dangerous assailant tries to make Cory choose between the welfare of her patients and her own life. A chilling read."

Kris Neri,
Agatha-nominated author

"Riveting, tightly woven mystery screeches to a satisfying conclusion bringing together all the pieces of this intiguiging puzzle. A terrific whodunit spun around the dynamics of psychotherapy. This would make a terrific film."

Maryanne Raphael, Editor,
Writers World

"Of interest not only to psychologists and patients, but to mystery fans. It has all the elements of suspense and drama : a clever plot and interesting well drawn characters."

Andrew Duggan, M.D.

"Author Sandra Ceren draws upon her thirty years of clinical work with crime victims to bring a degree of realism and accuracy that is rarely matched and never surpassed."

Midwest Book Review

THE DR. CORY COHEN MYSTERIES

- *Prescription For Terror*
- *Stolen Secrets*
- *Imposter for Hire* (coming soon!)

Learn more about Dr. Sandra L. Ceren, read blog postings, and the latest news at www.DrSandraLevyCeren.com

Stolen Secrets

A Dr. Cory Cohen Mystery

Sandra Levy Ceren

Modern History Press

Library of Congress Cataloging-in-Publication Data

Ceren, Sandra Levy.
  Stolen secrets : a Dr. Cory Cohen mystery / by Sandra Levy Ceren.
      p. cm.
  ISBN-13: 978-1-61599-068-9 (pbk. : alk. paper)
  ISBN-10: 1-61599-068-2 (pbk. : alk. paper)
  ISBN-13: 978-1-61599-069-6 (hardcover : alk. paper)
  ISBN-10: 1-61599-069-0 (hardcover : alk. paper)
  1. Women psychotherapists--Fiction. 2. San Diego (Calif.)--Fiction.
I. Title.
  PS3603.E697S76 2011
  813'.6--dc22
                              2011005842

Distributed by Ingram Book Group (USA/CAN), Bertram's Books
(UK), Hachette Livre (FR)

Modern History Press, an imprint of
Loving Healing Press
5145 Pontiac Trail
Ann Arbor, MI 48105

Psychologists open their doors to troubled patients,
each a puzzle to solve, and a life to live better.

⫻ 1 ⫻

A loud jangle brought Morgan out of the haze the sleeping pill had provided. She fumbled for the phone "District Attorney Heller," she muttered, for a moment too groggy to realize she wasn't at her desk.

"Lola, precious Lola, it's so good to be near you." The voice was unfamiliar—deep and soothing—and called her by the name she used for herself in her fantasies. She must be dreaming. Too tired to hang up, she dropped the phone on her pillow and dozed off.

"Lola, sweet Lola, precious Lola." The voice repeated, lulling, hypnotic. "Talk to me, Lola."

"Hmm," Morgan sighed, drowsy and floating.

"Lola, Lola, Lola. I'll pay double your fee to make you sizzle. To stroke your soft skin."

She could almost feel his caress. She heard him breathing hard and she began to moan.

"Yes, Lola. Good. Very good, Lola."

She stayed in the dream, allowing her arousal.

"Lola, Lola, Lola," he whispered. "The time has come for you to know." His voice rose. Your dirty secret is out."

"What?" she said, suddenly awake.

"Gotcha!" he shouted. Then he laughed. The line was dead.

Morgan opened her eyes and rolled over on the phone beside her. It slid off her pillow and clattered to the floor. She hadn't been dreaming. The call was real. She switched on the light and slammed the phone down on her bedside table. The digital clock blinked 2:10 AM.

Who the devil was the caller? How did he know about her sexual fantasy? Was he after more than phone sex?

Her legs shaky, she slid out of bed to check the security system. It was armed.

She staggered to the window and peeked through the shutters at a dark sky and a deserted street lit by a lamppost. She checked the alarm system again. Then she stumbled to the shower. The warm water poured over her for a long time, long enough for the water to turn cold; but she couldn't wash away the shame.

Morgan covered herself with a robe, closing it high under her chin, yanking the belt tight. She pulled off the bed linens and tossed them into the washing machine. Trying to go back to sleep in her bed would be futile. *Not now.*

Groping her way into the dark living room, she reached the couch. Wrapping herself in the blanket she kept on the armrest, she closed her eyes, but couldn't sleep.

At seven in the morning, she grabbed the phone. Her unsteady finger punched in a number.

"Cory Cohen, here." A familiar woman's voice. Comforting.

"It's Morgan. I need to see you as soon as possible." There was a tremor in her voice.

"You sound frightened. What's wrong?"

"I'll explain when I get there."

They made an appointment for eight that morning.

When Morgan hung up, she was shivering. Maybe it was a mistake to call her shrink—the only one who knew about Lola and the sexual fantasy. Could Cory have betrayed her? But Cory had been her sister Liz's psychologist and Liz had recommended her. Cory already knew about their screwed up family history.

But maybe Liz was a naive academic, untouched by corrupt doctors, CEOs, lawyers, politicians, whereas she herself had seen it all. Wasn't that why she had left that fancy-shmantzy job in a prestigious law firm to work as an Assistant District Attorney? She had told herself she didn't need a six-figure salary to be happy. Measuring her worth by her billable hours wasn't what she wanted. She wanted to right some wrongs. And there was plenty wrong in the D.A.'s office—misplaced files, lax supervision, a few people working their butts off while others goofed off. Now, when she was about to fulfill her ambition, her armor had come undone. She shuddered, afraid of what could be next.

⸗2⸗

Morgan's call surprised Cory. Although Morgan suffered from anxiety, this was her first request for an emergency session. Was she upset about something that could compromise her candidacy for San Diego District Attorney? Recent voter polls showed her in the lead over the other candidates: prosecutor Jim Solas and Judge Ellis Crandall.

Was it a problem with the shelter?

Only a few social workers knew Morgan was the benefactor of the hide-away refuge for domestic violence victims, and that she gave free legal assistance to the residents by phone. Grandma used to say anonymous acts of charity were the best kind.

Cory jumped out of bed, showered and dressed, grabbed a muffin, and drove to the office.

Autumn rain, rare in southern California, began a slow and steady descent. Dark clouds masked the sky. The morning was fit for singing the blues to the monotonous beat of her windshield wipers.

Cory pulled into the garage. Morgan's dark blue Saab was the only other car parked there.

Morgan waited in the lobby, holding a newspaper in front of her face. When Cory called her name, Morgan stood up. Her damp hair hung loose. Her stark, pale face and the dark circles under her eyes broadcast terror. Cory put her arm around her for a moment before they walked together toward the office suite, their long strides matching. Cory watched their reflections in the emerald glass-walled foyer. Both women were tall and slender with long straight hair, but Cory had the Asian epicanthic fold and thick black hair, while Morgan had a narrow nose and auburn hair. Although Cory was over ten years older than her patient, the two of them could be mistaken for contemporaries—from a distance.

Inside, the office was cold and forbidding without Cory's part-time receptionist. Ann's smiling face, her fresh flowers, and the soft music from the reception room speakers would warm up the place at nine.

In the consulting room, Morgan settled on the couch, her legs trembling beneath a long skirt.

"I'm mortified. I don't know where to turn; who to trust." She cupped her hands over her face.

"Tell me."

Morgan looked up. "I had a frightening phone call."

"Threatening?" Morgan had once said that in the courthouse corridors, she was dubbed "Heller from Hell."

"No. That's why I didn't call anyone but you. This was too personal. It was lewd." Morgan bowed her head. "I know you think because I prosecute such offenses, I'd be used to them. But this was different. You see, he knows my disgusting fantasy." Tears rolled down her cheeks.

Cory handed her a box of tissues. "What do you mean?"

Morgan blotted her face. In a voice barely audible, she began to tell her what had happened. To better hear her, Cory had to lean forward.

"He even offered to pay me for sex, just like the fantasy I've told you about. The way I come across—how could anyone guess that about me?"

"Listen, Morgan. It's possible a mischief-maker hit a number at random, hoping to have some fun. You aren't the only one who fantasizes being a prostitute. Maybe he got lucky when he reached you."

"You don't understand. He called me Lola."

"Lola? Your fantasy name?"

Morgan nodded.

"No wonder you're so upset. How could he know?"

Morgan's face reddened. "I don't want to believe it, but maybe ... from here." She turned her head to scan the room.

Cory's stomach dropped a few notches. "I don't understand. My office is soundproof. If someone broke in, my alarm system would alert the police, and me too."

Morgan rubbed her temples. "Tell me how you handle records."

"They're locked in a cabinet except when I make notes during a session. I haven't filed any insurance claims for you, so our work is completely confidential.

"Have you discussed my problem with a colleague?" Morgan's eyes narrowed.

Cory took a deep breath. "No. Anyway, it isn't ethical to identify patients without their permission."

"You could have slipped up."

"No. I'd remember. I feel bad that your confidence in me is undermined."

"No. No. It isn't. I'm sorry I had to ask. It's just that I can't fathom how this happened.

"I understand. It's troubling.

Cory's sense of security began to unravel. For all her professional life, she'd been careful to shield her patients' secrets. If the leak came from her office, other patients could be at risk too. "Let's try to figure it out. Was there anything about his voice you recognized? A nuance? An accent?"

She squeezed her eyes shut. "No."

"Does anyone know you come here for therapy?"

"Only my sister. And your receptionist."

"Both trustworthy?"

"Cory, I didn't mean..."

"You were just being specific. You're a lawyer." Cory smiled.

"I'm afraid if people find out about this, I'll be disgraced."

"I understand your concern, but we don't know the caller's intentions. Maybe all he wanted was phone sex."

"The fact is I have prostitution fantasies. How will that play with voters?"

"Why would he be believed? And even if he were, fantasies confined to bedtime that haven't interfered with your work shouldn't be a big deal."

"*Should* is the operative word, Cory. I'm exposed, and I'm frightened. Lord, I'm fed up with myself. Why didn't I hang up right away?"

"He caught you off guard."

"Why can't I let go of the fantasy?"

"Listen to me, Morgan. We know you were programmed to view sex as a sin. When you imagine yourself as Lola, you're free to give in to normal urges and enjoy sex as you think she would. These fantasies liberate you, but you allow them to make you feel guilty and ashamed."

"Mother sure did a number on Liz and me. Those peepholes in every door. Even the bathroom. What was she afraid of? That we'd masturbate? Once, when I was little, I had an itch and she caught me scratching my crotch. She shouted at me and said I was dirty. She slapped my face right in front of my friend. I was humiliated." Morgan pounded the arm of the chair. "And now this. I should have slammed the phone down when he started with me; but no, I had to listen. I thought I was dreaming. I was spellbound. *She gazed into space as though in a trance*. I'm furious with myself for last night."

"You could be angry at the caller, but you blame yourself."

"Because I feel so wicked."

"Feeling and being are not the same. In reality, you are a good person. You go out of your way to help others. People are judged by their good deeds, not by their thoughts. And fantasies don't make you wicked."

"Yes, but... "

Cory held up her palm. "Everyone is entitled to them, even the next District Attorney." She reached over and patted Morgan's hand. "If everyone's fantasy was prosecutable, your job would be impossible."

"But I feel so awful afterwards."

"Because of the conflict between your desire and the belief that it's wrong. Fantasies aren't felonies. They're not even misdemeanors."

The agitated woman gave a little smile. "I have to stop thinking about it."

"Remember how you've made your obsessive thoughts stop? Like changing the TV channel?"

"Yes, I know. I can't prevent what enters my head, but I can end it before it goes too far."

"Good. That proves you do have control."

"Right. I'll start by changing my phone number. It's unlisted, but now it'll be under my uncle's name."

The rain trickled down the window near Morgan's chair. As she traced a raindrop's descent with her finger, her troubled look faded. She dug a barrette from her purse and clasped back the long wisps of her hair that had fallen over her cheeks. She sat erect, ankles crossed, and folded her hands on her lap—a pose that would have pleased her mother. "Maybe I am making too big a deal of the call. Who'd believe the straight-laced *me* is a closet call-girl?"

Her wristwatch beeped. "I've got to muster up some energy for an arraignment at ten. I suppose you know that hotshot defense attorney Dale Rothenberg was arrested on Sunday. Big, burly, Rothenberg nearly killed his petite pregnant wife. Poor woman hemorrhaged and lost the baby."

Cory shook her head. "I heard the news. Sickening!"

"Well, if I have my way, he'll stay locked up. His ten-year-old son witnessed everything. He's the one who called 911. Poor kid is at the shelter now. I hope his mother will be out of the hospital soon."

"That's terrible. Such a big trauma for a little kid! He'll need counseling."

"I arranged for it," Morgan brushed her hands.

"Proves what I said about you, Morgan. You do whatever it takes to help others. Remember that battered woman too ashamed to go to the ER? She'll probably never forget you drove her there. You've got a big heart; and then setting up the shelter with your own money."

"It was worth every dollar. I've no time or interest to waste money on frivolity.

Cory made a note to follow up later on what Morgan had just said about frivolity.

"You are quite a person." Cory smiled. "A genuine *mensch*."

"Thanks. Back to Rothenberg. He's one guy for whom I haven't a drop of compassion. When I saw the photos of the battered wife, I was boiling mad. Jim wanted to take over for me, but I refused his offer. He said I was too emotionally involved and had to distance myself. That's a man for you."

"I think it's good to be passionate about your causes."

"I'm sure Jim dislikes Dale as much as I do, but he doesn't get worked up over it. We understand that a defense attorney is supposed to make sure the client is treated fairly; but when his clients are monsters and are acquitted because of his lack of scruples, there's public outcry. I'm determined to bring Rottenberg down." She slapped the seat of her chair.

"His name is Rothenberg, isn't it? You called him Rottenberg. Perfect slip of the tongue." Cory leaned back in her chair and laughed.

Morgan nodded. "That's true. Lord, the scum he's defended—some of them can't possibly afford his fees—they must compensate him in other ways. I suspect he uses them to threaten potential witnesses before they can testify against his clients; but we haven't been able to prove it. That slime!" She stood, smoothed the folds of her skirt. "Thanks for the early session. My regular time next week will be fine." She hurried out of the door.

Cory rested her chin in her hand. The timing of the troublesome call came when Morgan was most vulnerable—in the middle of the night; in the midst of her campaign.

7

When Morgan had decided to run for D.A., she had described her opponents to Cory as forthright and beyond reproach. Jim Solas, another prosecutor, hadn't impressed Morgan as ambitious, but he had gone along with his family's plan for his political future. Judge Ellis Crandall, a religious zealot, was not respected as a jurist. Few people took his candidacy seriously. Morgan was confident she'd win the election.

Morgan never mentioned being afraid of someone she had prosecuted; but was she naive? Could some felon have found a way to get to her?

Rain had cleared away smog from the horizon. Cory had an hour before her next session. She changed into red sweats, pocketed her cell phone, and set off for the beach.

The tide was high. She changed course and ran along the quiet coastal road toward her favorite place to meditate. A cyclist, a surfer, and an occasional camper shared the road with her.

"He called me Lola," echoed in her ears.

⫸3⫷

Cory neared the grounds of the Self-Realization Fellowship. Sparks of sunshine bounced off the gold and blue dome. Slowing her pace, she entered through the wrought-iron gates. Perhaps the serene setting would refresh her and give her the clarity to figure out how her patient's privacy had been penetrated.

She headed toward the well-tended flower gardens and settled herself on a bench under a rubber tree. Raindrops from the morning rain clung to the petals of the pink begonias surrounding a pond. Deep in thought, she watched the Halloween-colored koi swim around the rocks.

Finding no answers there, she climbed to the terrace overlooking the ocean. As the waves rolled along the shore, she considered the duplicate appointment book, the one Ann so carefully guarded. She hadn't told Morgan about it. The book listed patients' names and their phone numbers next to their appointment times. Ann stored it in her locked desk drawer at the office. The keys to the drawer had never been lost, and Cory hadn't seen the book out of Ann's reach, but she couldn't be certain that was always the case.

Had Morgan said anything that could be a clue? What about the time when Morgan had talked about her conflict between religious doctrine and her sexual fantasies? She'd suggested that Morgan confer with a priest. Had she done it? If Morgan had confessed her fantasies to a priest, could someone have overheard? Unlikely, but not impossible.

As far as she knew, she and maybe Liz were the only ones privy to Morgan's fantasy. Liz, had been her patient in New York years ago. The root of their problems was the same, the form different. Fragments of Liz's sessions duplicated Morgan's: "No matter how hard we tried, we couldn't please mother. She searched our stuff for pornography."

Liz and Morgan: sisters, best friends. Frequent phone calls to each other bridged the geographical gulf. They shared secrets not shared with others, perhaps not even with Cory.

She recalled Morgan's saying, "Mother's rages... if not for Dad, I think she'd have killed us. Lucky for us, he worked at home." Their father was a psychiatrist who edited a well-known journal. A journal.

That could be it. Morgan had begun writing into her private journal when she started therapy. If she had misplaced it, someone could have read about her sexual fantasies.

Cory checked her watch, pulled out her cell phone, and keyed in the code for Morgan's office.

"Ms. Heller hasn't come in today," said Morgan's secretary.

"Maybe she went directly to court," Cory suggested.

"No. Mr. Solas had to take over for her."

Cory's stomach knotted. "Has she called?"

"No."

"Please ask her to reach me as soon as possible."

It should have taken Morgan about fifteen minutes to drive downtown. If she were delayed, she would have called her office from her car—unless she had a bad accident. Was she more distraught than Cory had figured? Was she hiding?

Cory glanced at her Timex. *Time to get back to work.* As she walked toward her office, she thought of a couple of possible scenarios for Morgan's no-show in court: The obscene caller could have tailed Morgan and abducted her. But people who made such calls seldom followed through.

Morgan had seemed dazed this morning. Cory had attributed it to emotional fatigue and lack of sleep. But Morgan said she felt powerless—spellbound by the caller's voice. In that case, could a post-hypnotic suggestion lead her to a rendezvous?

Cory stopped at a bus-stop shelter and rang Morgan's house and cell phone. No response. She phoned hospital emergency rooms. No victims fit Morgan's description. She continued to walk and think. Dale Rothenberg, wife-batterer, could have had Morgan captured. It wouldn't have guaranteed his freedom from prosecution, but it may have delayed it and perhaps given him time to escape.

She rounded a corner and looked at the street sign. What the heck was she doing on Calle Abogado? It was hard to forget that address. Translated from Spanish to English, it meant "Lawyer Street." And it was Morgan's street. One of the rare times Morgan had laughed was when she had mentioned that she lived at Numero Uno on Calle Abogado or Number One Lawyer Street.

"Don't go to her house, Cory. It's unprofessional," Grandma, the voice of her conscience, cautioned. Cory knew her passion for excite-

ment and intrigue sometimes overshadowed her judgment, but she continued walking along Morgan's street.

Flanked by two olive trees, Numero Uno, a single-story white stucco cottage had a gray tile roof and a tiny lawn in front. A light ocean breeze blew through Cory's hair as she pressed the doorbell. She waited a few minutes. Nothing. She knocked on the door. Then again, louder. Finally, she pounded; but to no avail. Aware of Morgan's penchant for privacy, Cory noticed the open shutters. Shielding her eyes from the glaring sun, she looked through the slats at the neatly arranged furniture. Nothing appeared amiss.

Across the street, a car door slammed, making Cory jump. She hurried to the rear of the building. Crushed beneath her feet, eucalyptus leaves gave out a pungent scent. Peering into the windows of the tidy kitchen and family room overlooking the garden, she saw movement—shadows. She froze, then spun around. What she had seen was a reflection of foliage swaying in the breeze—the tall pines that eclipsed an ocean view. The glint of the sun made it hard to see. She couldn't check the rest of the house. As she stepped back, her heel grazed one of the potted red geraniums lining the patio and she almost lost her balance.

Cory wanted to see if the Saab was parked inside the garage, but behind the small grimy window, there was only darkness. She tried the side door—locked.

When she returned to the front to try the door again, she noticed a white card stuck into the jamb. She snatched the card and read the scrawl: *Please call immediately.* Flipping the card over, she saw the blue logo and read the text:

San Diego Police Department.
Sergeant Stanley Kipinski, Investigator.

She shoved the card back.

"Hey, what are you doing?" A man called to her.

She whirled around, and faced a tall, muscular man dressed in shorts and a tank shirt. He gripped the leash of a brown Labrador Retriever.

"Have you seen the woman who lives here, today?"

"No. Who are you?"

"An associate." She should have listened to Grandma's warning.

11

The dog tugged at his leash. After a minute, the man walked on. At the corner, he turned and scowled at her as his pet sniffed around a tree. She'd better get out of there—*pronto*! No doubt the D.A. had notified the police to check on Morgan when she missed her conference. *Stop playing Sherlock Holmes*, she scolded herself. *You're her therapist, not a detective.* But detection is part of the process—to plumb the unconscious for concealed messages and motivations, put things together from observations and clinical impressions. Now, she came up empty.

She shouldn't let other people's problems become her own. It was a bad trait for a psychologist even if it gave her the illusion of control over their emotional pain.

She walked back to the office with a gnawing feeling in her gut that Morgan had truly vanished.

❖4❖

Cory stepped into the reception room and found Ann frowning. Cory held her breath. "Oh, my! A problem?"

Ann shook her head, blonde curls springing to action. "Nothing out of the ordinary of late."

Little did she know..., Cory thought, exhaling slowly.

"It's just that as managed care grows, the number of your appointments shrinks. It makes me consider changing my goal." Ann reached into the cabinet and removed a bottle of plant food.

"But you'll make a really fine therapist, and you're so close to graduation, it would be a shame to quit now." Cory sympathized with Ann's kvetching, but she didn't want to discourage her from pursuing her dream. Ann's work allowed her time to study for a doctorate and freed Cory from some clerical chores.

"Quality doesn't count with managed care."

Cory sighed. "By the time you're a psychologist, managed care may be out of business and you can join my practice."

"Hah! From your mouth to Her ears," Ann said, staring at the ceiling. She poured some plant food into the watering can. "I can always work as a gardener. Anyway, your four o'clock had to leave town and will call to reschedule, and Morgan's three o'clock slot is empty. But there is good news. At least for today. You have two o'clock with that hunk, Alan Olsen."

"That's reassuring." Cory hesitated, wanting to be diplomatic. "Talking about sessions, have you ever misplaced the appointment book?"

Ann scowled. "No. I'd have told you. It's kept locked in the drawer until you ask me to add or change someone's time. And then I lock it up again."

"That's what I thought."

"Is something wrong?" Ann asked.

"Not with the appointment book. You're a great warden." She checked her watch. "I'd better get ready." She wanted to share more with Ann, but professional ethics stood in her way.

For the second time that morning, Cory hopped into the shower, grateful for her office amenities. Water pouring down her back, she imagined the possible scenarios that could have played out for Morgan after her session. Cory started to shiver and she turned the water faucet toward hot. By the time she'd dried off and dressed, she had talked herself away from panic-ville and was ready for her other patients.

While waiting for Alan, she leafed through his chart.

His freelance work as a building contractor allowed him time to philander, but his wife's tolerance of his infidelity had eroded and she had booted him out. After their recent three-month estrangement, she had agreed to reconcile, contingent upon his promise to work on his problems with a psychologist.

Cory glanced at the wall clock. Alan was tardy again, as he had been the last few sessions. He was probably ambivalent about therapy.

At two-twelve, Ann buzzed and, with a lilt in her voice, announced Alan undoubtedly one of the most attractive men ever to stride across this threshold. Tall, trim, having striking green eyes, and a cleft chin, his photo could easily be featured on the cover of a romance novel. Easy to understand women swooning over him, except now that his breath reeked of alcohol. "Here I am, late again. Going to bawl me out?" he asked, sprawling on the couch.

"Do you think I should?"

"Well, I dunno. Should you?" True to his style, he answered questions with *questions*.

"So, why are you late, Alan?"

"Could be that I think this is pointless." He examined his fingernails.

"That's honest."

"I know you try to help, Doc, but I'm stuck."

"Alan, you get a payoff from your actions. Why would you want to change?"

He paused, staring at the floor. "Yeah. Sexual adventures are what I get, but I pay a price. I hurt my wife with all my women. I don't keep promises. Maybe I'm a misogynist."

Was a glimmer of insight seeping in? "Sounds like you're figuring it out. Let's find out why you hate women; but first tell me where you were before our session."

"How did you guess?" He rubbed his chin.

"It is what I sense," Cory replied.

"Hah! Sense. Scent. My breath. You picked it up, didn't you, Doc?" Alan spoke rapidly without slurring his words.

Cory figured he wasn't drunk and they could continue the session. "That's correct." She leaned back in her chair and folder her fingers into a steeple.

"Well, here I go with a shocker for you, Doc." He inhaled deeply as if smoking a cigarette, then exhaled slowly. "Caught a porno flick. Had a couple of beers. I never told you about that stuff, did I?"

"You said you rarely drank—never to excess. Why now? Does it go hand in hand with the porno flick?"

Alan chuckled. "Doctor Cohen, you're a funny lady."

The porno stuff reminded Cory that Morgan had mentioned sex today, too. Wasn't it curious that in the course of her twenty-five years of practice, there were many occasions when several patients on the same day presented similar dreams or material? Science offered no explanation for this phenomenon other than coincidence. The day that Morgan told her of the obscene phone caller, Alan wanted to speak only of sex. Monday is *wash day*. Tuesday must be *sex day*.

"I'm surprised, Alan, that the cast of women you seduce isn't enough to gratify you. You need Rosie Palm, too?"

"I guess I'm over-sexed. I like to experiment. I enjoy novelty. Nothing too kinky, though. Are you ready to hear it?"

"I'd rather find out why you want to tell me."

"Well, isn't my sex life important in therapy?"

"It could be, but I'd first like to get some answers."

"I don't get it, Doc."

"Do you want to shock or arouse me—or yourself, again?"

"I just want you to know I'm not involved in any S and M stuff. No bondage. I'm a nice guy who gets off on pleasing women. Lots of them. I like *ménage à trois*." He stared into her eyes.

She stared back, reminded of a game youngsters play—whoever blinked first was the loser. After a few moments, Alan turned away, flipping his dark hair away from his eyes. Although she never allowed herself fantasies about patients, she questioned her motives for not allowing Alan to discuss his sexual behavior. Was she avoiding titillation?

Cory was reviewing charts when Ann knocked on the door and poked her head inside. "Ready to go?"

"In a minute." As she did every night, Cory locked her notes in the file cabinet and crammed her appointment book in her purse.

"Two cancellations today. It's not good, Cory."

"Strange. Seldom do we have only one cancellation in a day. If I get one, invariably another one cancels, too."

"A good research topic," Ann said.

"Yes. At times, patients won't show up when you're on to something they don't want to face."

"I've been giving a lot of thought to this work. I worry about the potential danger of it."

"I don't understand," Cory said.

"You're alone in a room with a patient who can hurt you." Ann armed the alarm system and snapped the door shut.

"I suppose it is possible, but unlikely. Many disturbed people don't become patients, and we can refuse to see violent ones."

"True—if you know their history ahead of time," Ann countered as they reached their cars parked side by side. "Maybe I'm just looking for reasons to quit school. Most of your patients seem normal and well-functioning. Anyway, thanks to you, I'm learning to protect myself. I'm really getting into karate. You're so good at it, it must be in your genes."

Cory winced. Ann's words felt like fingernails scraping a chalkboard. Abandoned at the age of three by her Japanese mother, Cory was raised by her Jewish grandparents. Bi-racial, she suffered feelings of alienation from her community. Despite her own psychotherapy, emotional scars clung to her like barnacles to a boat. She still felt uncomfortable when reminded of her Japanese genes. Her ears grew hot as she unlocked her old BMW and turned to face Ann. "Almost anyone can be good in karate with practice," she said, climbing into her car.

She headed out of the garage, followed by Ann's blue Camry. Pink and orange rays streaked the sky. The sun glared unmercifully in Cory's eyes as she drove west toward the ocean.

Cory had never considered the possibility of a patient hurting her until Ann mentioned it. It was odd for her to take comfort in Ann's razor-sharp mind, but she did. Cory hoped when Ann finished school and no longer worked for her, the barrier would be lifted and their friendship would flourish. Apart from psychology, they had much in common. Both were divorced, mothers, and middle-aged with similar tastes and values.

Cory remembered Morgan saying that she admired her own secretary, Sara, with whom she had dined and shopped a few times, but their work situation prevented them from becoming friends. Now Cory regretted a missed opportunity. Had she explored why Morgan admired Sara, she might have gained a greater understanding of her patient.

~5~

Driving home, Cory tuned the radio.

"… breaking news. The nude body of an unidentified woman was discovered washed ashore on the Coronado beach. A spokesperson from the Medical Examiner's office stated that the condition of the body suggests the victim was recently drowned. She appears to be in her thirties. We're following the story. Details will follow when available."

Could it be Morgan? The report indicated the woman was in her thirties, but there were many women of that age. Just because Morgan seemed to have disappeared didn't mean she was the victim. And wouldn't a candidate in a current election be recognized, especially by police with whom she worked?

Distracted, she missed the turn-off and had to make a U-turn. She clicked on several radio stations, all discussing the upcoming football season. She gave up and shoved in a cassette of Vivaldi's Four Seasons. Neither the music nor the surf view calmed her.

At the corner of Via de La Valle and Camino del Mar, the signal light turned red. She picked up her cell phone to call Morgan's home. Still no answer. Morgan probably hadn't had time to change her number before her disappearance. The car behind her honked. The light was green. She shoved the shift to "Drive."

"Morgan hasn't drowned," she repeated like a mantra all the way home.

Cory shut off the house alarm and prayed for a message from Morgan. When she bounded upstairs and checked the answering machine, the little red light wasn't blinking. She tossed her things on the bed, washed her trembling hands, and changed into a pair of sweats.

Downstairs in the den, she poured a glass of Merlot to still her shakes, then flicked on the local TV news station and began to prepare dinner. While listening for additional information, she created a rhythmic chop of garlic, red pepper, and ginger.

There was no mention of the missing prosecutor and no further details of the unidentified body. "She appears to be in her thirties," rang over and over in Cory's head as she slowly sipped the wine. She shut off the TV.

Cory heated a wok, drizzled a few drops of olive oil, tossed in the vegetables, and stirred. As she mulled over her snooping adventure at Morgan's house, Cory reproached herself for her repeated impulsiveness. "Stop it. Exercise self-control. Trust others to do their jobs!" She muttered. Another little voice in the back of her head said, "No, Cory. Don't trust others until they're proven as trustworthy."

Food particles began to spring from the pan as her frustration transformed her stirring into whipping. She turned off the burners, put down the wooden spatula, and set the table for one. The conspicuous absence at dinnertime of her grown children made her think of them. The house was too quiet without their cheery voices.

She switched on the radio to Jazz 88, sprinkled rice vinegar on a green salad, and sat down to eat alone. She heard Grandma's words: "As you grow older, a companion is comforting."

Grow older! She felt better than she did twenty years ago, but she had to admit that a companion would have stopped her from ruminating about Morgan.

She switched the station to local news and learned that prosecutor Jim Solas had made an impassioned plea to deny bail for Dale Rothenberg, but Judge Crandall Ellis had ignored him. Rothenberg's attorney stated the defendant had a prominent law practice in the community, was not a danger, and had promised to appear at the preliminary hearing. Rothenberg was released on bail.

"That idiot judge has just lost his slim chance to win the election," Cory muttered.

The commentator continued: "A spokesperson for the National Victims Rights Group, outraged by the judge's decision, remarked that Rothenberg could escape trial by leaving the country on his private plane despite the confiscation of his passport."

"*Oy vey!* What a rotten day this has been!" Cory sighed.

Out came her bongos, and on came a Tito Puente disk. She played along to Mambo Diablo. When she finished, her hands tingled. Drumming hadn't helped shake the creepy feeling that Morgan had met her own—*diablo.*

⚌6⚌

Jaime rewound the videotape of his very first anger management workshop from three weeks ago. Although he was well-trained and had earned Professor Blum's confidence and support, he remembered how nervous and worried he had been.

That first time he had arrived at the twelve-by-twelve window-less room donated by the YMCA to San Diego State University's pilot project, it had seemed as if the heat and humidity could peel the paint from the stark white walls. The heavy rank air had reminded the young social work intern of a men's locker room and nauseated him. He remembered the constriction in his vocal chords as he had scanned the circle of men perched on metal folding chairs, their sullen faces peering at him, awaiting his direction.

Now Jaime pressed the PLAY button and settled back to watch the videotape.

"Hi. My name is Jaime and my job is to help you gain control of your anger. The video camera is taping these sessions for educational purposes only. As we go around, each of you, please give your first name and state why you're here."

"Name's Tony. Wife, the bitch, called the cops 'cause I gave her a little shove. The court ordered me here," said a heavyset man with long dark hair.

"What happened before you got angry?" Jaime asked.

"The friggin' boss let me have it because I make one little mistake, so I took off work early and come home to no dinner. I got pissed."

"Sounds like your anger was meant for your boss, but you let it out on your wife. She didn't have dinner ready because she wasn't expecting you."

"Yeah, maybe so, but she didn't have to call the cops."

"Was this the first time this happened?" Jaime asked.

"No, but she never called the cops before."

"Was she hurt?" Jaime asked.

"No more'n usual," he cackled, turning to the man seated next to him. "You go, mister."

"I'm Melvin," said the short, thin young man wearing a Detroit Tigers cap. "My girlfriend likes to cut marks on her arm with a penknife. I can't stand watching her do it, so I ups and takes the knife from her and does it on her myself. She screams so loud, the neighbors call the po-lice. So, I come here 'cause the po-lice makes me. She ain't got no business doin' dat. I was only tryin' to get her to stop it."

Jaime had learned about self-mutilators. He visualized Melvin using the knife on the woman, and he shivered again, just as he had in the session.

The men continued to introduce themselves and offered their tales. Each felt justifiably provoked by a wife or girlfriend. These eight impulsive, angry men needed to take responsibility for their actions and they desperately needed the tools Jaime provided.

Only one man, Horace, said nothing apart from his name. He sat mute, his face vacant of expression. He shrugged in response to the intern's probe, as though challenging him. Jaime had decided to leave him alone.

The intern passed out notebooks and pencils. "This will be your journal. You will make notes in it.

"You mean like a diary?" Melvin asked.

"That's right. You should list all situations that trigger your anger and the ways you handle them. Soon you will learn to see the flares coming and you will find better ways of coping when it does," he said, walking toward the chalkboard. "I'm going to write down anger management tools that have proven to work. But, they will only do so if you continue to apply them. You must be consistent."

"Consistent. Is that like constipated?" said a baldheaded man with a youthful face.

Laughter ensued. Jaime joined in. "Let's say your aim will be to constipate your impulses."

"Huh?" asked the bald man.

Another man chuckled. "I get it! Clever, Jaime!"

"Thanks. Now, let's do it!" Jaime liked the upbeat way he'd said it. He reminded himself of his swim coach.

"Read what I'm writing. First say the words to yourself; then copy them. We will refer to each tool frequently as we practice it. You will start to feel in control. I promise you that is one great feeling!"

A man chuckled. "Not better than sex."

Challenged to transform this group of men, he began to scrawl: *I CAN CALM MYSELF BY BREATHING DEEPLY.* The chalk made an irritating sound. *I CAN CONTROL MY MOUTH AND MY*

BODY. Jaime wrote a few more sentences. "You must commit the list to memory."

"Yeah, commit. I'd like to commit my wife to the cemetery," a fat, heavily tattooed man mumbled.

"I'm glad you told us," Jaime said. "It's better to put your feelings into words than act on them. It's a step in the right direction. We'll go into this later."

After forty-five minutes, he had called a ten-minute stretch break.

Jaime shut off the videotape. In the company of volatile men he was prone to sweat heavily, and remembered rushing off to the restroom to clean up. He had watched the men in the courtyard collect around Horace, the man who had sat mute in the group.

At the session today, when the men had gathered in the courtyard for smokes, he overheard someone talk about a plan to ambush the battered women's shelter. This alarmed him. He had to learn what they were up to.

Someone was screaming. Cory clutched her chest. Her heart hammered and her throat hurt. The screams were hers and had come during a nightmare in which she and Morgan were buried at the bottom in a cold, dark pit. They had tried to scale its slippery walls, but every handhold broke and sent them sliding back to the bottom.

Cory knew the best way to induce sleep was to rewrite the dream with a good ending. She closed her eyes and imagined they were back in the hole. This time they found some protruding roots and easily clawed their way out into daylight and freedom.

Cory went back to sleep, but her project failed. The dream reoccurred two more times with the same bad ending. "Well, it works sometimes," she muttered.

By the time dawn peeked in between the slats of her window shutters, Cory awoke too weary to exercise. She had no appetite and didn't want to bother with her usual oat bran breakfast. Nor did she want to hang around at home.

She arrived at work earlier than usual even after stopping at Starbuck's for coffee and a couple of biscotti.

The phone rang as she unlocked the door. Making a dash for it, she caught it on the third ring.

"Morgan goes. You're next, you lousy bulldyke," a raspy masculine voice said, followed by a click. The coffee sloshed in her stomach. Why hadn't she left the phone to the answering service? She had her hand on the phone to call the police, when Ann came in.

"Oh, Cory! I didn't expect you here so early. Anything wrong?"

"I just got a threatening call."

Ann's eyes widened. "What did he say?" She set her purse on her desk.

"Why do you assume the caller was a guy? Never mind. It was. He called me a lousy bulldyke and said Morgan's gone and I'm next."

"What the heck is going on here, Cory?"

"I wish I knew." Cory shrugged, helplessly.

"A friend of mine had nasty calls. The police took a report and told her to call the phone company. In no time, they fixed her line to trace the call. Once the police are involved, it's easier to prosecute."

"This is very upsetting. I'm glad you're here, Ann. Would you please take care of it for me?" Cory snatched the newspaper from the reception room table, then slipped into her consulting room, and closed the door.

Leaning back in the chair, she closed her eyes. She tried to figure out who would threaten her and how he knew Morgan was her patient. She drew a blank.

Cory turned to the newspaper for news of the drowned woman. A description appeared on the second page:

About 35 years old, 5'10", 150 lbs., auburn hair, and hazel eyes. No clothes or other items were found near the nude body. No identification has been made.

The hair on back of her neck stood at attention. She removed Morgan's chart and checked her height and weight. She was 5'9" and weighed 135 lbs. Perhaps she had gained weight and it wasn't noticeable under her loose clothing. But if the victim was Morgan, someone would have recognized her as the prosecutor from her TV appearances or from her photograph in the newspaper.

Cory paced the office, afraid that she could be wrong and no one had spotted a resemblance due to the condition of the body. She considered a trip to the morgue, but even in death, the patient holds the confidentiality privilege. *Poo!* Ethics was her excuse to avoid the grisly visit. She made up her mind. If no one identified the body by tomorrow, she would step forward. She filed Morgan's folder back in the cabinet.

Advice from someone trustworthy and knowledgeable about crime was what she needed. Who better than George Lewis, a lieutenant in the Sheriff's Department? They had become friends after her role in a serial rape investigation last year. She called his office and was told he was unavailable for the next few days. "Damn!" she cursed.

On an off chance that Morgan had returned, Cory phoned the D.A.'s office and reached Sara.

"Morgan was called out of town suddenly with a family emergency," the secretary replied.

"You spoke to her?" Cory asked.

"Uh-huh," Sara replied.

Cory sighed in relief. "Do you have any more information about it?" she asked, amazed that Morgan hadn't notified her before the sudden departure, especially after their troubling session.

"No, I don't." Sara sounded bored. Cory imagined her checking her manicured fingernails.

"Did she leave a number, or say when she'll return?"

"No. It was pretty indefinite. If this is about a case, Jim Solas is handling her work until she comes back."

"That's okay. If you hear from her, please ask her to phone me immediately."

Cory marched into the reception room as Ann put a textbook aside.

"Morgan has a family emergency. Please cross out her sessions until further notice."

Ann stared at her. "You look like you need a break." She checked her watch. "You have an hour before your next session. Go hang out at the Plaza. If the nasty caller does his number before the phone tracking system is on, I'll bust his eardrum with this." She jingled a brass whistle on her key ring.

"You've grown tough, Ann."

"I have a good role model."

Cory smiled, snatched the latest copy of *The New Yorker*, and slung her purse over her shoulder.

She walked the few blocks from her office to the Plaza and climbed upstairs. Potted yellow mums and birds of paradise lined the terrace overlooking the ocean, but the splash of color didn't perk her up. A strange feeling that she was being watched came over her. She looked around. Apart from a gardener watering the plants, she saw no one.

Heading for the alcove, she passed three attractive, dark-haired women clustered around a small table at an outdoor café. Hand gestures accompanied their musical Italian tongue. Cory figured they were tourists. She stepped inside Café Pacifica and ordered orange juice and a muffin. Seated at a patio table, she listened to Billie Holiday on the cafe's stereo. Two men seemingly engrossed in a game of chess, sat at an adjoining table.

Cory thumbed through the magazine, but couldn't get interested in the cartoons or the stories.

Leaving the cafe, she again felt someone was watching her. She peered around furtively at a few shoppers minding their own business.

She returned to the office for her appointment with Jolene, of Jolene and Carlos Sanchez, a middle-aged couple. She expected Jolene would be a challenge.

Carlos had recently learned Jolene had stashed away ten thousand dollars of her earnings in a separate bank account. Feeling betrayed and concerned that she was planning to leave him, he had initiated therapy for himself. After the first session, Cory had suggested the couple attend sessions together, but Jolene had been evasive during their session. At that point, Cory had asked to see them individually and Jolene seemed relieved. Today, she'd meet with Jolene alone.

Ann buzzed. "The phone deal is done and Ms. Sanchez is here."

Cory hardly recognized the woman she greeted in the reception room reading a fashion magazine. Beautifully coifed, perfumed and manicured, her lipstick and nails matched her rose-colored suit, a startling contrast to the jeans and sweatshirt she had worn at the previous session.

"Jolene, you look stunning."

"Thanks, Doctor Cohen. I'm a big shot at work, so I have to look the part. Sure glad you suggested seeing me alone." She closed the magazine and arranged it neatly on the stack.

Inside the consulting room, Jolene squirmed in her chair. "I need you to help me break some news to Carlos," she said in a southern drawl. "I want out of my marriage."

"Why, Jolene?"

"Oh, my word. How shall I ever begin?" Her eyes glistened. "When Carlos and I first got together, he sure 'nuff wasn't perfect, but his love-making was sen-sa-tion-al. He took his sweet ole' time; showed how much he wanted me. That's why I married him. I'd make him do." She drummed her fingers on her lap. "Carlos is a fine fella. I don't want to hurt him, but why in the world should I be with a man who no longer excites me?"

"When did that stop?"

Jolene cupped her chin in her hand and paused. "It was gradual. Let's see. After he left print journalism to be on TV... you know, he's an investigative reporter. Well, he began to withdraw from me; became self-centered; hired someone to recreate his image; and goes to bed early to get up in time for his workout with a big ole muscle man." She shook her head. "And when he isn't in the field snooping for a story, he's home with his nose buried in papers. Fah too busy for me. Sex is… oh my word… Dull. But now with Alan, it's dynamite!"

"Alan?" Cory felt her eyes widen and hoped Jolene didn't notice.

"The contractor we hired to expand our offices. We hit it off instantly. Every time I see him, my lil' ole heart thumps so hard, I'm afraid someone will hear it. He makes love to me with his sexy eyes. They're penetrating. A wonderful shade of green. He could charm the dew off the leaves." She stroked the chair in a seductive way. *If it were an animate object, it would surely climax*, Cory thought.

"Is it worth losing Carlos for this romance, Jolene?"

"I know I sound like a silly love-sick schoolgirl." Jolene fluttered her thickly mascara-coated eyelashes. The gesture appeared comical and Cory cleared her throat to stifle a laugh. "Be respectful," Grandma's voice scolded.

"Do you want more than an affair, Jolene?"

"I love Alan for now. I don't know about the future." Her drawl sounded soft and sweet—marshmallowy.

"Sometimes we confuse sexual passion with love, Jolene."

The attractive woman raised her eyebrows. "Whatever do you mean?" She paused. "Ah, yes, I do see. I love it with Alan and sure enough don't with Carlos."

"There's more to a relationship than sex. How was your marriage before his new job?"

"Acceptable." She furrowed her brow. "Lordy, Lord. Whatever, am I doing?"

Cory marveled at this prominent businesswoman who made headlines as CEO of a growing company, but was unable to apply her savvy to her personal life.

At the end of the session, Jolene admitted that throughout her life, her need for instant gratification had caused her grief. She opted to hold off leaving her husband, and to work on her problem. The notion that it was possible to rekindle her passion for Carlos, who was eager to improve their marriage, was an added incentive. She admitted it would be difficult to give up Alan.

Jolene's lover fit the description of Alan, Cory's patient. She would make sure their appointments wouldn't occur back to back.

A refrain from a calypso ballad played in her head, "Back to back and belly to belly. I don't give a damn, I'm done dead already." The grim image made her shiver.

⸗8⸗

Barney Blum hurried through the door of his office and hastily gathered papers from his desk, jamming them into his briefcase. Young Jaime was the best intern he'd trained in years. He showed great intelligence and Blum had been confident he'd be able to handle difficult situations. Now however, there was a problem. And he himself had gotten Jaime into it.

To meet the requirements for the anger management project, they had needed an additional member. Blum took responsibility for his error in adding Horace Johnson to the group.

The felon's record showed a history of arrests for his involvement in planned robberies, but only a single conviction for assault. On several occasions, for reasons unknown to Blum, the charges were either vacated or reduced to misdemeanors. Each time Horace remained a free man on the condition that he would attend a therapy program. Three attempts at both group and individual therapy had failed to benefit Horace, according to all indications.

Unlike the other members, self-control was not Horace Johnson's primary problem. And unlike them, he was devious. His assaults were not impulsive, explosive outbursts, but well planned. Blum had no expectation that the group would help Horace to change, but he didn't expect to hear the news Jaime had brought him in the hallway.

Now Morgan Heller and her shelter were in imminent danger. He had to act. As soon as Jaime left, Barney punched in Morgan's cell phone number. It rang a few times until a recorded voice answered, "The voice mail box is full."

Blum phoned Morgan's office and reached Sara, the flake. He couldn't understand why Morgan kept that seductive bitch around.

"Well, hello, Professor Blum," she murmured. "So nice to hear your manly voice. I'm sorry but Ms. Heller is unavailable."

"When do you expect her?"

"I really don't know, seems she's taken off for a while."

An alarm bell rang in his head. "Just like that? No other information?" An assistant district attorney running for political office doesn't just take off for a while at such a critical time. Something was wrong. Very wrong.

"I'd like to speak to a detective from your office, please. This is urgent."

"Sorry, no one is here. Just this female presence."

"Please have someone call me back as soon as possible." He left his phone number.

"I'll convey the message, Professor." She sounded sarcastic, but Blum was never sure about Sara's responses, certain that she was disingenuous.

He couldn't sit still and wait for a detective to call him back, nor could he reveal Morgan's connection to the shelter to anyone. He even feared sharing the information with one of his law enforcement contacts. Presented with a vexing problem, Blum examined his watch. With little time to spare before his next class, he hurried out of his office in search of Jaime. He needed him to take over the class.

=9=

Since two days ago, when Jolene had admitted her infidelity, Cory dwelled on the probability that her patient Alan could be the other man. Jolene's description of her lover's appearance and his occupation left little doubt.

But today, Friday, Cory grappled with the problem frequently known to marital therapists: Carlos suspected his wife of infidelity. Cory knew it was true, but telling him was against the rules. Jolene would most likely reveal it to him soon enough.

Cory became busy with her usual roster of patients and their usual beefs. Fresh attempts to help them change challenged her and for a while kept at bay her anxiety over how Morgan's secret had become a secret no more. Cory had exonerated herself from any professional misconduct.

Between sessions, Ann buzzed. "Your friend Marci in New York is on the line."

Marci's birthday celebration was coming up and Cory had chosen a mobile phone and phone service for her gift. She could hardly wait to see her friend's happy face when she opened the package. Smiling, she picked up the call, eager to hear her old friend's voice.

"Hey, I'm calling to make sure you're coming to my big bash. I've done up the extra bedroom."

"Of course. I made my reservation last month and I'll be there in time to help. I hope you've made a list of chores for me.

"That isn't necessary, Cory. It's all under control."

"Well, there are usually some last-minute things. I'll be there a day early."

"Great! You still have my key, don't you?"

"At home in my top desk drawer left-hand corner," she said, imagining Marci rolling her large gray eyes.

They shmoozed a little longer. Before they disconnected, she gave Marci her flight number and time of arrival. A native New Yorker, Cory was starved for a culture fix. She looked forward to Marci's birthday party and her annual pilgrimage to the Big Apple. She could go more often, but prudent with her time and money, she rationalized that she was needed here, where there were enough thrills from work.

Yes, thrills. She chuckled, recalling a patient who had refused a suggested appointment time because it conflicted with her favorite soap opera time. "Don't you watch it?" the woman had asked.

Attending to the drama-filled lives of her patients, Cory had no need to watch a soap opera. She regarded herself as one of many socially accepted voyeurs who lived vicariously through work. Snug in a comfortable armchair, she listened to other people's adventures. She was safe. She wanted to make her patients safe, too. She'd had enough excitement to last a lifetime and not all of it good. However, from time to time, intrigue or some brouhaha would stir her and she would break free from her self-imposed exile.

Cory pictured New York in autumn: leaves turning color, crisp air, cultural events, and old pals. Her mouth watered as she recalled the savory marinara sauce at Bruno's in Greenwich Village. She saw herself strolling Fifth Avenue, meeting friends at the Met and listening to a concert at Lincoln Center.

She bounced into the reception room and filled a cup with ginger tea. She asked Ann to confirm the travel arrangements and to phone Joe to see if he would cover for her. Thinking about New York raised her spirits. She needed the escape; escape from alarming messages which increased her belief that Morgan's absence wasn't family-related. She had vanished after receiving calls from someone privy to her fantasy. Now someone linked her to Cory who hadn't a clue about the culprit. *What did Cory know of Morgan's associations anyway?*

She pored over Morgan's chart for information about the last boyfriend, but found nothing to identify him. Cory reproached herself for failing to ask his name. Morgan had reported they'd met at a charity function and dated for about a month. When he demanded more time—a scenario all too personally familiar to Cory—Morgan had lost interest. The man appeared to have taken their break-up in stride. There was no mention of any harassment. Reading through the notes, Cory found no leads. She slipped the folder into the cabinet as the phone rang.

"I confirmed your reservation for an aisle seat up front and ordered a vegetarian meal," Ann told her.

"You sure have my tastes down pat, Ann. You're terrific."

"That's what my mom says. Once a year on Mother's Day."

Cory chuckled.

"I spoke to Joe. He's glad you're taking a holiday and wishes he and Roberta could join you; said he'll mind the store. They have a surprise and invited you to dinner at their house tonight at seven-thirty. I didn't see anything in your book for after six, so I said it'd probably be fine. Is that okay?"

"You done good, Ann. Thanks."

The next couple of hours were like many with resistant patients. Lots of "yes-buts." Between sessions, she couldn't get Morgan out of her mind. Maybe Cory had jumped to conclusions based on limited information. Perhaps Morgan really did have a family emergency and was so involved, it hadn't occurred to her to call her therapist. Maybe Cory wasn't as important to her patient as she had thought.

But the bizarre phone message frightened her and the remark about homosexuality perplexed her.

Ann stood at the open door. "I'm going for lunch at the deli. Can I pick up dessert for you for tonight?"

"Great! Thanks." She smiled thinking how lucky she was to have thoughtful Ann around. If not for her, Cory would have the daunting task of scrounging around for the right bottle of wine for dinner. Dessert was better for the occasion—more New York style. She figured the surprise would be a tasty dish inspired by Roberta, a health-conscious gourmet cook. Her rumbling stomach reminded her that she hadn't eaten since early morning. Consulting her watch, she realized she had twelve minutes to grab something before the next session. She foraged in the office fridge stocked with finger foods, snagging carrot sticks, nuts, and grapes.

Cory plopped on the couch, newspaper in one hand, plate in the other.

As she turned the page, the plate took a dive. She began clearing the mess. Grapes rolled under the couch. Poking around for them, her finger touched a tiny metal object stuck to the bottom of the couch. What the devil was it? She peeled it loose and examined it. The size of a shirt button, but heavier, it had a bit of wire attached to it. Cory sat on the floor, staring at the object in her hand, too stunned to move. It looked like a tiny microphone with an antenna.

꞊10꞊

Barney found his intern seated behind a stack of books in the library.

"Jaime, I need a favor. Can you please take over my urban culture class? It starts in fifteen minutes."

Jaime checked his watch. "Sure, I know the room. I can make it."

"We're on chapter seven. Thanks, Jaime. See you later." Briefcase in hand, Blum rushed out the main door.

He jogged to faculty parking without breaking a sweat. At forty-five years old, physically fit, he prided himself on his ability to win tennis matches with younger men and to attract younger women. He smiled, thinking how lucky he was. But now, he realized his luck was running out, along with his judgment.

Blum chastised himself. He should have realized that Horace's placement in Jaime's group would lead to grave consequences.

He had tried to alert Morgan, but when Sara said she had "taken off", Blum was stymied. He hoped somehow someone had warned Morgan of the threat and she was lying low; but he feared that wasn't the case. Blum considered the greater possibility—her capture—her ultimate fate. He was afraid that under torture, she would break and reveal the location of the shelter. His sole option was to warn the shelter about the planned ambush.

Blum unlocked the door of his Volvo, climbed in, and clicked the shelter's number from his car phone, the only phone he could use that the shelter's monitoring system would accept.

"Hello," a woman answered.

"Hi. This is Beebee, he announced. "Listen carefully. Some men are planning an ambush to swipe their kids."

"Holy Mother of God!" she shrieked. "Are you sure?"

"Not absolutely, but you should be prepared. Is there anything I can do?"

"Not that I can think of now. I know how to reach you. Thank heaven, yesterday we installed an invisible fence that surrounds the property and we've got guard dogs everywhere."

"Good. I'll call the police here and tell them to keep an eye out."

"Thanks for calling," the woman said in a shaky voice.

Barney Blum opened his briefcase in the dimly lit faculty garage. With his flashlight in his mouth, he thumbed through the files until he found what he wanted. He pressed the number of the law enforcement officer assigned to Horace Johnson.

"He called me Lola." Finally, the haunting words made some sense. Someone had planted the microphone to harvest secrets from the couch. It had hurt Morgan. Who would be next? Cory felt a whopping headache coming on. She sat in her office, massaging her temples.

She didn't want to breach ethics by hiring a detective. Was there another choice? She couldn't sit idle. On her own, she'd try to find out who could have planted the device. The eavesdropper had to be someone motivated by curiosity, or blackmail, or someone vengeful.

The object, so tiny, so lethal, stayed on her mind, encroaching on her work, but her patients didn't seem to notice.

Toward the end of the day, she heard from Morgan's secretary, Sara Jaspers.

With a hint of urgency in her voice, the woman said, "I need to see you."

"Can you tell me what this is about?" Cory asked.

Sara's voice took on a conspiratorial tone, "My work."

Curious, but prohibited from treating someone close to her patient without her patient's permission, Cory hesitated. "I'm sorry, but I'm not taking new patients now. Would you like a referral?"

"Can we discuss that at your office please?"

Cory thought it was an odd request, but Sara had hooked her. Maybe she'd blurt out something to help her find Morgan. Cory compromised and agreed to an assessment and referral.

At the end of the day, Sara Jaspers, a dazzling spectacle, sailed into the office. Morgan's description of this woman had not done her justice. Sara was a knockout. Late afternoon sun filtering through the window reflected on her highlighted blonde hair. Her perfect features were enhanced by full lips, but it was the woman's eyes that most struck Cory. The color of Sara's expensive cashmere dress, they resembled aqua glass marbles. Shuffling on the chair, Sara crossed her long, shapely legs. With such glamorous women visiting her office, someone could think that Cory ran a modeling agency.

"Oh, this is cozier than I expected," Sara commented, turning her head to survey the room.

Apart from her framed licenses and certificates, Cory had furnished it much like her den at home: comfortable, contemporary beige-tweed chairs, and matching sofa surrounded a teak coffee table. Teak bookcases, desk, and file cabinets formed an L shape in a corner. Impressionist art posters hung on the wall for warmth and color. And fresh flowers from Ann's garden stood in an art-glass vase.

"My last therapist had high-tech furniture. Glass and metal. Cold like him. Couldn't get much from him except an occasional nod. The nerve of him suggesting I see a woman shrink."

He probably needed a steel suit and nerves to match for protection from her, Cory thought, waiting for Sara to launch into her spiel. Cory rubbed her cold hands together. "Tell me about the office problem?"

"It's Morgan."

"Have you heard from her, again?"

"No."

"So then what is it?"

"I'm afraid people at the office know Morgan is in love with me."

Sara's words felt like a sliver of ice sliding down Cory's back. Collecting her thoughts, she jotted down on her notepad "paranoid projection." She looked up from her writing. "What does she do that gives that impression?"

"When she looks at me, there's desire in her eyes."

"Oh?"

"She's also in love with you."

"What makes you think that?"

"When she's on the phone with you, she whispers like she's talking to a lover. Like she's saying something affectionate."

Cory had to keep her distance and remain formal with Sara. "Women can have respect and fondness for each other without any sexual feelings, Ms. Jaspers."

Sara smirked. "Oh, I doubt that."

"Let's do that referral now. Okay?"

"No. I'd like to be your patient."

"I'm sorry, but as I've said, I'm not taking new patients."

"Maybe you only treat lesbians like Morgan and her sister."

Cory raised her eyebrows. The woman in front of her seemed delusional. Was she the same woman Morgan had praised? Wouldn't Morgan have noticed Sara's deterioration?

"Where have you gotten this misinformation?" Cory asked.

"It's true, isn't it?"

"No. It is not." Cory didn't lie. The Heller sisters were her patients, but weren't lesbians. "What do you really want here?" Cory asked.

"Well, I was hoping if you won't take me as a patient, we could be friends."

"Friends? I'm sorry, Ms. Japers. That's not possible."

"Why not?"

Cory knew she should stop the session, but she persisted, trying to learn if her initial diagnosis was correct or if Sara was putting on an act.

"Friendship takes time to develop. I don't have time."

"So no new patients and no new friends, huh? Ah, crap! Double rejection. Can't you see I need help?"

"Yes," Cory said, thinking Sara could use a judgment implant. "I'll refer you to a therapist." She stepped to her desk and thumbed through her directory.

Sara lifted her hand, gesturing Cory to stop. "Why do I get rejected? I'm tired of being wanted for my body. And after we're through, they toss me out like a drained beer can."

Maybe because she was just as hollow. And if she really was tired of it, why flaunt herself?

"I know a lot about a lot of people, like you and your two kids. I know you're some kind of karate expert and you play drums. And you're Jewish, too, though you don't look it!"

Cory stared at her. "How do you know all this?"

"When I admire someone, I find out things."

"How?"

Sara hesitated. "Oh, I have ways."

"That's a provocative answer."

"Oh, I'm just kidding. I ask around. I'm curious about you because you're smart, attractive. A true professional." She played with her earring. "I read biographies. I like to find out about people."

That Cory, a middle aged woman, generated Sara's interest to this extent suggested she sought someone to fill a void she saw in herself. A hole in her ego. *Typical of a borderline personality*, Cory reasoned. Most patients evoked her sympathy. But not Sara. Grandma would have said she had chutzpah. Sara sure did have a helluva nerve. Cory had made up her mind that under no condition would this woman become her patient. Empathy had taken an early flight shortly after her arrival.

Cory walked her to the door.

Sara stood, grinning. "No harm done. At least I got to meet you."

After she left, Cory added to her notes: provocative, inappropriate, manipulative, narcissistic, and either delusional, or feigning deeper problems to spark psychologist's interest. Likely projection of her homosexuality. Provisional diagnosis: Histrionic or Borderline Personality.

She wondered if Sara kept her provocative behavior undercover during work, or did Morgan secretly admire it? Sara was a prototype of the woman Morgan fashioned herself as in her fantasy—her complete opposite.

After stashing away her notes, Cory thoroughly inspected the chair Sara had used. Apart from two pennies and a bit of lint, she found nothing. No bug. She was baffled as to why Sara had really made the appointment.

⸗12⸗

When Horace didn't show up for Jaime's anger management group, none of the members mentioned his absence, but it allowed them to bond. They began to see their particular red flags—the triggers that made them angry. Many of the triggers were universal—like rude people who push ahead of you on line or tailgate on the freeway, or inconsiderate bosses who change your schedule without warning. Slowly, the men were learning to control their impulses. Jaime would be patient.

And now they began to share their feelings:

"I miss my little boy so much, I can't stand it." Lonnie wiped tears from his eyes.

"Man, I know how you feel. My daddy was sent away when I was little. My momma said it done tore him up to be away from me," declared Melvin, a childless man. "Write him a note. My daddy wrote me one and I kept it forever."

"He's just a baby. He can't read," Lonnie objected.

"You can write to your wife, and in her way, she'll let your baby know," Jaime suggested.

"No. Account of her, I can't see the baby."

"No, it's account of you. You blew up and hit her. Wadja expect?" Melvin said.

Lonnie's face reddened. He leered at Melvin, but controlled himself. "I'll send him a great big teddy-bear."

"Looks like you were angry just now, but you controlled yourself. That's a good sign. You ought to feel proud," Jaime observed. He too felt proud to have created a trusting atmosphere.

When they took their break, Melvin caught up with Jaime in the restroom.

"Horace hasn't shown up. Is he in trouble?"

"I don't know, but you did the right thing telling me about him, Melvin. I'm proud of you and I liked the way you helped Lonnie today. You're going to be fine."

"Lonnie ain't. I just heard he's goin' along with Horace to raid the shelter."

"Thanks, Melvin," Jaime said, rushing off to telephone Professor Blum.

⸗13⸗

From the moment Cory had discovered the microphone, conflict and anxiety plagued her. On her own, could she learn who planted the device? If it became necessary to hire a professional investigator, could she do so without breaching her patients' privacy? She decided to discuss the problem with Joe, her old buddy and respected colleague.

A quick shower, a change of clothes, and she was ready to leave for Joe and Roberta's when the phone rang, startling her. She jumped as she picked it up.

"Hi Mom, it's Rachel. How are you?"

Cory breathed a sigh of relief at her daughter's comforting voice. "Glad you called, sweetie."

"Mom, I miss you. Can you come up for the weekend?"

Cory heard laughter in the background. "Sweetie, a drive up the coast to see you would be a pleasure."

"We're planning a barbecue for Sunday. It'll be fun."

Rachel loved to be with people. Cory missed her and needed the distraction "I'll leave tomorrow morning after my workout. What should I bring?"

"Your smile and your cranberry nut bread. You don't sound so hot, Mom. Is something wrong?"

"How did you pick that up?"

"I'm your daughter, remember? Must have inherited a gene marked 'perceptive' from you."

"It's just my work. Sometimes it gets to me."

"Not managed care again, Mom. That's bad news. It's also boring when you perseverate."

"Perseverate? Where did you hear that word?"

"Probably from you. It means you go over the same territory ad nauseam."

"Thanks for telling me. I'll keep it in mind. I guess that's what daughters are for—to keep mothers balanced."

"Are you angry with me for telling you?"

"No. At myself. I do get riled up. I ain't poifect."

"So, you know what to do about it, don't you?"

"It's not that simple." Rachel was a comfort. Sensitive, smart, she made Cory proud to be her mom.

"If it were, you wouldn't be in practice, Mom."

"Smartass! I'd like to talk more, but I'm running late for dinner at the Klein's. I'll see you Saturday, before noon. I love you."

"I love you, too, Mom."

"Kisses, sweetie."

Rachel was right. Injustices upset Cory a lot. As a kid, she defended the weak and had gotten several bloody noses and a black eye to show for it. Her efforts had probably made the bullied feel even worse for not fighting back. Grandma would say, "That's what you get for being a yenta. Mind your own business."

Like Morgan, Cory got fired up and wanted to fix things. She preached that anger wasn't always destructive. It was also the engine for change. After checking her appearance in the mirror, she grabbed the cake and set the alarm before backing out of the garage.

Off she went, heading south on the coast highway to Joe and Roberta's house. Inspired by a silvery moon and a sky ablaze with stars, she sang "Stardust." She imagined Hoagy Carmichael wincing at her slaughter of his tune.

Cory thought of her two friends, who had perfected the art of hosting at their swanky digs. She had become close friends with Joe in grad school, a time when he sported a full crop of brown hair, was pencil thin, and wore shabby jeans. Now the hair circling his balding pate was gray. No longer thin, he opted for expensive dark suits.

A year ago Roberta and Joe moved from a classy Manhattan co-op to a secluded La Jolla mansion protected by state-of-the-art security and a pair of German Shepherds. The dogs had two personas: well-behaved pets and trained watchdogs who responded to commands in German. Graduates of canine finishing school, they were playful inside the house, but outside—trespassers beware!

The new, rich lifestyle gained from his wife's investments didn't taint Joe. This wasn't the way Cory cared to live, but she wasn't knocking it either.

Fifteen minutes was the average non-rush hour time from any starting point to most destinations in San Diego. In exactly that time, she reached the walled estate, a three-story pink stucco with a red-tile roof on a hill surrounded by tall pine trees, a few palms, and an assort-ment of blooming foliage. Many of the homes in the neighborhood were California-Mediterranean. This one occupied the entire block and had a spectacular setting on the bluff overlooking the pounding surf with white caps illuminated by the moon.

When she pulled up to the gate, a car resembling Morgan's dark blue Saab slid to a stop across the street. Morgan? No. It couldn't be! Cory shuddered, wondering if she had been followed. In the shadows, she couldn't make out the driver.

Her fingers trembled as she keyed in the entry code, silently begging the gate to hurry and open. Her request was answered. The driver of the Saab revved up behind her as she raced in. The Saab backed up, made a U-turn, and sped away.

What was going on? Was the driver lost and needed room to navigate the narrow cul-de-sac street? Cory parked in the circular driveway and sat in the car for a few minutes, trying to compose herself. She rolled down the windows and inhaled the sweet scent of the night-blooming jasmine.

The crunch of footsteps on the terra cotta stones startled her. A man approached. Cory jumped and reached for the horn.

"Are you okay?" Joe asked.

"Phew! Now, I am. Why did you come out to meet me?"

"I watched you on the video screen racing in as the car behind you was about to slam your tush. I figured you'd like an escort."

Cory rolled up her windows and stepped out of the car. "Thanks. What a crazy thing! Did you happen to catch the license number?"

"No, but maybe it's on tape. How long were you tailed, Cory?" Joe took the cake box from her hands while she locked the BMW. He gripped her elbow, guiding her toward the house.

"I don't know. It's spooky. My patient has a Saab that looks just like it. She disappeared a few days ago."

Joe whistled. "Saabs aren't popular cars around here. We'd better call the police."

"She doesn't want them involved. She's a high profile person."

"Big deal. You're the one I'm concerned about."

"I'm not sure it was her car."

"Come on. Let's look at the tape."

They hightailed it down a long wide hallway to the library where several video screens displayed areas outside the house. One viewed the gate entrance. Joe fiddled with controls. Cory's BMW flashed on the screen. She recognized herself behind the wheel. The Saab turned so

42

quickly that only its side was filmed. They couldn't make out the driver or the license plate numbers.

"Can we save the tape, Joe?"

"Sure."

"I didn't notice the Saab on the freeway. I don't know who would follow me, or why."

Joe frowned. "Well, you know what to do if you see it again."

She nodded. "I'm in big trouble, Joe. I've had a threatening phone call."

"What?"

"I've reported it and my line is monitored now, but that's nothing compared to this." Cory whipped out the item from her purse and handed it to Joe. "I think it's a microphone."

Studying the gadget under the lamp, he shook his head. "You need a private detective," he advised, returning the item.

"That's what I think, but only to check for more bugs." She dropped the microphone into her purse. "I don't know what to do. I can't give information about patients to an investigator."

"You're forgetting something, Cory. Confidentiality is already compromised." His words chilled her.

"But not through my instigation. I'll do the sleuthing myself, but maybe a detective can discover who bought this and from where."

"I hope so, but it may be a long shot, Cory."

Just then, Roberta came into the library. The two women exchanged kisses. Roberta slipped her arm through Cory's and led her to the candle-lit dining room. Invitations to Roberta's home-cooked meals were a treat.

Roberta used to feel threatened by Joe and Cory's enduring friendship. For years he had tried to assure his wife the relationship was platonic, but friendship between a man and a woman was alien to Roberta, and she'd scoffed at it. After she finally accepted it, she and Cory became close friends.

Cory stared at the Christmas colored salad of spinach and tomatoes sprinkled with Feta. The dish should have whetted her appetite, but she couldn't stop thinking about the microphone.

"Aren't you hungry?" Roberta asked.

"Sure." Cory filled her fork. "Just as delicious as it looks. Any new acquisitions in the gallery?"

"Yes. An eighteenth-century... oh, you're just being polite, Cory. You aren't interested in antiques."

"I wasn't until your enthusiasm rubbed off."

"Glad to hear it." Roberta passed a platter of steamed baby vegetables and rice pilaf.

"You know, Ro, when I look at antiques, I imagine what it was like to live in that era. History seems to cling to the stuff."

Roberta smiled. "Say, if you're really interested, come to my lecture a week from Sunday."

"I'd love to, but I'm going to a big birthday bash in New York."

"That's a treat."

"So is this dinner," she praised, polishing off her poached salmon.

"I love to cook for you. You're so appreciative," Roberta said, gathering the dishes. She started toward the kitchen.

Cory began to help, but Roberta waved her away. "Go into the living room while I get dessert."

Joe ushered Cory to the grand room. Silky oriental rugs partially covered gleaming black marble floors. Furnished with antiques from Roberta's upscale gallery, the room reeked of richness that made Cory feel out of place in her plain duds. She plopped into a plush blue velvet sofa.

Roberta soon wheeled in a cart and served slices of the chocolate mousse cake as Joe poured coffee. Cory felt grateful for Ann's wise dessert choice.

After they finished, Joe moved aside a huge Chinese lacquered folding screen fronting a grand piano. "Our new addition. Now, Roberta will give us a little concert."

"I'm a bit rusty," she said. Seating herself on the piano bench, Roberta flexed her slender fingers and started playing Rachmaninov's Third Piano Concerto.

This was the first time Cory heard Roberta play. Carried away by the flawless rendition, Cory closed her eyes, allowing the music to transport her to another time and another place when Grandma and Grandpa had taken her to her first concert—a precious memory from a childhood riddled with feelings of alienation. The incongruity of her Asian features and her Jewishness had often amused other Jews and she sensed their hesitation to accept her as one of them. A lump of sadness, like a dike holding back a deluge of tears, formed in her throat. She

44

swallowed hard. Music always aroused her emotions and evoked memories.

Cory was lost in thought until she noticed Roberta had finished playing. "Bravo!" Cory applauded. "Flawless. Your playing carried me away. You're an exceptional pianist, Ro."

Roberta rose and took a bow. "Thank you. It's been years since I've played a concert, but I was once quite good."

"You still are." Cory wondered why Roberta had put her talent aside.

"Joe bought the piano and insisted I go back to it."

"I'm sure glad of that," Cory said, stacking the dessert dishes. She was tempted to ask Roberta what had made her give up music, but she wouldn't probe without being invited.

"It's the housekeeper's time off, and I actually like kitchen work, so please let me do it alone. You two wait in the library while I clean up."

They were the only people whom Cory knew with a separate room, called "The Library". That's what Grandma had called the bathroom.

"Ro, you've done more than enough. Please let me help," Cory begged.

"Go already!" Ro insisted.

"Roberta knows I want to talk to you," Joe said, as they traipsed down the hall to the library, where they plopped into two large armchairs opposite one another. "I'm worried about you, Cory. How can you do a good job when you don't feel safe?"

"I blot it out when I'm working. Later, I feel vulnerable." Threatened by her situation, Cory was also intrigued and excited. And ashamed of those feelings.

"Even before this problem came up, I had an idea that I discussed with Roberta. I'm tired of the isolation of private practice and now it seems you need a safe haven. Here's a solution. Share my office."

Cory pictured the situation. "It's very appealing. We could bounce cases off each other, just like old times. Ann plans to leave soon, anyway."

Joe proposed a remarkably low rent.

"That's very generous. It's tempting, but embarrassing for me to pay so little," she said.

"Your office would be smaller than what you have now and I'd continue to use it for my paperwork. I can't charge for the rest of the place because I'd use it anyway," he said.

Cory figured he was trying to justify his generosity. "I appreciate the offer, but I need time to consider."

The conversation turned to Roberta's former life as a concert pianist. Joe explained that before they had met, she had terminated her career because it was too stressful.

Cory checked her watch. She didn't want to intrude on their time. "It's getting late." She rose from her chair.

They walked back to the kitchen where Roberta was vigorously shining the granite counter with a terry towel.

"Thanks for a wonderful evening, Ro." Cory hugged her.

The trio linked arms and marched to Cory's car.

"Be careful driving home. Lock your doors and keep your windows closed."

She checked the batteries in her heavy flashlight and started the ignition.

⸌14⸍

Horace wanted to haul off and punch everyone at the police station, but he couldn't do that. Fighting would make it worse for him. Anyway, his hands were cuffed.

"This is a frame," he shouted. "You're gonna pay for this false bust. You know I had no coke in my possession when you arrested me. I want a lawyer."

"In due time," the investigator said.

Horace slouched in his chair, seething. He'd been here before, but Mr. Rothenberg, the attorney who had always worked magic for him, had his own troubles and couldn't rescue anybody. Hell, nobody even knew where he was!

Rothenberg's partner, the prick, wasn't interested in swapping services with Horace, and wouldn't lower his big fat fee.

Now, Horace had to wait for the court-appointed lawyer. He figured the guy would be an asshole, a just out of school kid, who wouldn't do him any good. *Shit!* Of all the unfairness! When he had done the crime, he'd paid no time. Now he hadn't done it, and was falsely accused. Probably because the cops wanted to hang him for getting away with shit in the past, they'd purposely planted the coke on him when they knew his lawyer couldn't help him. Yep, cops were like that.

"I need to take a piss," Horace griped.

"In a minute." The investigator smiled.

Horace figured the cop got off on watching him suffer. "Shit! All you know is time."

Horace squirmed in his chair thinking about the fun he was missing. Rothenberg had rigged a scheme to kidnap his wife and son from the shelter, but it wouldn't work with Horace's only recruit, Lonnie, in charge.

Horace figured Lonnie was jiving him or was too stupid to pull it off. The horse's ass was too weak to act alone and no one else had the guts to do it. A bunch of wimps! Thought they were tough, beating up their women. Shit, any little fucker can do that! Doesn't take smarts or brass balls like Rothenberg's. Shame such a smart man lost his cool. At least he had enough bucks and flew the coop.

Horace had to hand over his cell phone and pager to the cop. Now, how in the hell could Rothenberg contact him with instructions?

Horace checked his watch. *Shit, where was that free asshole lawyer?* It was a day of surprises. Maybe he was in store for a good one.

≈15≈

Cory rubbed her eyes and awakened from a dream in which a group of formerly missing persons stood on the stage of a grand concert hall applauding successful detectives. *Classic wish fulfillment*, she thought, turning off the static from her bedside radio.

She slid out of bed, stretched, and padded to the front door to fetch the newspaper. After putting up coffee, she spread the paper on the dining table. As she flipped a page and bit into a sesame seed bagel, a headline caught her eye:

CORONADO CORPSE CLAIMED

The nude body of a woman found on the beach was identified as Terry Salmonica, 34, of Augusta, Georgia, a naval officer missing from the North Island naval base for three days.

A photo of the woman taken in uniform accompanied the article. With her short-cropped hair and officer's cap, she could have been mistaken for a man. The article made no mention of a suicide note, a history of depression, or whether her clothes were found. Cory wondered where the woman could have stashed them and why she had disrobed to drown herself or if she really had committed suicide.

Although relieved the dead woman wasn't Morgan, she choked up with sadness for Terry Salmonica, and her loved ones.

Cory's over-reaction to the death of a stranger was a good reason to call Harold Greenwald, her former teacher and long-time friend. She keyed the memorized number on her phone pad.

"Hi, Harold. Cory Cohen here. How are you?"

"As well as expected from a man nearly ninety. I'm as busy as I like. These days, it's not too much. And you?"

"Fine physically, but I'm not sure of my emotional health."

"Are you still a psychological hypochondriac?"

"Could be, Harold. I'll be in New York next weekend and would love to see you. Do you have any time?"

"For you, yes. How about ten on Saturday?"

"That's great. Thanks a lot. I'm looking forward to it."

She hung up. After exercising to a video, she hopped into the shower and dialed the massage mode. The strong pulsating warm water struck her back and the nape of her neck, and relaxed her muscles. She stepped out tingling and toweled off. She pulled on jeans and Rachel's UC Irvine sweatshirt, tossed a couple of loaves of frozen cranberry-nut bread into her bag, and headed to Rachel's student apartment.

Cruising north along the Pacific Coast Highway, she opened the sunroof and a warm ocean breeze blew through her hair. Another day in paradise.

Cory shoved in a cassette and listened to Stan Getz's sax croon, "Autumn in New York". Her memories of that time of the year were of a prelude to gloomy gray, short days and frigid evenings, but here in Southern California, seasons gently melded into each other: eternal spring with flowers blooming year round and winters warm enough for a swim.

A car pulled out from a space near Rachel's house. This was a bit of luck. Cory zipped in. Nubile, tanned beach-goers crowded the Newport Beach Street. Some whizzed by on roller blades, as joyful and colorful as carnival participants.

After exchanging kisses with Rachel, Cory noticed they wore the same duds and today they had styled their hair in ponytails, but Rachel's was light and curly just like her brother Noah's and their father's. Cory loved her daughter's large blue eyes—always intense, yet warm. She loved everything about her.

Rachel and her roommates had invited a large group of people. Many sat on the crowded floor, munching veggies. Cory smiled and waved to familiar faces. Two young men played chess in one corner. In another corner, four people engaged in animated conversation. Rachel directed her to an empty seat next to a young man.

"Mom, this is Tim, the electronics maven." Off Rachel went to answer the door.

"Is that your claim to fame, Tim?" She felt fortunate to be seated next to someone who might explain the tiny mechanism in her purse.

"Rachel kids me about it since I fixed her stereo and computer."

"That's impressive. I'm sure she appreciates that."

"Well, she's always good for a home-cooked dinner. She fills up my fridge with her famous chocolate chip cookies." He smiled.

Cory was eager to pick his brain. "Have you always been interested in fixing stuff?"

"Yeah. When I was a kid, I took things apart to see how they worked. My folks encouraged it. Dad's an engineer. We worked on stuff together. He said I was a natural. I guess parents like it when you take after them."

"Sure. It's fun sharing interests. Are you familiar with miniature electronics, Tim?"

"My specialty. You interested, too?"

"Well, I came across something odd. Maybe you know what it is. Just a sec." She fished through her purse and handed him her find.

He rolled it over in his hand and examined its heft.

"Interesting. This cute little unit contains a miniature microphone, amplifier, and antenna for the narrow band FM broadcasting of voice signals. See here," he pointed to the attached bit of wire, "this is the antenna."

"Interesting. How close must the receiver be?"

"With this high quality? Maybe as far as across the street. Someone could listen from a car stereo or any other wireless FM receiver."

"Hmm. A wireless FM receiver? What could that be?" She paused, cupping her chin in her hand. "Say, would a personal radio with earphones work?"

"Oh, easily."

A chill surged through her. "Can anyone buy this microphone?"

"Yeah. You don't need a license." He smiled. "Just need to know where it's sold. There are plenty of spy shops around." Scrutinizing it again, he said, "I'm not too sure about this one though. It looks better than any you'd buy on the street. Sometimes they sell stuff in the back room that is stolen from government agencies."

"Black market? Do you think this one is?"

"Could be. The regular ones are made small enough to hide, but this baby is so tiny that it could be a government issue. Don't quote me on it. It's just a hunch."

"So FBI or CIA…"

"Or maybe ATF, DEA, or Secret Service. Where did you say you found it?"

"Uh… in an office building."

An attractive young woman crossed the room, smiled at Cory, and came toward Tim. Cory hoped the pretty woman would rescue her. She didn't know how much longer she could contain her horror.

Tim smiled and the look in his eye suggested he was happy to see the young woman, too.

"I'm really sorry to interrupt what looks like an intense conversation, but my car is acting up, Tim. Would you please take a look?"

For a moment, Cory felt sorry for Tim and hoped women liked him apart from his value as Mr. Fixit.

He rose to leave. "Nice talking with you," he said, rushing out the door.

Cory planned to ask Rachel whether Tim knew she was a psychologist. She realized she'd become a bit paranoid and didn't want him to link the microphone to her work.

Cory hoped kitchen activity would dissipate her rotten mood. She grabbed a wooden mallet and pounded two dozen chicken breasts into paper thin slices. Just as she finished, Rachel walked in and wrapped her arm around her mom's waist.

"I'm happy you're here, Mom," she said, kissing Cory's cheek.

"Me too."

Cory carried the platter to the patio and Rachel stoked the charcoal under the grill.

"Tim's an interesting guy. Is he majoring in Electrical Engineering?"

"Uh-huh."

"Does he know what I do for a living?"

"I don't know if I've told him."

"I guess there's no need to, unless one of your friends is a psych major."

"Hey Mom, what's going on? You're jumpy."

"Nothing, pussycat. I like your friends. And this is a fun party."

"Okay. You'll tell me when you're ready."

Cory winked. "Sometimes I think we do a role-reversal."

The noise from the stereo began to irritate her. "And sometimes I feel like one of the gang here until your music jars me back to reality."

A straight-ahead jazz aficionado, she missed Ron and what they'd had—the shared passion for music and each other. He was the only guy who'd interested her since her divorce eight years ago. Cory felt she had messed up. Perhaps they both had and were too stubborn or fearful of a future together to fix it. They were at different stages in their lives. She was twelve years older than he was, divorced, and had two grown children. That hadn't bothered him, but he had no patience for her obsessive attention to problems. In the end, she was left with mixed feelings: relief and sadness.

When the time came for Cory to leave, Rachel walked her to the BMW. "You seem uptight, Mom." She furrowed her brow. "And the way you whacked the chicken… something's bothering you, huh?" This was her second attempt to draw her out.

"A difficult patient," Cory said, confident that Rachel wouldn't probe.

"Take care, Mom. Don't let it get to you." Her outstretched arms invited a hug.

"Thanks, pussycat." Reluctantly, Cory broke away from the embrace.

Heading home, Cory tried to put things in perspective. Family and friends were important. Her work shouldn't place first. Being a therapist satisfied and challenged, but now troubled her.

She couldn't get the microphone out of her mind. Clearly, someone had learned about Morgan's fantasy from it. Who had planted it? A patient? The person who had threatened her on the phone? She would never know all there was to know about anyone. Sometimes knowing herself was hard enough.

She was hounded by the fear of patients finding out someone else had heard their sessions, although so far, no one had reported anything unusual to her. Perhaps the microphone was specifically targeted for Morgan.

She stopped at a jazz club in Dana Point to join an open jam session. She brought out her bongos from the trunk of the car, and took a place at the rear of the stage.

The guy on saxophone reminded her of Ron. Holding back her tears, she concentrated on the rhythm. Her hands worked a fast-paced Latin beat and she allowed the music to carry her away.

After they finished playing, the musicians thanked her. She went home exhilarated.

Cory rested her head on the pillow, preparing to dream about the jam session. She wondered if artists dreamed in color and musicians dreamed in sound.

She wondered if Morgan had good dreams, too.

꞊16꞊

Early Monday morning, Cory arrived at the office ahead of schedule and was greeted by the scent of orange spice tea.

"Hi, Ann," she called out.

Ann bounced and clutched her textbook to her chest. "You scared the daylights out of me. I didn't expect you until much later. Is something wrong?"

"I'm afraid there is," Cory said, sliding into a chair in Ann's office. She pulled out the microphone from her purse. "I found this stuck at the bottom of my couch. It's a microphone."

"What?" Ann stared at the item in Cory's palm. "You're sure?"

"I verified it."

"What a bummer!" Ann said. "This place grows scarier by the day."

Cory shook her head. "For twenty-five years, I had a smooth practice."

"Any idea who could have planted it?"

"Not a clue, Ann. Do you?"

"Only knowing your patients casually, I'd place my bet on Kevin Holloway. That guy gives me the creeps. All the patients greet me except him. He ignores my offer of tea or coffee. Seems lost in his radio..." Her voice trailed off. "This can hurt patients and ruin you. What are you going to do?"

"I'm not sure," Cory said. "I've left a message for George Lewis."

"Good you know a cop." Ann fidgeted with a pen. "This does it. I'm going to consider another career. Is it worth potential lawsuits when you can't even make a living under managed care? They don't give a damn about health, only about profits!" She slammed a book on the table.

"You're right. Under managed care, you can't make a living. You'd make much more in sales or law, but you chose psychology because you want to help people improve their lives."

"Sermon 101 you've preached to me so many times I can't count. You spend half your time on clerical stuff. Let's face it. Your earnings don't match your education and experience. It's not fair."

"Whoever said life is fair?" Cory sighed. This conversation was a replay of others they had which invariably ended in frustration and anger at a system gone amuck.

Ann's face flushed. "I see how much it costs to run a practice. By the time you're through, what do you have?"

"Bupkis, nada, zilch!" Cory nodded. "One day, with government intervention, mangled care will vanish."

"Seems to me I've heard your song before."

Cory sighed.

"Okay. I'll change the subject. Have you heard the latest local scandal?"

"No. What's up?"

"Have a seat. I'll fetch some nibbles."

In a few minutes, Ann returned with a platter stacked with fig bars and two cups of tea. "Mayor Nelda Evans was accused of welfare fraud."

"Are you kidding?"

"According to the paper, years ago, she used several different names and social security numbers to collect a lot of money from welfare. Of course she's denied it and hired a high-powered legal defense team."

"That's what I get for listening to music instead of news, Ann."

"I wonder if your friend Lieutenant Lewis is involved in the case?"

Cory shrugged. "How was the scheme uncovered?"

"An anonymous tip to an investigative reporter." Ann sipped from her Orphan Annie mug.

Noticing Ann's resemblance to the cartoon character, Cory grinned.

"Yesterday, Nelda's grief-stricken photo made the front page," Ann said. "The Trib always supported her. They'd never print anything negative without verifying it. Amazing, isn't it?"

"I'll say." But Cory still couldn't stray from the microphone. "Listen, we should see if there's another bug here."

"Way to go, Miss Marple."

For the next hour, they tore the place apart, turned furniture upside down, tossed cushions, and peered in every corner and behind framed diplomas and prints. The search was futile.

The wall clock chimed. It was too late to ask patients to meet her at Joe's office. She knew she had unconsciously delayed the decision.

At first, Joe's offer had seemed great, but later, ambivalence set in. Although she enjoyed his company and professional expertise, she didn't want to feel beholden and preferred working on her own turf.

Until she was certain that there weren't any other hidden microphones in her consulting room, she would use Ann's office for sessions. She would tell patients there was a construction problem. Ann's office could accommodate two people comfortably and Cory hadn't planned to see couples or groups that week. They rearranged the furniture, exchanging Ann's desk for two chairs from the reception room, where Ann would work until a surveillance expert pronounced the place clean.

"I'll take the portable phone, Cory, and tap on my—excuse me—your door when you have a call."

Glancing over Ann's shoulder at Tuesday's appointments, Cory noticed Kevin's name wasn't on the calendar.

"Did Holloway reschedule?"

"No. When he broke his appointment, I suggested a new one, but can you imagine he had the nerve to shout at me? Brr!" She shivered. "He sure is strange."

The phone rang. Ann left to answer it, then barged into Cory's temporary quarters. "It's Lewis."

Cory grabbed the receiver. "Good to talk to you, George. I need to see you as soon as possible. It's urgent."

"I'll be right over, Doc."

"No. Let's meet for coffee at the Pannikin in what—ten minutes?"

"Okay, Doc."

She hung up the phone and grabbed her purse. "I'll be back before my session. Hold the fort, Ann." She dashed out the door.

On the balcony of a small upscale shopping center in horse ranch country, the Pannikin cafe shared space with a bookstore. The changing display of art work and weekend live music made it a desirable neighborhood hangout, but it was usually quiet at this time of day.

Colliding at the entrance, George and Cory laughed. They plopped into comfortable chairs in the rear of the café away from view and earshot of the few patrons.

George's dark hair, usually worn in a crew cut, needed a trim, but he was clean-shaven. Since last year, he had made overtures of

56

friendship, but Cory resisted because she didn't want to be reminded of how they'd met: a rape and murder investigation in which her patient had been the victim. He was sensitive, but seemed able to keep his feelings in check about the grim aspects of his work. In time, Cory would heal and they'd be friends. She didn't want to base a relationship on her need for protection, or his need to protect, but that was precisely why she'd called him.

"What's wrong, Doc?"

"I found this stuck with Velcro on the bottom of my office couch," she said softly, handing him the microphone. "And one of my patients has vanished."

George examined the gadget in his palm. "You know this is bad news."

She nodded. "I'm scared. I need someone to check over my office."

"You know we don't have surveillance detection stuff or I'd do it for you, Doc." He poked at the bug. "This is quite a sophisticated device. You used your noodle meeting me here. Where are you seeing your patients?"

She told him about the office exchange with Ann and about the bizarre phone call.

"Not good. Your best bet is to hire a private investigator."

"Can you recommend one?"

"Yeah. A new P.I. in town. Like us, from New York, you know. Super smart. Went to City. John Jay Criminal Justice. Also Fordham Law. Did a stint with the FBI, but gave it up. Prefers independence. If he's available, he'd be perfect, Doc. He's an electronics specialist. We had a few beers together. I like him and I think you will, too."

"Sounds like a great endorsement. What's his name?"

"Ben Fortuna." Lewis scrawled the name and number on a paper napkin.

"Hah! Good fortune."

"Yeah. Better than Mal Fortuna," he chuckled.

At the counter, she ordered two coffees and bagels. Lewis pulled out his wallet.

"This is the least I can do," she refused, her hand on his arm.

"I miss you at karate, Doc. Heard you and Ron broke up. Is that why you're making yourself scarce?"

"Yes, Sherlock." She spread a thin coat of marmalade on the bagel with a plastic knife.

"He looks forlorn, you know. Never smiles," Lewis told her between gulps of the dark brew.

"He didn't smile much when we dated, either."

"Hope you don't think I'm nosy, Doc."

"No. It comes with the territory." She sipped the strong coffee. "I bet people have similar reactions to detectives and psychologists. They think we can detect their secrets."

"Yeah," he smiled. "Listen, Doc. You'll need to investigate your patients, you know."

Cory sighed. "That's another problem. It isn't ethical for me to hand over a client roster. Do you think a detective would show me how to investigate?"

He raised his eyebrows. "Hmm. You know, Doc, if I had time, I'd teach you, but I'm swamped. Working too many hours." He peered at Cory over the rim of his coffee mug. "You know, this is my first break since... I can't remember. Oh, yeah. Two weeks ago at karate. At the rate I'm going, I'll lose my nice shape. Then what will the girls—uh—women say?"

"They'll say, 'George is a gem. A hero.' Listen. I bet you're feasting on fast food." He smiled. "You are a good detective."

"Let me make you dinner and there will be some leftovers for a few days. How about tonight?"

"Thanks for the offer, Doc. Can't have tonight, but I'll take you up on it when I can. Call Ben. He'll help. He's probably not busy, yet. You know, being new here, he may be able to give you more attention than someone else."

She folded the napkin with the name and number on it and stuffed it into her jacket's pocket. "Thanks for meeting me. I appreciate it."

"You know, I do know that. When I can squeeze in a home-cooked meal, I'll be in touch."

They left the cafe together and walked to their cars. Before turning on the engine, Cory called Ben Fortuna from her cell phone.

He answered immediately. Probably eager for work. She explained the situation and recited her office address. He said he'd be there within the hour.

Cory returned to the office, stowed the files of the day's patients into her briefcase, and wrote a note to Ann:

"Shush! There may be other bugs here. Ben Fortuna, a specialist, is on his way here to inspect. Write notes to me if you need to say something private."

She handed the message to Ann.

"What's this?"

"*Shh*," Cory whispered.

Ann rolled her eyes, read the note, and nodded acknowledgment.

Noticing a small vase of flowers on the table in the temporary office, Cory smiled. "Thanks for the cheery buds, Ann."

The door to Cory's new quarters was ajar. Soft classical music wafting in from the reception room served as an additional sound barrier.

About twenty minutes later, the outside door of the suite swung open and Cory caught her breath at the sight of an attractive, middle-age, tall—maybe six-three—well-built man, carrying a briefcase. His hair was thick and dark, and his complexion, olive.

Hearts may not really leap, but Cory's did.

The man handed Ann a card and she nodded in Cory's direction. Cory stepped out of the office and extended her hand.

"Mr. Fortuna? I'm Cory Cohen and this is Ann Abrams, my assistant."

"It's a pleasure to meet you," he said. His smile was broad, his teeth, perfect.

Shaking his strong hand, Cory felt charged. She motioned for him to follow her into the office.

He sat opposite her and when she looked into his warm brown eyes, she almost forgot his mission. Ben Fortuna reminded her of her former English professor at Brooklyn College. Whenever she ran into him, she would forget what she was doing.

Clean-shaven and immaculately groomed, the private investigator wore a gray tweed sports coat, a light blue shirt, and a navy necktie that matched his tailored dark blue slacks.

"This will take about an hour." He placed his index finger on his lips, gesturing silence. From his briefcase, he removed an instrument and plugged it into the wall socket. "In case there are other listening devices here, this masks our conversation. Now, show me what you've found."

She scooped the microphone from her purse and handed it to him, feeling light-headed as her hand touched his. Rolling the device over his palm, he examined it.

"This looks like an FBI issue. You've probably had a patient connected with a government surveillance agency."

"None that admitted it."

"Good. They shouldn't. When I was an agent, we kept an inventory and had to account for every important item."

"Is it possible to find out who it was issued to?"

"I'll let you know, Doctor Cohen. Please show me exactly where you found it."

Crouching, she pointed to the bottom of the couch. He stooped beside her, his fresh herbal scent reminding her of a spring day after a light rain. Their knees touched. The feel of his trousers against her excited her. Quickly, she stood and watched him turn the couch on its side and examine it.

"There's another problem, Mr. Fortuna. I shouldn't compromise my patients by identifying them to you."

"Even though one of them might have violated your security?"

"A solution would be for you to teach me basic investigative techniques. I'd happily pay your going rate."

"I respect your ethics, but that's an unusual request. I'll have to think about it."

"As you can see, I'm in an awful predicament. I would be grateful to you."

Fortuna smiled in a way that made her think he could be easily convinced.

"I have a hunch we'd make a good team," she said, softly.

Fortuna hesitated, drumming his fingers on his knee "Okay. I'm sold. I'll offer direction. Unless it's life threatening, I won't invade confidentiality." He opened his briefcase. Items were neatly arranged in compartments. "Here's a contract." He pulled out two sheets of paper. Cory read the terms and found them easy to understand. The fee was less than she had anticipated. They both signed the documents and he gave one to her.

"Partners, Doctor Cohen." He held out his hand.

When she shook his warm, strong hand for the second time, she nearly melted.

"What's wrong with you? Falling for a man you've just met simply because he's attractive and hired to play your hero. For all you know, Mr. Fortuna could be married. Shame on you!" Grandma's haunting voice admonished her.

"I'll check over the whole place. It should take about an hour," he said.

She nodded and as he started his work, she crooked her finger gesturing Ann to follow her into the corridor.

Outside the suite, Cory asked, "What do you think, Ann?"

"About what?"

"Him." She pointed to the office. "I like his type."

Ann gave a sly smile. "I can tell. Your tongue is hanging out. And your eyes are bulging, too." She laughed. "I'm glad you find him attractive. We need to lighten up here. His name's a riot."

"I wonder if he has a sister, Felice," Cory joked.

"Good fortune and happy fortune. Parents could be comedians."

"Or gamblers."

They hung around outside the suite trying to make light of the situation until Ben Fortuna called them inside.

"Good news. No bugs."

"Phew!" Cory said as she and the detective entered her office.

"Who else has keys to your office aside from you and Ms. Abrams?"

"Janitorial and security. The building management."

"I should investigate them."

"Yes. Please."

"Has any harm come from this so far?"

"One of my patients has vanished. Her secretary said she was called away on a family emergency, but I don't believe it."

"Why not?"

"Because our last session was worrisome. I'm sure she'd have called me if she had more trouble." Cory avoided looking at him.

"When someone has a family emergency, calling a therapist may not come to mind," he suggested.

"True. But just prior to her last visit here, she received an intimate call on her unlisted phone. It frightened and upset her. The caller addressed her by the name she used during sexual fantasies. He must have overheard her sessions."

"Anything else?"

Cory told him about the threatening call she had received and the phone trace.

"Any idea who could have done this?"

"Not yet, but I'm working on it."

"First, I'll track down the device. Next, I'll investigate the building personnel. I'll need your schedule so I can check for bugs daily at the end of your last session. If I find another device, it'll narrow down suspects. You have a good alarm system here and I need the security code and permission to act as your representative should a break-in occur," he detailed, handing her another form to sign.

"Of course." She signed the document.

"As an added measure I'd like to install surveillance equipment in your office," he told her. "Don't worry, it's not voice-sensitive. A visual scan, for your eyes only."

Suddenly, she became embarrassed. Here, he'd know her every move. No more scratching private places or adjusting underwear. "Isn't your after-hours check sufficient?"

"No. Security or janitorial will come in later. I prefer thoroughness."

"But you'd see my patients."

"I doubt I'd recognize anyone. Anyway, your waiting room isn't strictly private. What they say inside the confines of your office is your concern, not mine. Mine is to observe movements."

Reluctantly, she agreed. She had to trust him.

"If anything comes up, call me. I'm easy to reach. My numbers are on my card."

"Thanks," she said.

"I'm going to like working with you, Doctor Cohen."

"And I, with you, Mr. Fortuna." She felt her face redden.

He smiled. "We'll talk soon."

After he left, Ann and Cory re-arranged the furniture back to its former position.

Relieved that Ben Fortuna was on the case, Cory was surprised at her sudden attraction. Such stuff is what close girlfriends ponder. Luckily, Betty would soon return from her holiday. Yearning for more than investigative techniques from this man, Cory realized she had turned her attention away from her problem.

⸗17⸗

Barney Blum clenched his fist. *Goddamnit! What the hell was wrong with his head?* First he'd screwed up by including Horace in the anger management group. Now he learns that the little rodent, Lonnie, has fallen prey to Horace. As an experienced social worker and a professor, he should have considered the group dynamics. Jaime wasn't conducting a kindergarten class.

The group was composed of disturbed men. Most of them were volatile and weak-willed. He knew the men would bond and he should have predicted the possible relationships that could spring up among them. It was too late to address it now.

He would have to contact Lonnie's probation officer and alert the authorities to keep an eye out. He wondered why he hadn't heard from a detective from the D.A.'s office. Are they so busy, or had Sara neglected to pass his message to them? So far the shelter hadn't been attacked, but he hadn't heard from Morgan.

He had begun to think of her frequently. Too frequently. It was distracting. He wondered why his feelings for her had changed from deep reverence to erotic. When making love to his wife, Morgan's image popped up. He imagined fingering Morgan's soft hair and caressing the planes of her face—a face a sculptor would love.

Blum struggled to see and feel what she would be like in bed, but it was too difficult. The image was elusive—vague—because Morgan gave no hint of what she covered up with those long loose dresses of hers. He figured she chose such a style to avoid sexuality. She was a study in contrasts: warm in her caring nature, but seemingly untouchable. Could it be that she was a late social bloomer and sex was not yet in her repertoire? She had shared enough about her background to make him suspect she was repressed.

He knew her sister was an academic—probably straight-laced—her father a non-observant Jew, and her mother a former nun. Morgan had given a rare laugh when he remarked that her mother had two Jewish husbands.

Blum vowed to give up contaminating her image with his lust. He would conjure up other women for that purpose. Now he would focus his thoughts on her good work rather than her eyes and her lips.

Among the few who knew the extent of her work with the underprivileged, she was regarded as a saint. With no expectation of praise or appreciation, she worked from behind the scenes. Blum regarded her as the quintessential altruist.

"I do it because it makes me feel good," she had said.

Was it because he felt responsible and worried about her fate that he thought about her so much, or was this another of his rationalizations?

At least he had used good judgment in choosing Jaime for the anger management project. The guy was smart, but so insecure, he ran to him with every little problem. Hell! This wasn't a little problem, but he had tried to rationalize it by minimizing it. Blum was good at after-the-fact self-analysis.

Barney Blum was convinced his judgment had eroded and he was in the throes of a mid-life crisis. He ought to make an appointment with a good psychologist.

≈18≈

It was Tuesday, the day Kevin and Morgan usually had their sessions. In the time reserved for them, Cory again pored through her notes in Morgan's chart to see if she had overlooked anything. As before, the effort yielded no clues and left her exasperated. She pushed the folder to the side of her desk, making room for her feet, leaned back on her chair, and begged the ceiling for help.

It was no use. To distract herself, she turned to the newspaper account blasting Mayor Nelda Evans. Evidence from ten years ago showed she had assumed seven identities and had filed fraudulent welfare and Aid to Families with Dependent Children claims for forty-five children. "Incredible!" Cory said under her breath.

Cory figured someone must be mighty miffed with the mayor to have dug up the dirt on her. She hoped the dishonest Mayor of San Diego, now serving her second term in office, would soon serve prison time instead. Too bad Morgan wouldn't be prosecuting her, but it was probably a federal case anyway.

Further into the column, Cory read that the mayor's younger sister was also implicated.

"Sister," she muttered. It brought to mind Morgan's sister Liz. She ought to contact her to check on Morgan.

Cory opened Morgan's chart and ran her finger down the page. The number should be listed under next of kin. Damn! The information wasn't current. Liz's permanent address was stored among the obsolete files in Cory's garage.

"I'll be back in half an hour," she told Ann, then headed out the door.

Tires screeching, she zipped out of the parking lot, and arrived home in a few minutes. Here, she rooted through the musty old files and located Liz's chart, copied the information, and dashed back to the office.

Cory settled herself at her desk and pressed eleven numerals on the phone pad. A recorded voice announced the number was disconnected. Slamming down the receiver, she remembered Liz had moved a few months ago when Morgan had gone to visit her. Cory couldn't recall the location.

She phoned information for each of the five boroughs and Westchester, Nassau, and Bergen counties. No listing. Damn! Cory remembered that Liz taught at Columbia University. She phoned the English department. "Professor Elizabeth Heller, please," Cory said.

"Not on the faculty. I'll connect you to personnel, perhaps they can help."

Cory drummed her fingers on the desk and waited. Finally, a man answered, "Personnel."

"This is Doctor Cory Cohen. I'm trying to locate Doctor Elizabeth Heller about an urgent family matter. I'd appreciate it if you would please call her and give her my phone number."

"That's not our policy," he said and disconnected her.

"What? Of all the nerve!" She felt her jaw tighten. She wanted to complain to a supervisor, but perhaps the rude man on the phone was a supervisor. She started to call again, but hung up to avoid fueling the fire raging inside her.

She turned her attention to Kevin Holloway's chart. He had begun therapy two months ago, but had missed several sessions due to work emergencies. Like Morgan, to assure privacy, he didn't use his insurance and paid for his sessions in cash.

On the confidential questionnaire, he had listed his social security, driver's license, and pager numbers, and at first, refused to enter his home phone and address.

"That's not acceptable." She had risen from her chair. "Sorry. Psychotherapy can't work in an atmosphere of mistrust."

He explained that he wanted to keep his business private from his housemate. He agreed to provide the required information upon the condition that he would be only be contacted via his pager.

How odd, she'd thought then, and now. Here was a guy making a decent salary as a computer consultant for the county, and apart from a mortgage, he was debt-free. Without an economic incentive, it made no sense to him to live with someone he didn't trust. She noted it on her agenda for his session.

Kevin booked weekly sessions for Tuesdays at four o'clock. Unlike most patients, when he canceled, he refused an alternate time. Was he so busy, or was he rigid?

When she'd asked who recommended her to him, he said a woman at a party whose name he'd forgotten.

Kevin sprinkled his pedantic vocabulary with pop-psych jargon. Allegedly, he sought help "to heal the wounds left by my dysfunctional family. That may account for my lack of success with women." He described his parents as "irresponsible, immature substance abusers."

Kevin said he was thirty-five years old, but the crows-feet etched at the corners of his small brown eyes and the few strands of gray threading his sandy-colored hair made him appear older. He had a crooked smile and a habit of poking his index finger into his wavy hair and twirling it. Though not an "Alan", who set the standard for "a hunk", his neat, clean appearance ought to be acceptable to women, but he reported constant rejection. Cory figured he provoked it. She recalled a session:

"W-women don't give a rat's ass about intelligence. They're too m-materialistic. They only go for rich, handsome guys."

"If you look around at couples, you'll see that isn't true," she'd said.

"Then why am I rejected?"

To find out, they'd reviewed his dating behavior. Kevin admitted he often made negative comments to women: "You don't sound like you graduated college. Are your teeth capped?"

"Designed to assure rejection," Cory had commented. To which Kevin had smirked. He was big in the smirk department.

"Want to find out why?"

But the topic had made him nervous and was put on the agenda for a later date.

Kevin's stuttering brought out her compassion, but she wouldn't let it stand in the way of figuring out his possible connection to Morgan.

Originally, Cory had offered him a session the hour before Morgan's. Kevin refused it, although he had time to arrive early and wait in the reception room where he supposedly tuned into his personal radio through headphones.

His rigidity about fixing the time for his appointment directly after Morgan's now became a red flag.

Noticing he had skipped sessions on the same days that Morgan had canceled hers, she slammed his chart on her desk.

Later that day, Ann interrupted Cory's paperwork with the announcement that Alan had arrived. Cory had dubbed him, "Alan the Philanderer."

She locked up the files she'd been working on and opened the door.

Alan strolled in, wearing a denim shirt and jeans, a western style belt, and work boots—the personification of rugged masculinity. A tweed jacket slung over one shoulder hooked his index finger. His dimpled smile was warm. It was easy to see how he charmed women. Alan always looked her directly in the eye. He had a particular kind of look that made her feel uncomfortable—as if he knew what she looked like naked.

He ambled to the couch and she caught a whiff of a pleasant spice-scented cologne or after-shave. Was he trying to seduce his middle-age psychologist? "Are you aware how you come across to women?"

"Ah, yes, Doctor Cohen. I know they fall for me. It's a kick. I'm like the guy in the New Yorker cartoon—the one where a woman asks a man if he loves her and he says, 'Of course I love you. I love all women.'"

"If that were true, you wouldn't hurt them." Cory crossed her legs, suddenly aware that she always chose slacks or long skirts on the day of Alan's appointments. "Let's talk about the first woman in your life. Your mother."

"I never laid her." He chuckled.

"Is that supposed to be funny, Alan?"

"Thought I'd shock you." He sank into the couch, draping his arm over the back.

"What would you gain?"

"I'm a big tease." He grinned.

Cory shook her head. "It's called resistance."

"Okay, Doc. You want to know about my mother. Well, so do I." He punched a couch pillow. "I haven't seen her since I was a baby."

"Who raised you?"

"She dumped me on her brother because he had room for me on his dairy farm in Minnesota. My uncle was a shy guy and never married." Alan paused, seemed to choke back tears. "He did the best he could for me."

"Did you get along with him?"

"Oh, sure. Uncle was the only family I had." His voice cracked. "He supported me through college. He was a straight arrow. I liked working with him. He was also a master electrician and taught me a lot about it. He died a few years ago." Alan's eyes moistened. "I hope I've repaid him for all he's done."

Cory found Alan's sentiment appealing. It probably contributed to his success with women. "The wonder and vitality of a child in his life must have enriched him," she said. "You both got something good from it."

"I'd like to think I took away his loneliness. Uncle was shy around the ladies. What I learned about them they taught me themselves. The first time I had sex was with an older woman. She said I had a special gift." He paused a few moments, perhaps slipping back in time to savor the memories. A sly smile dimpled his cheeks. "My fantasies have always been about older women."

Cory felt herself blush and she suspected he noticed.

"Actually she wasn't that old. I was fourteen and she was twenty."

"Today, that would be considered child abuse," she said.

Alan was a provocateur. Cory visualized him with his milkmaid and wondered with amusement how he would respond to someone like the flirtatious Sara.

"Do you think I take out my anger at my mother by screwing women?" He leaned back, stretching his long legs, and rested his head on the back of the couch.

"Perhaps that's why you disappoint them," she said, thinking that like Alan, she too had no clear memories of her mother. Her grandmother had been a fine replacement. Cory led a normal life with close friends and a successful practice. She had married, divorced, and was a single parent. Having grown up with emotional security from her grandparents and her father, she had no fear of intimacy or abandonment—only of making poor choices in the romance department.

Alan married and had a good career. Whatever fueled his lust for women, Cory was determined to help him find and temper it.

She couldn't ask him directly if he was Jolene's lover. She might be able to pry it from him, but her role was to help him, not to satisfy her own curiosity.

Three years ago, she had learned two of her patients were having an affair with each other. Neither had told the other they were in therapy with her. She'd found their sessions as intriguing as Kurosawa's *Rashomon*—each had given different versions of the same incidents.

From Alan's vignettes, Cory pictured his boyhood on a vast expanse of rich, green dairy land—the nearest playmate miles away. His sole and primary emotional support was his uncle, of whom he spoke tenderly. That relationship could have compensated for his mother's abandonment. But she knew individuals differ in their responses to similar experiences. Was Alan's hurt so severe that he would plant a gadget to catch women's secrets and take a hostage?

≈19≈

The final patient of the day had left. Deep in thought, Cory folded her arms and paced her office.

Since last week, the atmosphere had rapidly changed from that of a peaceful retreat—a sanctuary where problems were resolved—to one of a foreboding place; a place where unveiled secrets had taken root and rotted. She was convinced that the violation of privacy in her office and the threatening phone call from a foul-mouthed stranger were from the same source.

Whoever was responsible may have pegged her as a stereotypical Asian woman who was too frightened to act on suspicions, but he sure as hell had underestimated her.

"Damn! It can't be one of my patients," she muttered. She knew some of them had betrayed their mates, but this was different. Would a patient jeopardize her—a special ally?

She sat down at her desk, pulled out a sheet of paper, and drew three columns. She labeled them respectively: Carlos, Alan, Kevin.

Each man had the opportunity to hide the tiny microphone on the bottom of the couch.

As far as a reason, Carlos was suspicious of his wife and could have bugged the office in order to listen to her sessions. He could know about microphones because of his job on TV. He met the criteria for means, opportunity, and motive.

But why would he go after Morgan?

Alan was an electronics pro and had the means and opportunity. Adventurous and curious, he could have tuned in to Morgan's sessions. Challenged by her sexual conflicts, he could have captured her for sexual excitement. But 'could' didn't equal 'would'. Circumstantial. Insufficient. After all, many people enjoy sexual experimentation, but how many would go that far? More to the point, would Alan? She couldn't bring herself to believe it.

As she printed Kevin's name, she felt queasy and reached for a mint to still the wave of nausea. The glaring business with the headphones, the scheduled appointments and cancellations, plus his other odd behavior made her very suspicious of him. What was his motive?

71

Cory rubbed her temples and stared at the couch. An innocent piece of furniture had become a tool for treachery. Then it dawned on her. She'd had the couch cleaned last year. She dug around the office files and located a pink receipt from Clean Guardian. She phoned, but the number was disconnected. A check through the Yellow Pages yielded no listing. She photocopied the receipt for Ben Fortuna to investigate.

She drew a fourth column for Clean Guardian. The motive: fun and mischief.

Grandma used to say that Cory's refusal to accept help made others feel discounted. In order to become a mensch, she must learn when to take responsibility and when to ask for help. Grandma would be pleased if she knew Cory had hired Ben Fortuna and also had made an appointment with her old professor.

Ann popped in. "Your private investigator called. I told him we're done for the day so he's on his way here to check the surveillance tape. Do you want me to hang around?"

"If it's no trouble," Cory said, "Here, give this to him." She handed Ann a copy of the Clean Guardian receipt. "Please ask him to walk you to your car."

"It's obvious you're avoiding him."

"That's because I should maintain a business relationship, but I'm so damn attracted to him." She rummaged through her purse for her car keys.

Ann clicked her tongue. "You remind me of my old fashioned uncle." I remember his words, 'never dip your pen in the company ink-well.'" She sighed. "Okay, I'll stay to salve your conscience."

≈20≈

Fog had rolled in early Friday morning. Cory called the airline and was relieved to hear the flight to New York was on time.

On the way to airport, the mist dissolved. When the signal light turned red, Cory phoned Ben Fortuna mostly for the pleasure of hearing his voice. "I've left a copy of a receipt from the place that cleaned my couch last year."

"Yes. Ann gave it to me."

"I tried phoning them. I think they're out of business."

"I'll check it out. So far, the janitorial service is sanitary. "

"Hah. I'm off to New York for the weekend."

"I wish I could go, too." he said. Cory wondered what he'd say if her destination was Timbuktu. "Well, give my regards to Broadway. And have fun," he added.

"I'll call you when I get back."

"Ciao."

Cars jammed the freeway toward Lindbergh Field—a rehearsal for New York traffic. She switched from the jazz radio station to the news:

"... reputed to have taken bribes from attorney Lou Perry with whom she has a personal relationship. Perry has won all his cases in Judge Brenda Winter's court. Graphic photographs depicting their intimacy and records of his payments for her Mercedes and condo on Maui were submitted as evidence to the District Attorney's office for prosecution."

Cory was angry with a dishonest official and sad that Morgan wasn't around to prosecute a case that could have assured her election.

The city suffered from an epidemic of corruption. First the mayor, and now a judge. Both women, too. Cory worried the anti-fems would rant, "Give a woman power and she abuses it."

The airport was crowded. Grateful for a small carry-on, Cory navigated freely among unfamiliar faces to her familiar destination.

The plane trip to New York relaxed her, but the arrival at the airport amid the hustle and bustle proved grueling. Cory joined the long queue of travelers waiting for cabs. An attendant handed her a list of taxi fares from the airport to the city.

When she climbed into the cab, a well-known voice startled her:

"Halo. Dis is Docta Rood. I alvays say prectice safe sex. Now I vant you to be safe here, too. Sooo festen your seat belt," said the recorded voice of the famous sex therapist.

Cory giggled. "Must be the Mayor's idea," she said to the driver, then recited Marci's West Side address.

He didn't answer. She figured his comprehension of English was limited to local geography. He drove in silence threading his way through congested traffic. She marveled at the orchestration of vehicles in sync with each other's rhythm—like a fine jazz combo without sheet music.

She passed familiar landmarks and wondered about the crossroads in life and what it would be like had she followed a different path—a theme that reappeared whenever she was troubled.

New York had not changed much since her last visit. Motorists blared horns and graffiti splashed across highway signs. Shabby abandoned cars with missing tires lined garbage-strewn streets. And then the drive through Central Park, where beauty and tranquility replaced the unsightliness and noise.

The cab pulled up to the curb in front of Marci's high-rise apartment house. Cory tipped the driver and was surprised that he didn't thank her. His unpleasant job probably robbed him of civility. She gave him an A plus in Navigation and an F in Public Relations.

The desk clerk rang Marci, announced Cory's arrival, and pointed to the elevator. He didn't know that Cory had been a long-time visitor here. She pressed number *11* on the elevator panel and within seconds, she had arrived.

She rang the bell. Marci opened the door and they threw their arms around each other. Cory stepped back and looked at Marci's happy face. "It's good to see you," she declared.

"The pleasure is mine," Marci said. She grabbed Cory's overnight bag and led her into the guest bedroom.

"You've spruced up the place beautifully," Cory remarked, pointing to the new carpet and furniture.

"Cutting my sessions at the clinic, I needed something to occupy my time so I redecorated."

Marci gave Cory a run-down of the current New York cultural events, then asked if she was ready for dinner. "There's a new vegetarian café on Broadway."

"Sure, but you know the drill. My treat," Cory said.

"Okay, for tonight only. The rest of your time here, we'll split it."

"It's a deal," Cory replied.

They strolled up Broadway to the nearby café and looked at the framed menu posted in the window. The Greenery offered organically grown vegetables cooked Asian style.

"Looks good to me. What do you think?" Cory asked.

Marci chuckled. "Organic means sprayed at night?"

Cory shook her head. "It's certified by an agricultural agency."

"Do you really believe that?" asked her wary friend.

Cory shrugged as they entered the small café. A host seated them, followed by a reed-thin Japanese woman holding a teapot and a small chalkboard listing the specials. After a quick glance, they ordered oriental vegetables and cellophane noodles.

A harpist strummed *Clair de Lune* in the background. Once the server brought their order, Cory dug in, savoring the food. "I've never had a bad meal in New York."

Marci laughed. "You must have forgotten my cooking."

They finished dinner and strolled back.

Moonlight shone through the windows of Marci's apartment silhouetting a nearby forest of high-rise buildings. A perfect New York setting. It felt good to be home again.

⸗21⸗

The next morning, in the cool autumn air, Marci and Cory jogged along Central Park, the ground crunchy under their running shoes. Foliage, still green, clung to maple trees, providing a shield from the anemic sun. A breeze tossed red and yellow leaves. Varied colors on the same tree were like people developing at their own rate.

Manhattan's expensive high-rise, warm apartments and elegant hotels lined the park while homeless people slept huddled on cold, hard park benches.

A woman clad in a mink coat walked a poodle who wore a jewel studded velvet collar. The dog's ritzy image evaporated when he lifted his leg and christened the threadbare blanket covering a homeless person. The rude woman made no effort to pull away her pet.

Cory rushed up to her. "Such disrespect! How would you like to be in that man's place?" she chastised, glaring with mounting anger at the insensitive woman. She wanted to rub Ms. Hoity-Toity's nose on the poor man's urine-soaked shelter.

Ignoring Cory, the inconsiderate woman sauntered away, as if sticking her tongue out.

"You've no compassion!" Cory screamed after her. "You're an insult to humanity!"

Marci grabbed Cory's arm. "Hey, take it easy. You've forgotten the big city is filled with all kinds. You're so riled up. What's wrong?"

"Just stuff at work that I'd rather not get into. I was hoping to leave it behind."

"Understood." Marci frowned.

They went on jogging until Marci pointed to a cafe across the street. "How about breakfast?"

While waiting for a table, they stretched their legs. Patrons didn't linger and soon a table became available. Marci leapt to the self-service section, returning with two cartons of orange juice and one cheese and one poppy-seed danish.

Cory stared at the pastry and smiled.

"Come on," Marci said. "You're in New York. Where else can you get this?"

They were polishing off the last crumbs when the chiming of a nearby church clock reminded Cory she must hurry off to get ready for the appointment with Harold.

"Sorry, I can't linger. I have to see Harold."

"That's fine. What time should we meet at the Metropolitan Museum?"

"Would eleven-thirty be okay?" Cory asked.

Marci nodded. Cory collected their trash from the table, tossed it into the bin, and they hurried back to the apartment.

After a quick shower, Cory dressed and headed toward Harold's office.

New York was one of the best cities to ambulate. Her feet could take her almost anywhere, and often faster than a cab. Weekend mornings were different from weekdays here: quiet, apart from the loud hiss of bus brakes. Light traffic swished by. Unhurried pedestrians seemed lost in thought.

Cory knew the city's mores. Unlike San Diegans, New Yorkers didn't make eye contact with strangers—that would be an intrusion. Close physical proximity in the subway rush hour was intimate enough.

She checked herself in with the desk clerk, stepped into Harold's elevator, and pressed the button for the fourteenth floor. As the door started to close, a tall young woman flew into the lobby. The wind-swept auburn hair, angular facial features—Morgan? Cory started to rush out, but the elevator door shut in her face. She quickly pressed OPEN, but it was too late. The elevator lurched, then rose rapidly. She hit the button for the second floor. Seconds later, the door slid open and she raced downstairs to the lobby.

Cory scanned the area, but the Morgan look-alike was gone. Since Morgan's family lived in New York, the woman could have been Morgan. Then again, she could have been someone who resembled Morgan.

After Morgan's absence, Cory's frequent thoughts of her hadn't triggered any illusion. Why now did Morgan or her look-alike make a premier appearance?

She remembered other times when she thought of someone and suddenly he appeared. The experience seemed uncanny until she realized she must have seen him through the corner of her eye and hadn't paid attention until he came into full view.

The elevator stopped at Harold's floor and she stepped out. The front door to his suite was always unlocked when a patient was expected. Cory turned the knob and sure enough, the consulting room was ajar.

"Come right in, Cory," he called, hoarsely.

A dynamic man with a renowned sense of humor, Harold was the psychologist of other psychologists. He was best known for his early research on prostitutes. He had aged since she had last seen him, his hair, thinner; beard and mustache, whiter; and voice, raspier.

"How are you?" she asked, bending to kiss his cheek.

"Not bad for an old man. Aging is for the courageous. Enough about me. Let's hear about you."

She gave him a rundown on Morgan's obsessive sexual fantasies, her job, the calls on her unlisted number, and her subsequent disappearance.

"Cory, you'll always be a momma. To some it's an endearing quality, but others don't need it."

She figured he referred to her ex-husband who felt controlled by her mothering and had over-reacted.

"From what you've said, your patient can take care of herself. If she were in danger, she'd know what to do. She probably did have a consuming emergency. It could disrupt her sexual fantasies. You're not her priority. She puts hers in order."

"Not like me, huh?"

"I understand your concern, but it may be excessive."

Cory dug into her purse and pulled out the slip of paper on which she had scribbled the threatening phone message. She handed it to Harold and slumped back on her seat.

He hooked the stems of his eyeglasses around his ears, read the note, and handed it back to her. "Probably an adolescent prank."

"How did he connect her to me?"

"Perhaps a teenage neighbor followed her. He may have heard gossip about her family emergency."

"I suppose so," she said, finding it easier to dismiss the note than dwell on it. "Look, you're the expert in hypnosis. Morgan told me she'd felt mesmerized by the caller. What about a post-hypnotic suggestion?"

Harold poured himself a glass of water. "It's possible, Cory, but her secretary may have told the truth."

"Her secretary is bizarre." She related the session with Sara.

"Too bad you can't take her on. You like a challenge."

Cory rolled her eyes.

"Why are you so sure your patient would have contacted you?"

"She's a responsible person who disappeared right after telling me the caller knew the name she called herself in her fantasy."

"Now that is interesting, but you have no proof of foul play."

Cory felt flushed. "Yes, I do. I found a tiny microphone stuck to the bottom of my couch."

He raised his eyebrows. "You're sure that's what it was?"

"A bit of wire attached to it made me suspicious, and an electronics expert confirmed it. It can pick up sounds from across the street."

Harold shook his head.

"You see why I'm alarmed?"

"Of course. Who do you think put it there?"

"One of three patients."

"Three?" Harold shuffled in his chair. "Who is the most likely?"

"Kevin. His session follows Morgan's. There's no indication they know each other. If he were a felon and she recognized him in the reception room, wouldn't you think she'd have told me?"

Harold shrugged. "Maybe she didn't notice him. People with pressing problems tend to be oblivious of others."

"He's the only one who wears headphones in my waiting room. The damn thing could be a receiver for the transmitter. Ann says he usually arrives early, as much as forty minutes. That's plenty of time to eavesdrop."

Harold clasped his hands over his middle. "Who referred him to you?"

"A woman he met at a party whose name he didn't remember. Or so he said. Probably Ms. Yellow Pages."

"Could be."

"He hasn't been in since I found the microphone."

"Ah hah!"

"Last week I hired a private investigator. He checked the office and didn't find any other surveillance gadgets. He said the microphone looks like an FBI issue. I don't know anyone who worked for the FBI."

"Patients in sensitive jobs keep quiet about their work; even in therapy. Tell me more about Kevin."

"He sprinkles his speech with psycho-babble. I have a hunch he fabricated a story about his dysfunctional family as a ruse to see me."

Harold sat silently, stroking his beard. "Have other patients complained of anything suspicious?"

"Not yet. Ann says Kevin gives her the creeps."

Harold raised his palms in a gesture. "Bad guys look normal and many are amiable; even good-looking, like Ted Bundy. And those who seem strange may not be. Perhaps Kevin reminded Ann of someone she didn't like." He wiggled his gnarled index finger at Cory.

"Right, but you taught me to use my third ear."

"I accept your gut feeling, but why would he target Morgan? What's their connection?"

"I'm thinking about it."

"He could have planted the microphone during the first session," Harold said. "And later listened somewhere near your office. He wouldn't need to continue a charade with you."

Cory cleared her throat. "At the end of each session, I ask patients for their home and office numbers when I confirm the next appointment. If he had eavesdropped, he'd have heard her number." She rubbed her throbbing temples. "Whoever knew of Morgan's disappearance made a bizarre call to spook me."

"Could be. How would Kevin know of her appointments with you?"

"Maybe he stalked her." She sighed. "I'm not even sure Morgan was abducted." She poured a glass of water and rummaged in her purse for a packet of Advil.

"How did he know you had an opening after her session? And why would he scare you?"

Cory leaned forward, her hands on her knees. "Here's my theory: Kevin saw Morgan somewhere, took a fancy to her, and followed her around." She let her words sink in while she massaged the back of her neck. "He tailed her to my office for a few weeks. Figured she was a patient. He waited around to see if anyone came in after her. No one had, so he reasoned the hour after hers was free." She swallowed hard. "He manufactured a reason to see me in order to snoop on her. He didn't want to chance listening from a longer distance."

"What's his motive?"

"Don't know. Perhaps they had contact; she rejected him; and he's getting even with her by scaring me. Is it far-fetched?"

He shrugged. "In our work, we see strange things. So what can you do?"

She swallowed what tasted like bile. "Check his identity. If it's counterfeit, confront him."

"Too dangerous."

She nodded, sank back into the soft, safe cushions of Harold's old familiar couch, wishing she could stay there for a long, long time.

"Listen, Cory. You don't need this patient. Your security and peace of mind must be paramount. Find a reason to terminate his therapy. We're not compelled to treat everyone who asks."

"As usual, you're right. If he wants another session, I'll say I can't work with him because of his inconsistent appointments. I'll suggest a referral to a less rigid therapist." Rehearsing the scene in her head gave her a sinking feeling in her stomach. "I must admit, I'm afraid of his reaction."

"What's his diagnosis?"

"You taught us not to pigeon-hole people."

"True. I dislike categories that change every few years."

Cory flashed on the shelf of books on diagnosis collected during the last two decades: The Diagnostic Statistical Manuals revised every few years.

"I also don't like being called a provider," he snapped.

"Me, too. Techs with six months training and brain surgeons are lumped together as healthcare providers, now. May as well call the prostitutes you wrote about sex-care providers."

He chuckled. "So your patient imagines call girls enjoying sex with their clients? They don't."

"If I told that to her, do you think it'd make a difference?"

"Try it."

"I hope for the chance." She sighed. "Kevin is hard to diagnosis. Maybe he's a pathological liar. He shows borderline features. It's possible he has a multiple personality. A dissociative identity disorder."

"On what basis? There are few well-documented multiple personalities, Cory."

"I know. But the conflicting stories he's told about his family leads me to think he lied or built up an imaginary life much like multiples do." She rested her head on the back of the sofa. "There's another clue. Many times when she'd canceled, he did too."

"You've got a headache because this is unsettling and you don't accept coincidences."

"You've said there are no coincidences in psychotherapy, Harold."

"Yes, but as Freud said, 'Sometimes a cigar is just a cigar.'" He shifted in his worn, black leather chair, which looked larger than she had remembered.

"I was hoping you'd help me." Cory felt the blood rush to her face. "I'm so obsessed with Morgan, I even thought I saw her in your lobby."

"Take it easy, kid. You don't hallucinate. You probably saw someone resembling her."

Cory closed her eyes and felt Harold staring at her. "I have to find out if Kevin planted the bug."

"How?"

"I'll tell him I found this little item under the couch and figured it fell from someone's pocket. I often ask patients if they've lost a pair of sunglasses."

"Sunglasses are one thing, but a microphone?"

"I'd only ask him to see his reaction."

"Why would he admit it? You can make a better plan."

"How's this? I'll verify his employment. If his identity is bogus, I'll stop therapy."

"And if it isn't?" he asked, brushing aside a strand of his silver hair.

"I'll refer him for a psychological evaluation."

"What if he refuses?" Harold's voice was fading. He popped a lozenge into his mouth.

"A good reason to end his treatment."

Harold clasped his hands behind his head. "Hmm. It's interesting to speculate about his connection with Morgan."

"Finally, I gotcha!" Cory cheered, raising her fists.

"An intriguing situation. And you like drama."

"It's a comfort that you know me so well." She grinned. "Since it's unethical to give the detective a roster of patients to investigate, is it okay for me to do it under his supervision?"

"In a dangerous situation, ethics are a luxury."

Cory was sure Harold had noticed something in her manner when she'd spoken of the investigator. "I had an instant attraction to the P.I."

"You're alive!" He clapped. "Wonderful!"

She smiled. "You may remember that after my divorce, I was celibate for eight years until Ron came along, but that's over and when that P.I. sailed into my life last week... Wow! What's happening to me?"

"Nothing to worry about. It's normal. The door to your libido is open. Enjoy. Don't lose your perspective. And don't let your professional life screw up your love life."

"You're good." She kissed his cheek again before leaving.

⹀22⹀

Cory hopped on the bus and rode through the park on her way to the museum. With time to spare, she strolled on Madison Avenue, passing trendy cafes, antique shops and a gallery featuring African masks—symbols—perfect for a psychologist's collection. Although tempted, she couldn't justify an addition to her cluttered wall and moseyed on.

The headache remedy kicked in twenty minutes later, and she spotted Marci seated on the crowded steps of the Met.

As they poked around the Egyptian room, the session with Harold began to haunt her. Perhaps she had made a big deal over coincidences because something was missing in her life—not drama—a sense of belonging to an extended family. Her kids were grown and attending school away from home. They would probably find careers elsewhere. She knew she couldn't keep loved ones close to her bosom forever.

She wondered if she'd created a drama about Morgan in order to cover up her growing despair by bringing excitement into her life.

No. This time her professor was wrong. The tiny microphone and the threatening phone calls couldn't be denied.

The birthday party that evening brought friends she hadn't seen in several years. They swarmed around the catered buffet of bagels and lox, turkey, roast beef, salads and Viennese pastry like buzzards over a carcass. They toasted Marci with champagne and played charades.

After the last of the guests had hugged Cory and Marci goodbye, Cory placed her gift on the table. She was busy cleaning up the living room when Marci spied the package. "Oh!" she said and smiled. She read Cory's card and tore open the box. "How did you know I wanted a cell phone?" she screeched. "You really are a mind reader." She scanned the phone service contract. "And you got phone service for me, too. You shouldn't have spent so much money."

"The phone is free with the service."

Marci kissed Cory's cheek. "Thanks a lot!"

Marci's joy was contagious and Cory was glad to have pleased her friend.

When the weekend came to a close, Cory dreaded returning to San Diego to face her problems. Marci waited on the curb with her for the taxi to the airport.

"I'm going to miss you. I'm tempted to move back here."

"I've got room for you."

"I wish you'd visit me." Cory repeated this old refrain, knowing Marci wouldn't leave New York for California more than once every decade.

When the cab came, they did their warm good-byes.

During the trip to the airport, Cory peered out the window at the city's drawbacks. The air was damp and chilling; the sky, gray; the traffic, intolerable; and the noise, relentless. A bittersweet place. San Diego had a healthier climate and new memories to make. Cory prayed they'd be good ones.

During the jet's descent toward Lindbergh Field, she shuddered at the proximity of the high-rise buildings. Flying into San Diego—the scariest landing—had to be a pilot's nightmare. She squeezed her eyes shut.

꞊23꞊

Cory's heart raced. Swathed in bandages, she must have survived the plane crash, but was injured. Afraid to move a muscle, she remained still, slowly opened her eyes, and looked around, expecting to see an unfamiliar hospital room. To her relief, she was back home in her own bed, blankets wound tightly around her. The glowing green numbers on her bedside clock announced 7:10.

It was Monday morning and she had awakened from a hair-raising dream. A dream so vivid, so fraught with anxiety, she had experienced it as real.

She believed in dreams; she saw them as guideposts—Freud's royal road to the unconscious. She sat up and loosened the jumble of wrappings she had created from her tossing and turning. Her visit to the museum mummy display and Harold's reference to her as everyone's mommy had probably triggered the imagined bandages. They also symbolized how she felt tied up in knots.

Sipping from the glass of water on her bedside table, she continued to analyze the nightmare. Anxiety caused her to dream her plane had plummeted from the sky.

Grateful that it was only a bad dream, she crawled out of bed and was splashing cold water on her face when the phone rang. She toweled her face as she headed for the receiver.

"This is the answering service. Shall I put Kevin Holloway through?"

She cringed. "Sure. Good Morning, Kevin."

"Hey Doctor Cohen. I was out of town on personal business, but I'm back now. Hope you've kept my time open."

"Let's see," she said, stalling to regain her composure. "Yes. I have."

"Good. I'll be there. Bye."

Did he request the session to divert suspicion? Or did he realize the microphone was gone and he wanted to plant another? Perhaps she'd made too much of headphones and appointment schedules and he was completely innocent.

Over oatmeal and orange juice in the kitchen alcove, Cory read the newspaper, fascinated by more evidence about the judge and her lover-boy attorney. The gifts-for-favors scandal. The gender role reversal made her smile. The impending prosecution dragged Morgan to her mind again and wiped away the smile.

The sun cast a golden hue. Another warm day in Paradise and a perfect time to jog. She pulled on a tank top and shorts, tugged her hair through the hole in her red baseball cap, and started for the half-mile trek to the beach. She passed joggers and bikers. Women and young men returned her greeting, but older men ignored her—the invisible woman. A guy wearing headphones reminded her of Kevin. Anticipating his session, she had that butterflies-in-the-stomach sick feeling.

Cory headed home and got ready for work. Before leaving the house, she phoned County Personnel, identified herself as a loan officer from Bank of America, and verified Kevin Holloway's employment.

Kevin showed up on time without the headphones. He slumped on the couch and plunked a large ring of keys and his cell phone on the floor. Why not lay them on the coffee table? Was he considerate of the furniture or was he looking for an easy way to plant another bug?

He folded his brown leather jacket neatly on the couch and crossed his legs. His slacks were pressed and a silk designer necktie brightened his freshly starched shirt. What did his fellow workers think of his spiffy get-up? Unlike most computer pros, whose clothes were casual, he dressed in the style of an affluent executive. Things about Kevin didn't compute. Why did he choose a roommate he didn't trust? Was he desperate for money to support a drug habit or to help pay off a gambling debt?

While waiting for Kevin to talk to her, she studied him for sinister signs, recalling Harold's words: "Bad guys look normal, even good-looking."

"I just returned from Oklahoma," Kevin said. "My sister had emergency surgery."

"Sorry. How is she?"

"Recovering from an appendectomy. It's always hard for me to see her."

"Why is that?"

"I'm not a big shot like Rebecca, the prominent judge." He loosened the knot in his necktie. "She's my twin."

"Twin?" Cory looked up from her notepad. "You told me you had a sister, but I didn't know she's your twin."

Kevin shrugged. "She's ten minutes older than me. Hah! She acted as if it were ten years."

"Her competition with you started early. When you were ready to be born, she shoved you aside so she could go first."

"That would be just like her. She acts like a mother surrogate to me. Whenever I'm near her, I regress. Feel like a helpless kid again."

There he goes again with that psychobabble. Although he'd denied any previous therapy or interest in psychology, his vocabulary sure suggested otherwise. Cory wanted to discuss that discrepancy with him, but knew that psychotherapy depends on timing. She thought it wiser to keep him on track and follow his thread.

"What about your parents?"

"They were always wasted, so Rebecca took over," he snapped. "She grew up fast. Did our laundry. Made meals—such as they were. Peanut butter and jelly. Ham and cheese sandwiches. Cereal. Rebecca bathed me and shampooed my hair. Even laid out my clothes for school."

"She must have liked the mother role. Made her feel powerful."

"Oh, yeah. At seven or eight, she looked twelve. I felt like a total failure next to her." He rubbed his eyes. "She was way smarter and bigger, too. She's over six feet tall now." He wiggled his foot, the large deck shoes incongruous with his attire.

"Girls usually mature earlier than boys," Cory said.

"Everyone admires her. I was proud of her, but disgusted, too. That's why I moved away. Here, I'm not compared to the great Rebecca. Man, sometimes I hate her!" He gazed into the distance as though watching a movie of his past.

"This is the first time you've shared these feelings with me, Kevin."

"Well, it's been hard for me. I was going to quit therapy, but realized I have to deal with my anger at my family... and maybe myself for running away." He looked straight at Cory, a first-time eye contact.

"You were uncomfortable at home. A good reason to escape."

He bowed his head. "You don't know me... don't know how messed up I am."

"I've heard those words many times. Help me understand."

"I don't know where to begin."

"By being honest with me. Let's start at the beginning. How did you choose me?"

He stared at his fingertips. "I told you."

"Sometimes people are ashamed to admit they plucked my name out of the phone book. They may think it shows a lack of sophistication. You said someone at a party referred you after you'd told her you had a dysfunctional family. It's odd that you'd speak so openly with a stranger when you're such a private person."

"I don't know what you're talking about." He picked at his cuticle.

"You don't recall that?"

He shrugged his shoulders.

Was he embarrassed and pretending a memory lapse? Or could he have the rare condition of multiple personalities? She knew the theory that traumatized children developed other personalities to disconnect from horrid experiences. "How were you punished when you were a kid?"

"For what? I never did anything wrong."

"In an earlier session, you said your father was abusive and your mother wasn't protective."

"Did I say that?" He grimaced. Was he confused or fabricating a charade? His strange emotional landscape began to earn him the title of Cory's toughest case.

"Tell me about your parents."

"They hung out listening to bad music, smoked pot, and drank." His voice rose. "Those slime bags ignored us and didn't work. They lived off funds from a trust left by my grandparents."

"Oh?"

"Yeah. They owned oil wells. That's how I managed to leave Oklahoma. I have money from the trust." He bit his fingernail. "Rebecca gave me some of her share. She said I needed it more. Man, she sure made me feel inadequate."

"She probably meant well. After all, she took care of you."

"I know." His eyes glistened. "That's why it's hard to hate her."

"What happened to your parents?"

"Those stupid disgusting pigs had an accident. Their pickup turned over. The end!" He brushed his hands together. "We were grown by then."

"Did you have any friends when you were a kid?"

"Mario, but he moved away. I missed him," he recalled, bouncing his heels on the floor. "Rebecca had her own friends, all girls. They didn't want me around."

"Sometimes kids without friends create an imaginary one. Did you?"

"Yes." His face reddened. "I was about six or seven. I called him Mario. One day I pretended he was there and Rebecca laughed at me and said I was nuts." Kevin flashed his eyes at the door as though contemplating a getaway.

"You weren't nuts. You needed a pal. Missing the real Mario, you made him up. Kids do that. Do you have friends now?"

"Not really."

"What about your roommate?"

"Who, Kevin?"

"Kevin? So your roommate's name is Kevin, too?"

Flushing, he mopped his brow. His contorted face made Cory anxious. She expected a different personality to emerge.

"You're having a funny reaction to my question, Kevin."

"It's very warm in here."

"I'll lower the temperature." She walked over to a panel on the wall and fiddled with the thermostat already set to a comfortable seventy-two degrees. "Tell me about Kevin."

"There's nothing to tell. He's just a guy who rents a room in my house. That's all."

"Do you ever hang out with him?"

"I don't care for beer drinkers."

"Why do you need him there?"

"Let's change this ridiculous subject, okay?" His voice rose. "He's not important in my life."

Cory had clearly hit a sore spot. Kevin had exposed more of his feelings in this one session than all the rest combined. If she wanted to keep him in therapy, she would have to follow his lead. She would go for the innocuous.

"Have you ever had a pet?" she asked.

His face relaxed. "Yes, my dog, Amigo."

"Did he ever make you angry enough to hurt him?"

"When he was a puppy, he bit me," he said, squirming.

"What did you do?"

"I smacked him."

"How did you feel afterwards?"

"Like I taught him a lesson."

Cory felt empathy for the sad and lonely little boy who had wanted the dog's affection, but was bitten instead.

She gave him another appointment for the following week and watched him out of the corner of her eye as he snatched his stuff from the floor, preparing to leave.

When he had gone, Cory felt along the bottom of the couch and removed the cushions. She searched thoroughly for another microphone in vain. Distracted by his sudden openness, she had forgotten to schedule his psychological evaluation.

Ann poked her head in. "That Kevin is a strange character. I wonder why he's so contemptuous of me. I'd like to shadow him—see where he goes, what he does, but I know the rules. Too bad you can't break them and have Fortuna do it."

"You're looking for a new career? Ask Ben Fortuna how to become a professional investigator. Maybe we'll do it together."

<h1 style="text-align: center;">≈24≈</h1>

When Cory arrived the next morning, Ann waved a message slip at her. "A prospective patient just phoned. Here's his name and number. I told him you'd call soon."

"Thanks, Ann." She collected the little sheet of pink paper, stepped into her office, and called the phone number.

"Professor Blum here," replied a man with a Midwest accent.

"Doctor Cohen returning your call."

"Morgan Heller told me if I ever needed another dose of therapy, you're the one to see."

Cory's knees started to buckle. She grabbed her chair and plopped into it. "Nice to hear that."

"I've had therapy as part of my training. I thought all my kinks were ironed out, but I've developed a couple of problems that are interfering with my professional life."

They agreed to meet that afternoon. Cory was curious to learn his connection to Morgan.

Later that day, Barney Blum, a trim, light-haired, attractive forty-something man arrived a few minutes late for his initial appointment. "Sorry, it's like Los Angeles type traffic here in late afternoon." He extended his right hand. Cory shook it. In his left hand, he carried a leather planner. He had the demeanor of a self-assured man. Blum wore white jeans, a navy blue shirt, and a red sweater neatly tied across his shoulders. Very patriotic, Cory mused as he seated himself in the chair across from her.

"How do you know Morgan Heller?" she asked.

"She serves on a committee to help the homeless."

"You're on the committee?"

"I hope it's obvious I'm not homeless." He smiled.

She smiled back at the affable man, feeling at once comfortable with him.

"I'm a social work professor. Worked in the field for a few years until I caught the academic bug. It's been fine at the university until now. I'm here because lately I've made some horrific errors in judgment."

"Such as?"

"We have a grant that enables our students to provide anger management training to spousal abusers. The guidelines called for eight members, but we had seven. I took the liberty of interpreting the criteria a bit differently than what was intended. Not in terms of numbers of participants, but in the specific presenting problem."

Cory found the commonality of their language refreshing.

"I chose this guy Horace. He has a record of assault, but is not, in the strict sense, a proper candidate for the group."

She looked up from her notepad. "Why not?"

"The criteria specifically called for men whose impulse control problems resulted in an assault on their wives or girlfriends. To my knowledge, this man never had a significant other."

"But you needed a candidate to fill the slot."

"Yes."

"And he has a record of assault. That doesn't sound like such a terrible error."

"I failed to consider group dynamics." Blum toyed with his planner.

"Go ahead, Barney."

"None of the guys in the group have a backbone. They'll follow the leader. And this guy is a leader. I'm afraid he's dragging them down a path of terror and destruction."

"Are you sure of his plans?"

"Yes. He expects to lead at least one of the men in the group on a raid of the hide-away shelter that houses their women."

A chill raced through her. "That's horrible," she said. She wished they could join forces in pursuit of the man in question. "The address of the shelter is a well-kept secret. How would he know it?"

"That troubles me."

Me too, she thought. No one named Horace had visited her office, unless he was a maintenance worker who could have planted the bug.

"How have you handled it?"

"Personally, I'm guilt-ridden. Professionally, I have a privileged line to the shelter."

She figured he knew Morgan's connection to the place, but it would be out of bounds for her to mention it. Blum was a patient, not an ally.

"I warned them. So far, all is well. An invisible fence—the kind with electric eyes—surrounds the place and they have guard dogs. It's in a remote part of the county and very hard to find, but I'm afraid this man could know someone who worked or lived there at one time. He could have tortured her for the address."

Shivering, Cory rubbed her arms for warmth.

"I've taken some corrective measures. I've notified his probation officer. For the present time, Horace is out of commission. The other guy's probation officer and a detective are keeping a close watch."

"Sounds like you're doing a good job of fixing your mistake."

He nodded. "I've also come here for reassurance about another problem. I think I'm having a mid-life crisis. I'm forty-five years old and married to a fine woman. We have two great kids. I thought I was reasonably content, but with all the young, eager, flirtatious women in my class, I have fantasies."

"Barney, you know that's normal. As long as you don't follow through, you're okay."

"Nevertheless, it's disturbing. Lately, I'm having trouble keeping my mind on my lectures. Sometimes, I have to sit down—if you know what I mean."

The session continued in that vein, and Cory was certain Barney would be an excellent patient. He was intelligent and insightful. Unless something odd occurred, she was sure they'd wrap it up short term.

*　*　*

Alan presented a continual challenge to Cory. Gleefully, he related his sexual exploits perhaps to titillate, but instead he wound up amusing her. Today she would learn how far he would go in his adventures of the flesh.

"Ever been a Peeping Tom?"

"If I had the chance to see a woman disrobe, sure I'd watch, but I wouldn't go out of my way for it."

"When some people feel anxious, sex offers relief. Is that true for you?"

"I'll have to think about it." He rubbed his chin and laughed. "No chance to experience anxiety because of my active sex life."

"Which came first? The chicken or..."

Alan laughed. "I love your double entendre, Doctor Cohen."

"Do you consider the risk of sexually transmitted diseases?"

"Sure. Condoms are mandatory. I've always used them. It's my way of not getting too close. And I don't want to be slapped with a paternity suit."

Cory smiled her approval for his insight and caution.

"Ever fantasize anything strange or unusual?"

"Like what?"

"You tell me."

"Uh… maybe a new position—if I could find one. Let's see. Animals aren't my thing. Nor men. Only women. Often in pairs. And no bondage or rough stuff for this gentle guy. What's left?"

"Secrecy, Alan. It turns you on. Propels your infidelity."

"You've got that wrong, Doctor Cohen. I'm no good at it. My wife always finds out."

"Perhaps that's it. Her willingness to forgive you proves how much she loves you." *Or what a masochist she is.*

"I'm pissed at myself. I shouldn't need proof at the expense of her humiliation. No more!" He punctuated his decision by slapping the armrest. He seemed to slip into deep thought while Cory sat back and waited patiently for Alan's insight to grow.

"Now I get it. My involvement with other women prevents me from getting close to my wife."

"Right. You haven't expressed any emotional connection to your sex partner du jour either."

"Why do I do this?"

"Could be you're afraid to get close because you're afraid of rejection. Even a handsome hunk like you isn't immune to that universal fear."

"I suppose that's why I stay with my wife. No matter what I do, she takes me back. I force her to show how much she cares for me."

"It's time to quit making her prove it," Cory said.

Alan buried his face in his hands and sobbed. Cory resisted the urge to comfort him.

Two hours later, Jolene sailed in, delighting Cory with her sudden insight.

"Bless your heart. I've begun to understand myself. As I look back, I realize my teenage life was hell. I was a fatty. No boy wanted me and I was… oh, my, so intensely jealous of my friend Ruby Mae. She was thin, pretty, and popular with the boys. Many a night I cried myself to sleep while she was out on the town ready to brag about it the next day." Jolene blotted a tear at the corner of her eye. "After I learned to control my diet, I lost weight and the boys swarmed all over me, like bees on a hive. I loved the attention. Mostly to show off for Ruby Mae. I dated every guy who asked me, and I let them have their pleasure with me."

"Did you enjoy it?"

She shrugged. "I did it to make sure they'd come back for more."

Like Alan, her affairs were one-sided. Relating her past, she made no mention of her current lover, Alan.

"I do believe this therapy is working for me."

"Because you're ready and have good insight."

"Bless your heart." Jolene left the office with a radiant smile on her face.

But several hours later, Jolene called, breathless. "Sorry to disturb you, but I've just had a threatening phone call and I don't know what to do."

"Tell me," Cory asked, feeling as though she was in a bad recurrent dream.

"This dreadful man said he'd tell Carlos about my affair unless I give him ten thousand dollars."

The very same sum Carlos had said Jolene had concealed from him.

"I can't imagine who found out," Jolene said. "We've been ever so discreet."

"Have you told the police?"

"Heavens, no! Just when I think we can patch things. Carlos would leave me if he found out."

"One good thing has come from this, Jolene. Now you realize how important he is to you."

"That's why I called you. I don't want to be impulsive," she said softly.

"What are your options?"

"I can pay."

"Blackmail is dangerous, Jolene."

"Oh, I can't believe this is happening." Her voice trembled. "He told me to put the cash in a large envelope tied with a green ribbon."

"An appropriate color. Where and when?"

96

"Day after tomorrow, Thursday, three o'clock at the entrance to the main post office."

"If you comply, he'll probably continue to hound you. Maybe escalate his demands. If you want him stopped, notify the police."

"What if I don't pay, and he tells Carlos?"

"Unless the blackmailer wants revenge, he'd gain nothing, but you could help stop a crime. Carlos knows you betrayed him by hiding money and he hasn't left you."

"But my affair…"

"That doesn't always end a marriage. I can't predict he won't leave, but I doubt it."

"Oh, dear! You're surely right. Here I am, a hard-as-nails- business-woman, but in my personal life, a silly goose. I must stand tall. Thanks for your help. I'm sorry to have interrupted you."

"I'm glad you did," Cory said, wondering if Carlos had set up the blackmailing scheme—melodramatic enough for a TV show.

At the end of the day, Cory and Ann were in the reception room, checking the appointment schedule, when the front door swung open. In pranced Sara, strutting her stuff like a mannequin on a runway.

"I'm sorry, we're closing now," Cory said.

"No. I must see you. It's about Morgan."

Sara shut the consulting door behind her and flashed a satisfied smile. Cory expected her to say, "Gotcha." Noticing the look on Sara's face, Cory felt annoyed at herself. She should have remembered about curiosity and cats instead of letting that woman into the consulting room. "All right, Ms. Jaspers. What about Morgan?"

"First off, you need to know I'm psychic. I dream things that come true."

"You've come here to tell me your dream?"

"Correct. As her friend, or whatever you are to her, I thought you'd want to know. Morgan is in terrible danger."

From the smile on Sara's face when she entered the consulting room, Cory guessed she had made up the dream to spark Cory's interest. "Why come to me? Why don't you go to the police?"

Sara laughed. "They don't believe such things."

"Why do you think I would?"

"Because you trust me."

Surprised at Sara's flawed reasoning, Cory had to put her straight. "I don't know you well enough to trust you."

"If I'm your patient, you will."

"As I've mentioned before, I can refer you to several competent therapists."

"I don't want anyone else but you."

Cory sighed. "There's a fine psychologist, Betty Pepper. Her style is similar to mine." She reached into her desk drawer and handed Betty's card to Sara.

The persistent woman tapped the beige rectangle on her lap. "You're the only one who can help me."

"Why are you so positive about that?"

"I told you, I'm psychic. You're the best for me."

"I'm sorry, but I don't have time. There's nothing more I can do for you." Cory rose and opened the door.

Sara darted to the door, slammed it shut, and leaned against it, blocking the exit.

Cory's pulses throbbed with blood pounding through her veins. "What do you think you're doing?"

"I'm not ready to leave," Sara said, flopping on the couch, her short skirt bunching up to the top of her thighs.

"Then I'll call security and have you removed." Cory lifted the receiver.

"Oh, lighten up and hear me out; then I'll go and you can avoid an incident," Sara said in a commanding tone. "I know you don't like calling attention to yourself."

Cory's ears grew hot. Sara knew too much about her. "You can have five minutes."

"It's not only a dream, but it's real, too. My lover is jealous of Morgan and is out to kill her."

"I don't understand."

"My lover knows Morgan sizzles over me."

Cory felt she was imprisoned in a Grade B movie. Struck with Sara's bizarre tale, she could hardly wait for her to leave. "Your lover sounds paranoid."

"Oh really? Morgan has sent me love notes. My lover read them, became jealous, and has threatened to kill her. I dream about it every night and wake up drenched."

"A threat demands police attention."

"I've tried. They said there's no proof. They think I'm a kook because of all my psychic stuff and they don't want any part of a lovers' quarrel."

"When was the last note you received?"

"I don't know when it was written because I got it on e-mail and I rarely check.

"It's possible someone is playing tricks."

"Tricks?" Sara chuckled. "That's a good one! How'd you guess my night job?"

Cory raised her eyebrows. "You're a prostitute?"

Sara grinned. "I earn more money having sex than you do in your pathetic line of work. Ever have an orgy?" She rolled her tongue across her plump lips.

Cory was revolted by her gesture. Grandma would have called Sara Jaspers, a *tsatske*. A toy. Cory pointed to the wall clock. "You have two minutes left here."

"So soon?"

"This isn't a regular session." She noticed Sara's pupils were dilated. "How often do you smoke pot?"

"A few times a day. I do a line or two also."

"Hasn't anyone in your office noticed?"

"Why should I care if they find out? I don't need the job."

"So why work as a secretary? And if you're happy, why do you want therapy?"

"Good question. When I get crushes and am rebuffed, I fly into a rage. I scream and tear things up. And I despise women who are jealous of me when men want to jump my bones. Sometimes I want to shove their heads in the toilet. My problem is that I love and hate fiercely."

Her self-description fit the diagnosis of borderline personality, a condition difficult to treat. She needed a no-nonsense therapist, rigid in limit-setting, like Betty.

"Also, I get confused when both men and women turn me on. I guess I'm hypersexual or bi."

She hadn't answered the question about why she did secretarial work, but Cory didn't want to prolong the time with her and ushered her out the door. "I hope Doctor Pepper can see you."

Sara tossed the card in her purse. "I'll think about it." She sauntered out, leaving behind a musk scent reminiscent of a cat in heat.

Cory opened the window. She sat at her desk and added notes substantiating Sara's diagnosis:

> Borderline Personality illustrated by sexual escapades, daily drug use, need for excitement, erratic behavior, and over-idealization. Narcissistic features. Prognosis: poor. Recommendation: Referral to Betty Pepper, Ph.D.

Cory was not flattered by Sara's demand to be her patient. Such behavior was typical of borderlines. Their love changed to hate in a flash.

⸗25⸗

Jaime trudged to his car, the last session at the Y fresh on his mind. Several things bothered him that he had to review with Professor Blum.

Tony had picked on Lonnie mercilessly, calling him "pansy", and despite Jaime's intervention, the name had taken hold.

With growing concern for Lonnie, Jaime climbed into the Honda and started the ignition. Thoughts meandering, he started to pull out and was nearly sideswiped by a passing car. He blamed his poor concentration on his work problems. To calm down, he tuned his car radio to a soft rock station and hummed along.

The unusual light traffic allowed Jaime's mind to drift back to the group. He realized that Lonnie had become the whipping boy and he wondered how to handle it.

Jaime had grown less intimidated by the men and he regretted not having been firm with them. He worried that Lonnie would attempt to ambush the shelter to snatch his child to show the group he was a real macho man, but he couldn't do it alone. Would others join him? Was Horace involved?

Horace hadn't returned to the anger management group and no one mentioned his absence. His enrollment had insured the group's existence, but his attendance in it no longer mattered as far as the project was concerned. Nevertheless, Jaime toyed with introducing the subject of Horace's absence and exploring each man's feelings about it.

He considered his motive for doing so—a fishing expedition to catch information about a possible attack on the shelter—could be construed as professionally unethical. What a shame!

He wouldn't let on to anyone in the group that he knew about Horace's plan. If he did, the men would start to distrust each other.

Jaime was unclear how much of group therapy was appropriate in an anger management workshop. Group dynamics played a part, but he wasn't experienced enough to separate out the difference. He needed Blum's direction.

He pulled into student parking and hurried to Blum's office.

Jaime's jaw dropped when he read the note posted on the door:

Dear Students:
I'm sorry I must cancel today's classes due to an emergency.
Barney Blum, Ph.D.

≈26≈

"My nerves are sure frayed, Doctor Cohen," Jolene said softly on the phone. "I called the police about the blackmailer and they sent two detectives over to see me at my office. They advised me to follow his plan."

Cory began to believe her patients' lives mimicked a soap opera.

"When I arrived at the post office, those detectives were already there, pretending to sort mail. We waited almost an hour, but no one came for my package. They set a phone trap, but the blackmailer hasn't called yet."

"You did the right thing, Jolene."

"I can't go on without arousing my husband's suspicion. I have to get it over with and tell him tonight. After that, we'll need a joint session."

They agreed on a mutually convenient time.

After her last patient left, Cory dashed off a few notes. She expected Ben would come by to check the office and she was conflicted about running in to him and was ashamed her feelings for him would show. Tonight, she had a good excuse to avoid him. She'd made a date with Betty to hear about her recent safari. They'd meet at Jake's on Del Mar beach for a sunset dinner.

Heading toward the restaurant, Cory had to wait for a tow truck to get out of her way. Preparation for hauling the disabled vehicle seemed to take forever and she disliked keeping Betty waiting. She drummed her fingers on the steering wheel and decided to make the best of it by gazing out the window at a picture postcard pink and lavender sky. The colors merged into variegated shades of purple as the giant sun slowly slipped into the ocean. Soon the road was clear and she hit the accelerator.

Suddenly, she caught sight of a dark blue car drifting into her lane. Gripping the steering wheel tightly, she swerved to the side of the road just as a skateboard flew into the air.

Cory stepped on the brake. Within seconds, a boy, unscathed, got on his board and rolled away.

She turned her head to glance at the speeding Saab. The glaring red sun blocked her view of the driver, but she made out what looked like MR on the license plate. Now, she was convinced she was being stalked.

A few minutes later, she pulled into the restaurant parking lot and handed the car keys to the valet.

She scanned the crowded room until she spied Betty's copper-colored curls. The most stunning middle-aged woman in the place, Betty sat at table overlooking the ocean, her flawless face glowing in the candlelight.

As they hugged, Cory caught a whiff of her friend's vanilla scent and yearned for a chocolate chip cookie. "Sorry I'm late. A tow truck blocked my way."

"You missed a gorgeous sunset,"

"I caught it, but was too upset to enjoy it."

"Surely not because you're late?"

"No." Through the hum of the diner's voices, Cory shared her terrible news.

"My God!" Betty shrieked. "And I thought I had big problems. Did you call that lieutenant pal of yours?"

"Yes. He recommended a private eye."

Betty's jaw dropped.

"And what are your big problems?" Cory asked.

Betty leaned forward and spoke softly, "The woman who drowned in Coronado was my patient."

Cory shuddered. "That's awful! I'm so sorry." She patted Betty's hand. "Did you know she was suicidal?"

"I'm positive she wasn't. It's a bizarre story. You see, while Terry was in the Navy, she had to keep her sexual orientation private. She never socialized at work."

The server interrupted to take their orders for white Zinfandel and chicken Caesar salad for two.

"Dressing on the side, please," Cory called as the busy server hurried away.

Soon, the woman returned with a basket of hot sourdough bread and two glasses of white wine.

"Terry was a fine, ambitious person," Betty continued, sipping the wine. "She got involved with a woman she met on the Internet. After a brief affair, her lover tried to blackmail her."

Cory felt the blood drain from her face.

"What's wrong, Cory? You look like you've seen a ghost."

"Recently, one of my patients was blackmailed, too."

"For the same reason?"

"Not quite. She didn't recognize the blackmailer's voice. He threatened to tell her husband about her liaison."

"With another woman?"

"No."

"Oh, my! You know I can only handle one subject at a time." She clutched Cory's hand. "Let's finish my case first, and then I'm all ears for yours. As I said, Terry handled the threat well. She told the woman she didn't care if the Navy found out about their relationship because her tour of duty was almost done and she had accepted a civilian job."

"Good for her!" Cory broke off a small piece of bread, and lightly buttered it.

"Yes. Terry felt she'd be better off out of the military. She is—uh—was a computer programmer with excellent performance reviews and her new job was to start next month." Betty's tears rolled down her face, streaking her mascara.

Cory handed her a pack of tissues.

Betty wiped away her tears. "Terry had become reasonably comfortable with her sexuality, not depressed in the least. She'd come to me because she suffered anxiety about her career goals." Betty blotted her cheeks. "We'd agreed my vacation was a good time for a therapy break. We'd planned to tie it up after my return."

"You think she was murdered for revenge?"

Betty nodded. "What can I do? I don't know much about her lover."

"You've probably gone through her chart many times."

"And wracked my brain trying to remember something... anything that could help." She leaned her elbows on the table.

"Okay. Tell me everything about her lover no matter how insignificant."

"Knock-out attractive. Blonde. Probably bi-sexual. Hypersexual. Terry thought the relationship was great until she learned Sara did drugs and liked orgies."

Cory shivered. The profile of Terry's lover was all too familiar. It fit Sara's description to a tee.

"That kind of stuff upset her," Betty continued. "In her way, Terry was straight."

Cory grinned at the double meaning of the word.

"Terry couldn't tolerate Sara's wild lifestyle. She became disenchanted and ended the affair. She had coped well with the disappointment."

Slightly nauseated, Cory slid the wineglass aside. "Have you met Sara?"

"No."

"Well, maybe I have. She sounds like the woman I just referred to you. My Sara's borderline. Provocative. A tri-sexual."

"What?"

"She'll try anything sexual."

"I hope she calls."

"No. She's dangerous."

"You're right. I just realized Terry may have told her about me. Do you think she'd come after me?"

"It's doubtful, but don't take any chances."

"Maybe I should take karate. I'm serious. I need exercise." She patted her hips.

"I'm big on promoting self-defense. Come to the studio with me. Maybe we'll see Ron."

"Really? Have you run into that boychick lately?" Motioning the server, Betty pointed to the empty breadbasket.

"I've avoided it. I'm jogging for exercise."

The server brought the salads and more bread, but Cory had lost her appetite. To keep Betty company, she nibbled on a piece of crust. "I want to hear all about your vacation."

Betty took out a folio of photos of her safari and passed them to Cory.

Cory studied a glossy print and whistled at the close distance between Betty and a lion. "Weren't you scared?"

"No. On the photo that king-of-the-jungle appears closer than he actually was. He didn't gobble me up."

"You haven't touched your dinner," the server said, filling their water glasses. "Anything wrong with it?"

"No. I'm not hungry. Would you please package it for me?"

The woman scooped up the dish and hurried into the kitchen.

Betty polished off her salad and wiped the corners of her mouth with a napkin. She dug into her purse, bracelets jangling, and produced a mirror. "Why didn't you tell me I look a wreck?" She frowned at her reflection.

"You don't. Besides, no one here sees us. We're the invisible over-the-hill women."

"Cory, you've become a cynic. We can still attract men."

Cory studied her glamorous buddy—a Rita Hayworth look-alike. "I've no doubt you always will."

"You sure hit it off with Ron, but he wasn't right for you. Not because he was younger—of that I approve; but because he gave you a hard time."

"True, but now, I have the hots for someone."

Betty raised her eyebrows. "Oh? Who?"

"The private investigator."

"Ooo! What's he like?" Betty leaned forward in anticipation.

"Intelligent, attractive. Oh yes, very attractive." Cory felt her face flush.

"He sure juices up your pheromones." Betty grinned. "My-oh-my! It's a treat to see you so animated."

"A guy I hardly know traipses into a room and I'm ready to run off with him?" Cory shook her head. "So, what do I do? I avoid him. I feel like a kid. It's confusing, Betty. Maybe he's attached. I don't know where to go with this."

"Find out if your detective is available. If he is, make your move."

"But we have a business relationship."

"He's not your client. You're making excuses because you don't want to risk getting hurt. Be brave. Go for it!"

"I hear you. You're the *sexpert* in the romance department." Betty's love affairs were short lived, but she persevered and enjoyed life. Semi-annual therapy tune-ups helped her get over the man-of-the-season.

"Getting back to Terry, the cops will probably find out you were her therapist."

"I'd like to protect her privacy."

"At the expense of letting her murderer go free?"

"Definitely not," she said, over the rim of her wineglass. "It's just that Terry wasn't ready to come out. No one in her family knew she was a lesbian."

"Solving her murder may be all that matters to them."

"If only I could count on it." She paused. "Now, let's talk about your case."

Cory told her about Kevin.

"He sounds confused, but motivated for therapy," Betty decided. "A challenge. If you think he may be dangerous, you should insist that he take a battery of personality tests to substantiate your theory."

"I agree."

The server waltzed by with the check and Cory's dinner packaged in the form of an aluminum swan.

They paid the bill and waited outside for the parking attendant. Betty's car arrived first. She tipped the valet, slid inside, combed her long manicured fingernails through her lustrous hair, and waved goodbye.

As Cory waited, she nervously scanned the area for a Saab, relieved it wasn't there. Finally, the valet brought her BMW and she headed home, making good use of the rear and side view mirrors. All the talk about dangerous patients had made her more vigilant.

Approaching the house, Cory noticed a light on in her bedroom. Certain she had shut off all the lights, she froze.

⸗27⸗

Afraid someone was lurking in her house, she started to punch the emergency number on her cell phone. She stopped, remembering she had set timers on the lights.

Phew! That damn Saab has pushed my weird button, she told herself, stepping into the lighted house. As she fiddled with the security system, a waft of Ravel's Bolero welcomed her. She had set the radio on the timers as well.

Tonight was a night to slip into bed, prop up some pillows, and sip a large mug of triple strength chamomile tea with the latest copy of Ellery Queen Mystery as her companion. She read until her eyes grew weary.

Lost among tall trees laden with twisted vines, she squinted through the branches at the blinding sun, a huge orange ball ablaze in a clear azure sky. The sun, usually a gauge for time and place, offered no help, leaving her stumped and terrified.

Rustling foliage caught her attention. She turned and gasped at the sight of a stalking lion. Quickly, she hid behind a tree and held her breath as he stomped a few yards from her. He came upon a small animal—a strange looking species she couldn't identify—and he chased after it. She watched the agile creature scamper away and escape.

The regal hulk ambled toward her hiding place. In minutes, Cory would be his dinner. Her heart thudded like a herd of bulls. She scrambled up the vines of the tree and held on to a branch, just as the lion raised his head in her direction.

Awakened by her own screams, she shivered and reached for the extra blanket at the foot of the bed. She lay in a fetal position and reviewed the disturbing dream.

Her unconscious had blended ingredients from yesterday such as Betty's lion photo, the stalking Saab, the blinding sun into an anxiety-ridden dream. One of several lately.

Her sleep shattered, she switched on a local radio station to a talk show about the upcoming election. Several callers discussed the merits of the candidates for District Attorney. Morgan Heller was the front runner and her colleague, Jim Solas, her chief rival. The other contender, Judge Crandall Ellis had a slim chance. His notorious poor judgments were legendary—especially the latest fiasco with Rothenberg. *Go figure how he even got on the ballot*, Cory thought. The commentator's voice droned on, lulling her back to sleep.

The sound of tinkling glass, followed by a thud and the wail of the alarm system awakened her. Startled, she turned on the light and bolted out of bed. The glowing green digits on the clock read 4:30. She grabbed her hefty Maglite torch from the bedside drawer for protection.

The phone rang, giving her another jolt. It was Coastal Security asking if there was trouble.

"Yes," she said, pulling on sweats, "Send the sheriff."

Within minutes, she heard cars drive up. She ran to the window and saw two black and whites.

Cory opened the door to the officers. "Something crashed through my window."

"Ma'am, for your protection, wait inside my vehicle," a deputy said, as he and his partner drew their guns and entered the house.

In the back seat, Cory huddled for warmth and wondered how many bad guys had been there before her. Through the car window, she watched pink and gold slowly streak the sky, announcing daybreak—an eerie time to be out. Dew glistened on the grass. She spied a large footprint under the broken window and reasoned the vandal must have stood there when he had hurled something at her window.

About fifteen minutes later, the deputies filed out of the house and one of them beckoned her. She jumped out of the car.

"There wasn't anyone inside your house. This was what broke your window, ma'am," he said, holding a potato-shaped rock in his palm. "See. There's no soil clinging to it. I've looked and can't find any place around here where he could have picked it up. That suggests he brought it with him. Looks like someone wanted to scare you."

"Well, he succeeded." She hugged her arms for warmth and comfort.

"I taped a plastic garbage bag over the broken window. You'd better get a new pane. Fortunately, the splintered glass was confined to the bathtub or else you'd have to contend with a bigger mess. I've collected the major shards and wrapped them in a newspaper from your recycle bin. They're in your trash basket. Please be careful. I've printed 'CAUTION-BROKEN GLASS' on it. I advise you not to walk barefoot until every piece of glass is cleared away."

Some cops were kind and real heroes. "That's very considerate of you, officer. I appreciate it."

"Don't mention it, ma'am. You're lucky that the rock fell on the thick carpet and didn't shatter your tile floor."

"I'm grateful it wasn't a bomb," Cory said. "Before this incident, I reported a threatening phone call made to my office. You're quite right, someone wants to scare me."

"I'll make sure this is investigated."

"Maybe there's more evidence," Cory said, pointing to the patch of grass. "This looks like a recent footprint."

He smiled. "Yes, ma'am. It's mine. The rock was probably tossed from a car window."

"Thanks for your rapid response, and kindness," Cory told him, as they started off.

Amazed that none of her neighbors had come out to check on the commotion, she figured fear or disinterest had immobilized them. Perhaps they were heavy sleepers.

She went back to her bedroom and began to cry. "Why is this happening to me?" After washing her face, she moistened some paper towels and carefully sponged up tiny particles of glass.

When she finished, it was breakfast time. She toasted a bagel, brewed coffee, and collected the newspaper from the driveway. Thumbing through the pages, she read about the debate among the candidates for District Attorney scheduled for Thursday evening. The newspaper mentioned Morgan's inability to attend, due to her family emergency. Maybe it would instill sympathy for her among voters.

At eight o'clock, she phoned a glazier. He promised to install a new windowpane within the hour. Shivering, she checked the thermostat. It registered sixty degrees and she raised it. She hoped the window would be repaired in time for her to keep her first appointment.

True to his word, the man completed the job in forty minutes.

"Have you been busy with an epidemic of broken windows?" Cory asked, writing out the check.

"Not really. Two days ago, a kid accidentally broke mine with a baseball. I'm usually busy with construction. New houses. New windows."

Cory opened the door to let him out and a blast of cold air hit her. She slipped into her black coat and glanced at her reflection in the hall mirror. The coat looked fine over her gray wool dress. She jammed an apple and a plastic container of frozen vegetable soup into her briefcase.

After arming the security system and light timers, she climbed into her car and backed out the garage door. Whoa! Parked across the street with the motor running was a dark blue Saab.

Cory felt as though her stomach dropped ten notches. She craned her neck to make out the driver, but she couldn't. In seconds, she pulled back into the garage and pressed the remote. The door rolled down slowly. Her hands were still gripping the steering wheel when she heard the Saab's engine stop. In the darkened garage, she began to perspire. She was about to call the sheriff when she heard an engine start and race away. Releasing her grip, she blew out a deep breath and dashed into the house.

From the corner of her front window, she peeked at a vacant curb where the Saab had been.

Who was hounding her? Why? Cory couldn't think of anyone so angry with her to go to such lengths. Whoever planted the microphone knew it was no longer receiving. Did he think she figured out who did it and was he now was out to get her? It seemed far-fetched. The dark blue Saab that had drifted into her lane last night could have been an accident. There could be a reasonable explanation for a similar car outside her house and also one across from Joe and Roberta's. To avoid her candidacy as a paranoid patient, she told herself that all of this could be coincidental. Either dark blue Saabs had suddenly become popular or she had been oblivious to them until now.

Harold had said she took coincidences too seriously. But the rock crashing through the window? The threatening call? The microphone? The Saab? There had to be a connection.

⊰28⊱

Glad for a busy Friday, Cory rushed off to the office. It was easier to cope with a patient's woes than her own.

During a break between sessions, she nuked the soup and checked her mail. She leafed through workshop announcements, an invitation to hospital grand rounds, and a check from a managed care company billed six months ago. A handwritten air mail letter with a Greek postage stamp and no return address grabbed her attention. She ripped it open and read the scrawl:

> Dear Dr. Cohen:
> Sorry for not phoning you before my hasty departure. A doctor in Athens called, urging me to come immediately. My father had a stroke. I don't know how long I will be here. Everything's on hold until we get further details regarding his condition.
> Thanks for everything.
> Morgan

Cory flew into Ann's office waving the letter. "Read this," she said, handing it to her.

Ann slid her half-glasses above the tip of her nose and read the page. "I didn't know you needed proof." She looked puzzled.

Cory hadn't shared her suspicions about Morgan with Ann—only that she'd canceled sessions. Cory shrugged and dashed back into her office. She pressed Betty's number on the quick dial and shared the news with an answering machine.

She got lucky when she called Joe and read the note to him. "So, my missing patient really does have a family emergency. She's shelved her career for her father." Cory slipped the letter into Morgan's file.

"One puzzle solved, but there's still the microphone," Joe said.

"That remains a problem."

Ann signaled a patient's arrival. "And as we speak, I've got another one waiting outside. Talk later."

Kevin had turned up a few minutes late. Usually well groomed, he looked like he had just run a marathon. His hair was matted and perspiration stained the neckline of his gray sweats.

Cory waited a few minutes for him to start, but when he didn't, she finally said, "You seem different today. You're very quiet."

"That's because I'm galled." He mopped the sweat from his brow. "Tell me."

"It's women." A throbbing vein on his forehead drew her attention. "Specifically…"

"I can't even get a date. What do they want from a guy? I work-out. I'm presentable."

"Yes, very presentable. It's disappointing."

"You've got that right!" he said through clenched teeth.

"Have you changed your approach?"

"I've avoided insulting anyone. S-sometimes I want to bash their skulls."

"How do you handle your anger?"

After a long pause, he said, "T-take a run. L-like I just did."

"That's a good outlet."

"W-women make the rules," he mumbled, stooping to tighten the laces of his huge athletic shoes.

"That's not true, Kevin. Some women won't let a guy know they're interested. Just like men, they fear rejection."

He rubbed his watery eyes with his fists.

"You do have attractive qualities, Kevin."

"Oh, yeah. Name them. Go ahead and try." He smirked, crossing his arms over his chest.

"You're nice looking, well-groomed, intelligent."

Painful pauses punctuated the session and Cory found it hard to break through his wall of anger and resistance.

"How do you meet women?" she asked.

"Lately, the Internet."

"Do you find out much about them before you make a date?"

"Yeah. It's like an interview."

"Do you choose a particular type of woman?"

"Trim and tall."

"Any hair color preference?"

"I don't care. I prefer a pretty woman. What does that matter?"

"Maybe you're too particular. Or pushy."

"Not so. A lack of education or big bucks aren't barriers. In fact, I like them to know I'm better than they are."

"That's a quick way to get rebuffed." She waited for her statement to sink in, but he didn't respond. "Perhaps this has something to do with your sister."

He glared. "You've made your point."

"Surfing the net baffles me, Kevin, but your skills probably help you."

"What are you talking about?"

"Aren't you a computer consultant?"

He flushed. "Oh, sure. I didn't know what you meant." He grew silent again and toyed with his watch. "I've got to cut this short." He plunked down some folded bills and fled fifteen minutes early.

Five sessions had yielded no progress and Cory doubted he'd return. She chastised herself again for failing to ask him to take a psychological evaluation. Was she afraid of his response?

"Did Kevin make another appointment?" she asked Ann.

"Yes. Same time next week."

By the end of the day, Ann had left the office with the last patient. Cory waited for Ben Fortuna. She washed her face, applied lipstick, and brushed her hair.

He showed up whistling a refrain from "I've Got That Old Feeling."

"Glad you're here," he said. "I was beginning to think you were avoiding me."

In a pretense of shame, she covered her face with her hands, peeking through the spaces between her fingers.

He smiled. His sparkling eyes seemed to probe hers. Dare she imagine he was as interested in her as she was in him? Feeling her face flush, she told him about the broken window and the stalking Saab.

"Quite a scare! I'll trace that vehicle right away." He pulled out a notepad and wrote as he spoke, "Late model, blue with a partial MR."

"Thanks."

"Maybe we'll get lucky when I get more information on the microphone on Monday." He waited as she locked the office, then he walked her to her car. "Ciao," he said. "Have a good weekend."

She had probably mistaken his interest in her.

=29=

Cory awakened giddy from a romantic dream starring Ben. Heck, fantasy wasn't as gratifying as the real thing, but safer. You get to write and star in your own script.

After a quick breakfast, she decided exercising to an aerobics video would dissipate her frustration.

When she finished her workout, she switched on the TV and sat on the floor, stretching. She heard a familiar voice and there was Carlos Sanchez on the screen, reporting on the disgruntled views of motorists navigating the unnerving merge of two heavily trafficked freeways.

"Right! So what can we do about it?" she asked Carlos, who looked quite handsome in a new hairstyle. Or was it the TV makeup? Although she was his therapist, she really didn't know him well. For that matter, how much did patients really reveal?

Cory turned off the TV, showered, and slipped into her terry robe. She sat at the kitchen table, clutching a cup of tea, drawn to a newspaper headline:

D.A. CANDIDATES DEBATE

Frequent interruptions between Judge Crandall Ellis and Prosecutor Jim Solas clouded their respective positions on the three strikes law. Morgan Heller, the third candidate, was unable to attend due to her father's illness.

Jim Solas would most likely win without Morgan in the race. Cory recalled that Morgan had described him as a cooperative colleague with little ambition, who had become a reluctant candidate at the behest of his family.

From what Cory had read about Judge Ellis, he was a simple and religious man, not the type to have a rival abducted. Riffling through the paper, she came across another headline and read on:

ABANDONED BRIEFCASE
DISRUPTS SURGERIES

A briefcase left in the busy waiting room of Dr. Lisa Lopez of Women's Surgical Associates disrupted scheduled surgeries yesterday. No one remembered who had left it there. More than one dozen patients had to be wheeled into the street until the San Diego bomb squad X-rayed the briefcase and forced it open with a high-pressure stream of water. "Nothing but a hoax device set up to look like an explosive," concluded police Sgt. Dennis Murphy.

"This is not the first time my office has been threatened," Dr. Lopez said. "I'd like to stress that Women's Surgical Associates is not an abortion clinic." Authorities vowed strict prosecution once the culprit is apprehended.

Damn macho-creep, Cory thought, reading on:

MAYOR EVANS PROSECUTED FOR WELFARE FRAUD

This article reviewed Nelda Evan's fraudulent activities of ten years ago and strengthened Cory's cynicism of politicians. If Morgan were here, she'd win the election and would be one of the few honest elected officials. From what Cory read in the newspaper, San Diego citizens had responded like betrayed lovers eager to crucify the mayor.

The conspiracy case between the judge and the attorney also brought irate mail expressing discontent with the judicial system.

Thumbing through the local section, she read that a university chancellor had reported an attempted blackmail to the police. Her academic importance and demand for justice created a stir. Cory gave her a thumbs up.

In one day, five women had made newspaper headlines. Three were victims and two were no-goodniks.

Attempted blackmail brought to mind two targets: Jolene and Betty's patient. Were these events related? Terry's death, ruled a suicide, was no longer newsworthy. Cory knew that the passage of time weakened the apprehension of suspects. It was time to speak to Betty.

They made a date to walk on the beach.

Cory enjoyed autumn weather, but seldom experienced it in Southern California apart from a few trees that shed leaves. Flowers, always present, made fall seem more like spring. Here she couldn't gauge the time of the year things had occurred by the weather, and by the clothes she had worn. She checked the outside thermometer. A cool sixty degrees, crisp, and as close to autumn, as she liked. She pulled on green leggings and a red sweatshirt, headed out the door, and walked briskly into town.

Betty, sporting pumpkin color sweats, sat on the bench outside the Del Mar post office.

"Ready for Halloween?" Cory asked.

"Hey, Cory. You look ready for Christmas."

Chuckling, the two friends marched to the shore, skirted the waves, and watched a regiment of sandpipers dig for food.

"Have you done anything about Terry?" Cory asked, above the surf's roar.

"The police haven't contacted me, so I figured they closed the case."

"What? You didn't pursue it?"

"Don't jump to conclusions. I met the head honcho at Homicide division and told him I was positive she didn't kill herself. I described the woman who had tried to blackmail her and suggested they may be able to find her from Terry's computer files."

"That's terrific." Cory patted Betty's shoulder.

"They didn't seem impressed."

"It's too bad they dismiss help from the public, Betty."

"I know." She stopped to scoop up a seashell, rare on San Diego beaches.

"Hmm. I wonder if the other blackmail attempts I've heard about are related."

"You mean the chancellor? Maybe someone has it in for powerful women, Cory."

"Could be the same someone driving a dark blue Saab. I'm convinced he's after me."

Betty stopped jogging and stared at her. "It happened again?"

Cory told her about the broken window.

"Oh, Cory. This is way too much."

"And how! At least my alarm system worked. Of course I had to call Ben."

She smiled. "Just mentioning him, you're aglow."

"It's from jogging. Let's slow down to a walk. Guess I'm over Ron."

"You, my dear friend, are resilient."

"Am I?" She smiled. "Remember my difficult patient? Well, I found out his sister is a prominent judge and he's jealous of her. The other day he came in fuming with anger because women reject him. Why? He's intelligent, presentable and…"

Betty stopped walking. She placed her hands on her hips and frowned. "You suspect him of doing this bad stuff and you're still seeing him? What's wrong with you, Cory? Why not refer him to another therapist? What were the results of the personality tests?"

"Oops! I forgot to do it. I'm glad you reminded me." Cory hung her head.

"Oh my! When your conscience takes a break, I pitch in as a substitute."

"I feel kind of sorry for him, Betty."

She shook her head. "Sometimes you're too tender-hearted for your own good."

"At least I verified his employment."

"Not good enough. He needs that evaluation. Check courthouse records to see if he was ever charged."

"Great idea. I planned to go downtown to check out a new gallery, anyway. Want to come?"

"I'd like to, but I'm fully booked."

Cory knew why. Betty was the best in town. After leaving the beach, they strolled to the market, tossed down fresh-squeezed carrot juice, and parted.

≈31≈

The student lounge buzzed with a sickening rumor that Professor Barney Blum had a heart attack. Shaken, Jaime didn't want to believe it. He ran to the phone and called Blum's house.

Jaime was greatly relieved when Doctor Blum answered.

"No heart attack, Jaime. I appreciate your concern. I had pain in my chest, and at my age, it must be taken seriously. Fortunately, the tests are all normal and I'm fine. Thanks for calling."

Jaime didn't think his favorite professor sounded fine. Perhaps he had some other trouble.

A few hours later, he learned he could trust his intuition.

Someone in the administration office leaked a rumor that an undergraduate student threatened to sue Professor Blum for sexual harassment. Inflamed, Jaime and his classmates agreed to submit a petition in support of Blum citing his emphasis on political correctness in his lectures. The majority of student signatures would be those of women.

But first, Jaime, at the request of his friends, had to check out the rumor with Professor Blum.

Again, he called and explained his purpose. This time he learned the rumor was true; the accusation, obviously false.

"Please tell the students that I'm pleased to accept their support. You can imagine how upsetting this is. It's best for me to think about something else for a while. If you have time now, let's go over your notes on the anger management workshop."

Blum validated Jaime's concern about group dynamics and supported his rationale for a discussion about Horace's absence. Blum agreed it was against the rules to discuss an absent member; however, he was free to explore each member's feelings about anyone dropping out.

After the long conversation, Jaime felt confident he had the tools to handle Lonnie's situation. If he found out any additional information about a projected ambush, he would report it to Blum immediately.

⸙32⸙

On Monday, after her art gallery visit, Cory hoofed two miles to the courthouse. Stress etched on their faces, plaintiffs, defendants, and attorneys crowded the hallways. Cory threaded her way to the Records department.

She keyed in several spellings of Kevin's name and identifying data, and found no listing of any charges in San Diego. She checked Alan Olsen and Carlos Sanchez and got the same results. This could mean that they hadn't committed an offense in this jurisdiction, or weren't apprehended, or were innocent.

Cory cruised back in early afternoon traffic, singing along with Errol Gardner's piano rendition of "Teach Me Tonight". She had a lot to learn from Ben about investigative tools. Who was she kidding? She wanted to learn about him.

Ben was due to check her office and she was in a hurry to catch up with him. The speedometer read seventy until she reached the merge of the 805 and 5 freeways where traffic stalled. She played a Tito Puente cassette, drumming her fingers on the steering wheel to the Latin beat of *Mambo Gozon*. Since the relationship with Ron had ended, she had stopped her drumming regimen. The high spot in her week had been jamming with Ron and other musicians. To avoid him, she had eliminated her other passions: percussion classes and karate. Now she began to feel the stirring of a healing process.

Traffic started moving at a good clip and, finally, she made it to the office.

"Fortuna just left here and asked me to give you this." Ann handed Cory a slip of paper.

Cory unfolded the note and read:

Investigation of building personnel and microphone continues.

Tell you about Saab over dinner? Call me.

She tucked the message in her pocket.

"Good news?" Ann smiled.

"Sort of." Cory nodded, closed her office door, and phoned Ben. He picked up the call on the first ring, leaving her no time to mask the thrill of dining with him. "Can you make it for dinner tonight?" he asked.

"Sure. Where and when?"

"Up to you. You're my only client at the present."

Strictly business, she guessed. "Doesn't your wife expect you for dinner?"

"No."

What did that mean? "Oh, she knows you're on a case."

"No. I'm divorced."

"Sorry for being presumptuous. The dining room's quiet at L'Auberge." They agreed to meet at seven-thirty.

Cory and Ann waited twenty minutes for a new patient booked for the last session of the day, but he didn't show.

"Maybe he got cold feet," Cory said.

"I think it was a prank because when I called the number he gave me, it was disconnected," Ann said. "What a waste of time."

"I made the best of it." She had used the time to imagine her evening with Ben.

They left the office together and Cory headed home.

She showered, spritzed on a light herbal perfume, and wiggled into gray wool slacks, then slipped into a red silk shirt and a black jacket. For a change, she dolled up with cosmetics and scrutinized her reflection. Too sexy, too obvious. She blotted the lipstick and exchanged the red shirt for a black one.

The sedate Del Mar L'Auberge was comfortably furnished with soft carpeting, large stuffed armchairs, and just the right amount of lighting. Ample space between tables created ease for private conversations.

As soon as Cory spotted Ben perusing the menu in the corner, she got that-old-feeling.

He pulled out a chair for her. To Cory's surprise, he wore gray wool slacks and a black shirt and jacket, too, but he had on a white silk tie.

"A coincidence, I assure you," he said, pointing to his duds. He poured Chianti from the bottle on the table. Puccini's Tosca wafted from the sound system. Ben's duds and the ambiance were perfect for a gangster movie.

Patty, her favorite server, took the order for angel hair pasta with sun-dried tomatoes. "Pleased to see you, again," she said.

Cory smiled. "Pleased to see you, too."

From frequent dinners there, Cory knew men found Patty attractive, but Ben didn't give her a glance. In Cory's head, she heard the tune, "I Only Have Eyes For You."

"What did you find out about the Saab?"

"None registered in California with MR on the tag."

Fortuna could have written that on his note, but he had chosen dinner with her.

In a few minutes, Patty delivered their crisp salads.

"Almost certain that's what I saw," she said.

"There is one close—MB." He dipped his bread in olive oil. "Belongs to Marilyn Browne."

"Who is she?"

"An eighty-year-old retired physician and the sole driver. Her car hasn't been serviced lately."

The pasta arrived reeking with garlic and basil. Cory twirled it on her fork; sorry she'd ordered an aromatic dish—the Italian method of birth control.

"Maybe you'll get a better look, next time."

"So you agree, someone is stalking me."

"I never doubted you. Any idea who or why? A jealous ex-husband, lover, or a patient?"

"My ex-husband left here a long time ago. I don't know anyone angry with me."

"No one nuts about you?"

"Not that I've noticed."

"Well, maybe you should look a little harder." His eyes scanned her face.

She grew flushed.

"This isn't just a business meeting, Cory. I had quite a reaction when we met. It's been a long time since anyone gave me such vibes. I can't stop thinking about you."

If this was a line, he hooked her. "I'm glad to hear it," she said, swallowing hard.

"I want to know all about you." His baritone voice delighted her.

"Okay, you tell me first."

"I'm a fifty-year-old man who gets off on puzzles and can't tolerate idleness."

Cory stared at him. He could have said he was in his early forties and she would have believed him. His powerful physique and warm dark eyes melted her.

"Here's my life in capsule form: At twenty-one, I married a woman who hated my work. Maybe my guts too. Anyway, she wanted me to study law. Pushed hard. If it weren't for the kids, I'd have left. Twenty-five years later, she did." He wiped the corners of his mouth with a napkin. "Two months after that, she moved in with the lawyer of her dreams. Despite our family discord, my kids turned out terrific, to my credit. I spent more time with them than their mother did. They live on the East Coast, but we stay close."

"No women in your life."

"I've had a few dates, but nothing serious. Now tell me about yourself."

"I'm only a few years younger than you. I was married long enough to have two wonderful kids. They're young adults now. Away at school. My husband was a tyrant who flew into rages with no obvious provocation. I kept thinking he'd change. Doesn't say much for my judgment, huh? It took therapy to get me out of that situation." She took a deep breath. "After our divorce, he abandoned the kids."

"Your ex was rejected, so he took it out on his children? What an irresponsible, selfish guy!" Ben filled her wineglass. And her heart.

"In spite of him, they turned out great." Her eyes welled with tears of tenderness for Rachel and Noah.

"Any man in your life?"

"Not until last year. He was much younger. It didn't work out and now I'm over it."

"I see. I thought it best you know my feelings, Cory."

"I'm glad, because the feeling is mutual. I hope it won't get in the way of our work."

He smiled. "Makes it more pleasurable."

"Oh, yes."

After pasta, the server brought small cups of lemon sorbet. Cory was grateful for a breath freshener.

When they finished dining, Cory expected him to say, "Your place or mine?" But he didn't. He walked her to her car and kissed her forehead, the way her grandfather used to do.

"I'll call tomorrow," he said.

She shrugged her shoulders, wondering what was wrong with him.

⸗33⸗

The following day at work, Cory stared into the drawn face of Barney Blum. The dark circles under his eyes and the sad expression around his mouth gave him a scant resemblance to the attractive, self-assured man she had last seen.

"I've survived a narrow escape into a deep, dark hole of professional oblivion."

"Tell me about it."

"It's a common tale. Young female student senses her professor's attraction to her and tempts him with a request for an appointment to discuss a class problem. He agrees. She enters his office, closes the door, and practically falls into his lap. Despite his desire for her, he resists her seduction. She reports him for sexual harassment and attempts to cut a deal."

"What kind of deal?"

"She threatened me. Said if I didn't have sex with her, she would proceed with litigation."

"You're attractive, Barney, but for her to go to such lengths…"

"I know. Who would believe it? I think she'd planned to place me in an incriminating pose, and without my knowledge, someone would take photos."

"Why do you suppose she wanted to hurt you?"

"I don't think she cared about what would happen to me. She just wanted money. After my attorney had her investigated, he quickly disposed of the matter. You see, Darlene had tried the same bit on another professor in Oregon. Poor man was incapable of sex. To prevail, he was forced to disclose his medical condition."

"How is your wife coping?"

"With compassion and love."

Cory smiled. "You deserve each other."

"Thanks, Cory. It's no wonder I had heart palpitations."

"Have you seen a cardiologist?"

"Yes. Everything checked out fine. Probably anxiety. I was anxious about a possible assault on the shelter, and, then, this."

"Nothing about a raid in the news."

"As far as I know, the plot has dissolved. Horace is in jail. His buddy's girlfriend took their baby and skipped town."

Cory smiled her relief. "So what do you want to work on?"

"I'd like to sublimate my sexual fantasies with a little red Porsche."

At the close of her session with Barney Blum, Cory wanted to pop outside her office and catch a peek at the sign on her door. Under her name, she expected someone had added: "Sex spoken here."

Jolene and Carlos Sanchez followed Cory into the consulting room. The couple headed for the couch, sat down, and held hands. Their display of affection appeared phony. "We're planning a vacation in Hawaii. A second honeymoon." Jolene rubbed noses with Carlos. "We've patched things up. Haven't we, sugar?" She poked him gently in the ribs.

"Sounds like a great idea," Cory said.

Jolene turned to Carlos. "Sweetie pie, you know my infatuation wasn't serious."

"I blame myself. I've taken Jolene for granted and spent my energy on work."

"Why sugar, like you, I'm busy as a chigger at a picnic, but I stop for sex."

Carlos grimaced. "I don't want to hear about your exploits."

"That's not what I was referring to. Oh, what's the use, maybe we can't fix it, after all." Jolene scooted to the corner of the couch.

The buzzer rang, startling them.

"Sorry. This must be urgent." Cory snatched the receiver.

"The sheriff just called," Ann said, breathlessly. "Your house alarm went off. He wants you to meet him there right now."

"I'm on my way!" She grabbed her purse. "I'm sorry to dash, but I have an emergency. We'll continue this as soon as possible. Marriages take time to repair. I think you can work this out. I'll call after I take care of the emergency. You won't be charged for this or your next appointment."

"Don't worry about your fee," Carlos said. "Hope all's well."

Cory raced home with visions of her belongings tossed about the house and everything topsy-turvy. Biting her lip, she made a mental inventory of her art objects, Grandma's irreplaceable jewelry, and collectible phonograph records.

A black and white car sat in her driveway. The deputy, a handsome dark-skinned man with green eyes stepped out. "Please remain in your vehicle while I check your house. May I have the keys, ma'am?"

Cory obeyed. Looking out of the car window, she noticed the side door to her garage was open. Tools, an old bike, and obsolete files were stored in there.

A few minutes later, the officer came out. "We've had a few false alarms today, ma'am. That happens when the wind is wild. It whips at doors, setting off alarms. The house appears undisturbed."

"Thank goodness." She pointed to the garage. "I think someone broke in through the side door."

"Stay put. I'll check." He opened the patio gate, turned, and nodded his head. "Doctor Cohen, the locks on your file cabinets were broken and ransacked. Come here."

Her ears burned at the spectacle of yet another violation. The contents of eight file drawers were spread helter-skelter on the floor. "Who? Why?" she cried.

"The intruder probably was looking for drugs. He pegged you for a medical doctor."

"Several times I've noticed someone in a Saab following me. The other day, when I opened the garage door, there he was again, parked across the street. He must have noticed my file cabinets."

"Have you reported this?"

"Oh, yes. I've made statements about several scary incidents."

"I'll refer this one to our detectives. In the meantime, don't touch anything in the garage. They'll dust for prints."

"How soon? I have to go back to work."

"Ma'am, I'll get on it now. Please wait for the technicians to finish here before repairing the door."

"Yes. Thank you."

The officer took off and Cory entered the house. Her hands trembled as she phoned Ben. She told him what had happened and gave him directions to her house. Next she phoned Ann. "I'll be back in two hours. Please book an appointment for the Sanchezs as soon as possible."

"Was anything taken?" Ann asked.

"I can't tell yet. My old files were vandalized."

"What were they looking for?"

"I don't know."

At eleven in the morning, Cory sat in the den, drinking brandy, and listening to a tape of Chet Baker crooning, "I Wish I Knew." Eyes closed, she waited for the detectives.

Fifteen minutes later, Ben showed up, sporting jeans, a sweatshirt, and a tool kit, followed by crime-scene technicians who dusted the door and the file cabinet for prints. They were about to monkey around with the scattered papers when Cory realized the futility. "Officer, this looks like an overwhelming job. There's more than a hundred fingerprints here of former patients from the year one."

"We're not interested in every folder, ma'am. Judging from the yellow condition of these papers, the old prints would be long gone. We're looking for freshly done prints. You see, a suspect, naturally nervous, would leave marks that are bright and easily developed. Just point out the folders that were in the front of each drawer because it's likely he'd pull them out first."

Cory knelt on the floor using the eraser tip of a pencil to sort through the folders. Fortunately, the file drawers were divided alphabetically. She handed the technician eight folders she believed to be the first in each drawer. He proceeded to dust them.

"Hey, look over here," he said to another tech. "See these small smudges? They're from a leather glove."

"Right. I found the same marks on the file cabinets." He shook his head.

"Sorry, ma'am, but we're not able to get any usable prints."

"Because the vandal wore leather gloves?"

"Afraid, so," he said, nodding.

"Thanks anyway. If you were able to arrest the S.O.B., I'd like to force him to organize this mess."

The officers headed out while she scooped up the fading papers and tossed them in the drawers.

Ben examined the door. "Plenty sturdy. We'll need a new lock. A double-bolt. Where's the nearest hardware store?"

"I'll take you."

"Okay. Time for lunch, after?"

"Great."

Within a short time, he had installed the lock and handed Cory the key.

"There's something about a man fixing stuff that comforts me. And I'm supposed to be a feminist?" She shook her head.

He smiled and they trooped to The Sayonara Sushi Bar.

The server, clad in a peach satin kimono, ushered them to a quiet booth and filled their cups with green tea. Ben ordered steamed dumplings and Cory her usual inverted California rolls. The chef nodded to her from behind the counter and she waved to him.

"Here's an update, Cory: nothing to incriminate the building personnel. The owner of the company that cleaned your couch retired." Ben sipped from the steaming cup. "The microphone is too small to get a good fingerprint and appears to be government property, but serial numbers are usually etched into it. The FBI tried to get the number by X-raying, but it was scratched out by a professional."

"Intriguing."

"It could belong to the CIA. The agency conspires with private companies to provide a cover for agents. Agents never talk about their real work, not even to their therapists."

"I understand the need for government security, but the work we do is part of who we are."

"Right. It'd be better if all relationships were open and honest." Ben nodded.

The look in his eye and his words were like a magnet drawing her closer to him. Her hand inched across the table toward him, the moment interrupted by the server dropping off their lunch and chopsticks. With tiny steps, the petite woman shuffled to another table.

"It may be impossible for me to figure out who could be an agent, but you agreed to show me how to investigate a suspect. How about it?"

"Verify employment. Check criminal record. Check credit."

Cory gulped the hot tea. "I've done two out of the three. I don't know how to do a credit check."

"If you have an account with a credit reporting company, you supply the names and social security numbers." He scribbled on a page from his notepad and handed it to her. "Here. Use my account number. When I receive the report, I'll hand it over to you unopened."

"Thanks."

"How many suspects have you?"

"Three or four." She dipped the cucumber rolls into wasabi.

"Here. Try my steamed dumplings, Cory. They're outstanding." Adept with chopsticks, he grasped a dumpling and popped it into her mouth.

Warmed by his familiarity, she yearned for him and the look in his eye told her he knew it. Although he had spoken candidly about his interest in her, he did nothing about it. Was the ball in her court?

When they finished lunch and parted, Cory returned to her office. Although she had eaten well, she felt emptiness.

She turned her attention to the credit search.

⚡34⚡

At six in the cold, gray, foggy Thursday morning, Cory set out for her usual run. Visibility was poor and she barely made out the landmarks. She considered turning back, but the fog started to lift and the shape of trees began to take form. She trekked along the edge of the street next to the deserted golf course, curious about what she would learn from the credit report. She had begun to feel more like a detective than a psychologist, with less confidence in her new role.

When she reached the intersection, from the corner of her eye, she spied a dark blue car speeding down the hill behind her. Her heart slammed against her chest. Rounding the corner, she leaped off the pavement onto the grass and dodged behind a tree. Before she could get completely out of the way, the Saab swerved on the damp road and struck the tree. Cory fell to the ground.

Tires screeching, the car backed up and raced away. Trembling, awash in perspiration, she rolled on the grass. Her pulses throbbed so hard she felt the vibration in her ears. Though stunned, she managed to glimpse the letters MP on the license plate as the car sped down the street.

Afraid of fractures, she lay on the ground, hoping someone would come to her rescue. After a few minutes, she realized she'd better put a move on before the stalker returned to finish her off!

Slowly she stood. A pain crept down her leg. She leaned against the tree. Slapped by waves of nausea, she breathed deeply. The left side of her body stung and her pants were torn and bloody. She longed for the safety of home, where she would call the police. Could she make the quarter-mile trek home without incident?

She must use every bit of strength and not panic. On shaky legs, she hobbled to the corner to cross the street. Dizzy, she grabbed on to the STOP sign for support. A driver in a red Ford slid to a California stop, ignored her, and sped off.

The street was empty of life. No joggers or walkers, except for Cory limping along.

Suddenly a noisy flock of crows shattered the silence. "Caw-caw," the large black birds called, swooping down on to the tree branches. Cory slowly dragged herself home and called 911.

A few minutes later, she heard a pounding on the door. A heavy-set redheaded officer, his biceps bulging through his tan shirtsleeves stood in the hallway where he pulled out a little notebook to take her statement.

"I'm getting to be a habit with you guys. Someone driving a Saab has been stalking me… the same car that tried to hit me this morning."

"About how fast was it going, ma'am?"

"I don't know. It struck the tree. Maybe after you examine the area, you'll know more."

"Yes," he said, busily scribbling her statement.

"Two vandalism incidents… my files ransacked… a rock through my window." She stopped rambling and took a deep breath. "And now, this. What next?"

The officer looked up from his notepad and stared at her. "Do you need an ambulance, ma'am?"

"No. Thanks anyway. What I really need is for you to catch this guy."

"Did you get the license number?"

"It happened so quickly I couldn't get a good look, but I made out the letters M and P. At least I think it was a P."

"Are you sure he was after you? The car could have skidded on the damp pavement."

"That car was definitely aimed right at me!"

"Yes, ma'am. I understand, but with no witnesses and only a fragment of a license number… we'll do what we can."

"Listen. I'm sorry, but I must insist on a patrol of this neighborhood. It's obvious that I'm in danger. There should be an APB for a dark blue Saab with those letters on the license. And what about the skid marks? I want an immediate investigation of the scene."

"We do a routine patrol here, but I'll check with my superior. We'll probably send a volunteer contingent. As for the skids, I'll call for the techs now."

After she thanked him and he went on his way, she phoned Ben and, in a shaky voice, told him what had happened.

"Are you hurt?"

"Nothing broken."

"Listen. Call Lewis to make sure the scene isn't compromised. I'm on my way over. We'll check the skid marks. They could be dried up by now or erased by traffic. Then I'll take you to the doctor."

Cory shivered. "The motorist could have killed me before speeding away. Instead, he took a serious swipe at me. Did he want to kill me or terrify me?"

"Take it easy, Cory. I'll be there soon."

Soaked with perspiration she felt chilled. She filled the bath with warm water, climbed into the tub, and gently washed. Stepping out slowly, she wriggled into a terry robe.

A soft rain had sprinkled the windowpane. Would the tire tracks be dissolved?

Cory stood in front of the mirror and examined her body. A wide area of raw flesh covered her left side resulting from her fall onto the gravely ground. She applied Neosporin and felt a cool, soothing effect. She ran her hands down her legs and felt her bones. Nothing appeared fractured. Her knee was red, but not swollen. The palm of her hand was red and tingling. She slipped into a loose purple velour pants outfit and a pair of loafers, and tied her hair back with a purple satin bow. Sickened by the pale reflection in the mirror, she restored some color with a dab of lipstick and blush. In a few days, the bruises would match her costume. In a few days, she could be…

The doorbell chimed, interrupting her frightening thoughts.

Through the peephole, she saw Ben and opened the door.

"Poor Cory." He gently hugged her. "Did you reach George?"

"I left a message on his pager."

"Are you up to showing me where it happened? I'll take photos, then off to the doctor we go."

"But the rain…"

"Let's hurry!"

They drove to the crime scene in Ben's white Mustang. "No sawhorses. They haven't been here yet." He parked the car, jumped out, snapped some photos, and hopped back in.

"Were the tire prints preserved?" she asked.

"Barely."

"That tree saved my life." She turned to gaze at it. "I ran behind it when the car came at me."

"Now, you're a bona fide tree-hugger."

She smiled and gave him the address of the orthopedist.

After the doctor examined her and took X-rays, he assured her that she had no fractures. She hobbled into the waiting room and told Ben.

"I'm glad to hear it. We've had quite a scare, Cory." She liked the way he said, "we."

He wrapped his arm around her as they walked to his Mustang. "Listen. I'd like you to rent a car and I don't want you to stay in your house. Can you stay with a friend for a while?"

She wondered why he hadn't volunteered his place. Was it a mess? Did he have a roommate? A lover? Why hadn't he offered to stay with her? She told herself to concentrate on safety not romance. "I'm sure I can find a safe place."

"Good. I'll take you home and wait while you make arrangements and then I'll bring the film to the photo lab."

"No. Just drop me off. I can manage."

"I'd rather be there with you," he said.

"Thanks, but you have to take the film to the photo lab. I'll hurry."

"Call me as soon as you've made all the arrangements."

⚡35⚡

After Ben dropped her off, Cory sat on her bed, exhausted and ready for a good cry. She gathered her thoughts and considered who to stay with. Joe and Roberta and their fortress came to mind. She picked up the phone.

"Hi Joe! It's Cory. I have a favor to ask. I'm in trouble. Someone's tried to run me over."

"What? Where are you? Are you hurt?"

"Just bruised and scared. I'm afraid to be alone for now." She told him about the vandalism.

"Oh, my God. Come stay at the guest cottage. We'd love to have you," Roberta said, apparently from an extension phone.

"I appreciate this a whole lot."

"Shall I pick you up?" Joe asked.

"No thanks. I'll rent a car."

"Have dinner here," Roberta invited. "When shall we expect you?"

"Thanks anyway. I don't want you to wait. I'll eat out."

"We're staying in tonight, so come whenever."

"Thanks, you're a life-saver." Her words could very well be true.

She made arrangements to lease a late model, ubiquitous car, settling on a bronze Buick touted as having a great sound system. While waiting for the delivery, she called George Lewis. This time with success.

"Hi, Doc. Sorry haven't had time to reach you. How's it going?"
Cory explained.

"Geez! I'm glad Ben's on this. We're stretched today. The techs were probably busy elsewhere."

"Ben suggested I rent a car and stay at a friend's."

"Not a bad idea, you know. What'll you do about your office?"

"I'll use my friend's in Pill Hill."

"Thank God for friends, huh?"

"Yourself included. Have there been similar complaints to mine?"

"Yeah, Doc. A few. All from women big shots. None hurt, but damn scared. A broken window here, a blackmail there."

"What about a stalking Saab?"

"Nope, but I'm writing it down. Any chance you can make it to karate tonight. You're probably too bruised to work out, but we're having an exhibition at seven. And don't worry, Ron hasn't been there for a while."

"I'd like that. Maybe we can go for a bite after."

"That'd be nice, Doc."

After they signed off, she grabbed a handful of her favorite classical music, R&B, and jazz CDs, stashed them in a tote bag with the trusty Maglite, and shook her head in amazement at her priorities.

Dragging her travel-worn suitcase from her closet, she opened it up on her bed. She tossed toiletries and underwear into plastic sacks and neatly folded her clothes and apparel into the luggage. Confident that she was prepared, she struggled to close the suitcase, but couldn't. What had she done to be forced out of her house? With the weight of her body, she sat on top of the suitcase, forcing it to shut.

She activated the timers, notified Coastal Security, and left a message for Ben of her expected whereabouts.

As she carried the last of the houseplants into the garden, the bell rang. The car rental agent waited while she gazed around the house as though taking a last lingering look at a lover. Finally, she grabbed her stuff and locked up.

After dropping the agent off and signing the papers, she hurried off in the leased Buick to her afternoon sessions.

At the office, she crammed her current files into her briefcase and wrote directions to Joe's office, then stepped out to talk with Ann.

Ann looked up from her textbook. "What's wrong? You don't look so hot."

"I've got a big problem. Someone in a dark blue Saab is after me."

Ann grimaced. "Oh boy! That's scary."

"I'll stay with Joe and Roberta for a while and use Joe's office. Until this is settled, I'm sorry, but I'll have to give you some time off."

"Of course. I understand. Don't worry about me. I need time for a school project, anyway. But you be careful, Cory. Karate isn't enough to keep you safe." She paused. "Maybe you should take a vacation. Get far away from here. Tahiti. Israel."

"Thanks for your suggestion, Ann, but I don't want to disrupt my practice."

"What are you saying, Cory? It'll be worse for everyone if you get hurt."

"It's better for me to work, Ann. Please phone all my patients, except those coming in today. Tell them there's a construction problem here and give these directions to my temporary office." Cory handed Ann a sheet of paper. "Do me a favor. Please print enough of these to hand out to today's patients as they leave."

"Sure. What about the mail?"

"I'll ask the post office to hold my home and office mail."

"I'll pick up the request cards for you when I go to lunch. Shall I have the phone service transfer calls to Joe's?"

"Yes. Thanks," Cory said, just as Jolene and Carlos Sanchez stepped into the office.

Although the couple had managed to patch up their problem after the last session, Cory figured it was a mere Band-Aid. Carlos said he was simmering with hurt and anger and needed time to get over Jolene's betrayal. Jolene said he was making too much of her affair. Cory expected him to boil over, but his mask-like face didn't change expression. When she called it to his attention, he stormed out, leaving Jolene red-faced and Cory, surprised.

She thought about people who expressed themselves openly when they chose, but clammed up when their feelings were probed. She didn't like to stereotype anyone, but couldn't help thinking he was a typical reporter.

"Carlos is hard to know. Erratic. Maybe this marriage can't be fixed," Jolene said, resting her chin in her hands.

"It takes time to rebuild trust, Jolene. How do you think he felt when you said he made a big deal of your affair?"

"But it was only a fling. No biggie. Really."

"Betrayal is a big deal. It's a matter of trust."

"Well, I sure enough don't want to spend the rest of my life trying to earn it back."

"How much time is it worth to you?" Cory asked.

"I'm impatient."

"Do you want to work on that, Jolene?"

"Bless your heart. Of course, I do."

"By the way, did that blackmailer bother you again?"

"He sure didn't, but I thought of it when I read about that university woman."

"So did I."

The doorknob swiveled and Carlos returned. "I'm sorry I ran out. It was childish, but I can't stand it when you discount me, Jolene."

"Sugar, I'm truly sorry. Sometimes I'm plumb insensitive." She held her arms out to him and they embraced.

Carlos may have accepted Jolene's apology, but Cory sensed his restraint. "Have you ever felt like getting even with Jolene?"

His face reddened. "I've never cheated on her."

"That isn't the only way to even the score," Cory said softly.

Jolene raised her eyebrows. "I'm beginning to catch your drift, Cory."

"I d-don't understand." Carlos tapped his fingers on his knee.

"Blackmail, sweetie. Ten thousand dollars worth. The amount I squirreled away from you."

Carlos buried his face in his hands. "Oh, Jolene. It was impulsive. I felt ridiculous afterwards. I'm really sorry."

Jolene inched closer to him. "I suppose I deserved it. I'm truly sorry, too. We'll make a new start. No more games. Plain ole' honesty from now on."

At the end of the session, the couple left the office holding hands.

When the last patients of the day had left the consulting room, Cory locked the door, just as Ann put down a watering can. "Gave the plants an extra dose and I'll drop by to make nice periodically, okay?"

"You think of everything, Ann. I'll miss you. I don't know how soon things will return to normal." She hugged Ann.

"Normal is a joke around here, Cory, and I'll miss you, too. I knew I'd leave here when I finished school, but who'd have expected this? You'll keep in touch?"

"Of course." Cory snapped the door shut. Their heels clicked as they stepped downstairs to the garage. Ann approached her Camry, but tonight, Cory couldn't locate her BMW.

"Damn! Someone stole my car."

"No! Who'd want to steal an old car like that when there are new ones here? Maybe you forgot where you parked."

"I forgot all right. I forgot I rented a Buick to avoid the stalker."

Ann shook her head. "Be careful, Cory, and don't forget to call."

Cory hated saying goodbye to Ann and the office. She especially hated her role as a victim and the loss of her freedom.

Night had fallen when she pulled the Buick into the last remaining space at the Karate Institute parking lot. In the foyer, she kicked off her shoes abandoning them amongst several other pairs. The exhibition was in full swing. She spotted George sitting on the floor leaning against the wall. Aching with every step, Cory's bruises seared as she limped toward the lieutenant.

"Have you had X-rays?" he asked, a look of concern on his face.

"Yes. No fractures. Just a mess of flesh wounds."

"They'll look worse before they get better." He nodded, knowingly. "Too bad it happened to you. We've sent a volunteer patrol to your neighborhood. They'll report anything suspicious."

"Thanks. When are you doing your thing here?"

"You missed it."

"Damn! I am sorry. Just closed-up shop."

"Hey, it's okay, Doc."

"How'd it go?"

Grinning, he reached behind his back and held up a trophy.

"Congratulations. Let's celebrate. Where shall I take you for dinner?"

"Aw, you don't have to do that, Doc."

"Are you rejecting my offer, Lieutenant?"

"Okay. I like the Asian stir-fry at Pacifica Del Mar."

"Me, too."

"Hey, catch this kid coming on." He pointed to a scrawny boy of about twelve. "He's ready for his black-belt." The kid's agile movements, his swift kicks and stunning blocks, so much like a dancer's, sparked Cory's interest in karate again. She felt comfortable in the familiar dojo, but wondered how she'd feel if she ran into Ron. No one had ever aroused her as he had. Perhaps Ben could.

The exhibition over, George dashed into the dressing room.

In fifteen minutes, he came out, looking clean and fresh. "Okay, Doc. Let's dine."

They slipped into their shoes and stepped outside. A faint sliver of moon hung above like a surrealistic painting. "I'll drive." Cory strolled toward her rental.

"I'm not used to that, you know."

"Get with the times, George."

Soon they were in the restaurant, seated at a table facing the ocean, but the sky was overcast and the whitecaps barely visible. They turned

139

their heads to examine the new display of colorful sea creature sculptures on the wall. "Quite lovely, don't you think?" Cory asked.

"They're okay. Are you satisfied with Ben's work?" George asked.

"Yes. He's a real asset. I don't know how I'd manage this mess without him."

"I can tell a good guy, you know. Too bad the skid mark photos aren't usable."

She frowned. "That's a shame."

After the server took their order and brought bread, they dug into the basket. "Any more scuttlebutt about the mayor?" Cory asked.

George shook his head.

"The judge's conspiracy?"

"You see a connection, Doc?"

She nodded. "Three prominent women humiliated. Maybe I'm a paranoid feminist."

"The mayor and the judge deserved it, you know. Someone suspected the mayor of welfare fraud, sniffed it out, and reported it to the media."

He kept silent as the server dropped off their steaming dishes of stir-fry. "The conspiracy between the judge and lawyer came from an anonymous tip. There's a lot of evidence. It's all in the newspaper."

"How about the woman from the university?"

"A different kind of case. First she reported the attempted blackmail to the campus police, you know. The professor believes she was targeted because she's a woman."

"And what do you think?" Cory asked.

He shrugged. "There are plenty of women haters around, you know."

"Any suspects?"

"You know I can't say."

"Sorry. Consider this, George. Whoever planted a microphone in my office could have planted others in places where important women shed secrets."

George signaled the server who was rushing around the room with a steaming coffeepot. The waiter poured the dark brew into their cups and they thanked him.

"Look, Doc," George said over the rim of his cup. "We've examined financial records of the mayor, the judge, and the lawyer. No payments to psychotherapists."

"They're too smart to use insurance or personal checks and risk confidentiality. It's possible they paid cash. Without arousing their suspicion, can you find out if they were in therapy?"

"Interesting. I'll think about that."

"If they were, the defense would claim diminished capacity."

"Hey, Doc. You're a cynic, you know. Any idea who planted the bug?"

"I have a few suspects."

"What are you doing about it?"

"I've checked criminal records and verified employment. All clean, but I'm waiting for credit reports." She took a sip of coffee. "No prints on the bug."

"I'm not surprised. You know, you could change your occupation and become a private eye." He winked.

"Seriously, George. I really can imagine opening a detective agency. Ann and I would run it. We'd need someone like you and Ben to supervise. For a fee, of course. What do you think?" Cory asked, putting down her fork.

"Can't you tell I was kidding, Doc?"

"Sure, but it's an interesting idea. Ann has the smarts and is considering another career. We work well together."

"It's not as interesting as you imagine, you know. Long, boring stakeouts. Often a waste of time. Nowadays, people check stuff out on computers and the need for the gumshoe has lessened. You might not have enough clients to pay the rent." George said.

"Not much different in psychology these days, George. My career dreams are shattered."

After dinner, Cory dropped off George at his car and cruised to Joe and Roberta's. Trying not to focus on her precarious position, she flicked on the radio and heard a commentary on the upcoming election.

Cory shook her head. She just couldn't get away from her problems.

≈36≈

No Saab trailed her as it had the last time when the gate to the Klein's manse opened for her. Probably because she was driving a rental car, thanks to Ben's bright idea.

Fog had set in, but the drive was lit up and lights were ablaze in the main house. She parked in the long driveway and limped to the front door.

Before she could ring the bell, Roberta opened the door. "Hey, glad you're in one piece," Roberta said, her arms spread for a hug.

Cory stepped over the threshold and wrapped her arms around her friend. "Thanks for letting me stay here."

"It's my pleasure. There's a message from Ben. He said you could call him anytime," Roberta said. "There's a phone in the cottage. Have you had dinner?" Roberta's solicitude reminded Cory of Grandma and she loved it.

"Yes. With my friend, the lieutenant."

"Oh?"

"We're just friends, Ro."

"Too bad. After Ron, another romance could be the ticket."

"So now we have two psychologists in the Klein family," Cory joked.

Roberta smiled. "Someone else will come along."

"I wish that was my only concern, Ro."

"I know. At least you won't have to worry about safety here or in Joe's office. He's upstairs, sleeping. His first patient is at eleven, but he said he can leave early for you."

"We won't have to. I'm sorry if I made you wait up for me, Ro."

"You didn't. I wanted to finish reading this T. Jefferson Parker mystery, "Laguna Heat". A real page turner." She jangled keys in her skirt pocket and slipped her arm through Cory's. "The guest cottage is ready."

They stepped out of the house. Roberta whistled and called for Otto Rank. Sigmund Freud came running toward them, wagging his tail, followed by Otto.

"I swear these dogs rival like siblings." Roberta rubbed Siggie's head.

Otto nudged his nose under Cory's hand forcing her to pet him. She opened the car door and the dogs jumped in. Roberta sat in the passenger seat and pointed the way to Cory's temporary digs.

Cory parked in the short driveway of the guesthouse and pulled out her suitcase. Roberta unlocked the front door and flipped on the recessed ceiling lights. Colorful throw rugs warmed the hardwood floors.

"The design on the largest one reminds me of a Paul Klee painting, Ro."

"That's right." Roberta smiled.

A chocolate brown leather couch and an Eames chair provided comfortable seating in the living room. Assorted plants and a small ficus tree in a wicker basket gave the cottage a lived-in look. A TV, VCR, and stereo lined a wall. "Ro, you think of everything." Cory fingered through the compact disc collection of classical music.

Roberta crooked her finger for Cory to follow her into the bedroom suite, furnished straight out of a Laura Ashley catalogue, purple and peach dominating. Cory laid her suitcase on the bed. A Jacuzzi, a washer, dryer, and an efficiency kitchen added to the livability of the cottage. "If you want a nosh, help yourself." Roberta opened the refrigerator stacked with goodies. "Breakfast will be ready between eight and nine."

"A hostess with a perfect hideaway! I could stay here for a long time, but I pray to God it won't be necessary." Cory shuddered.

"Here's the key." Roberta placed it on the table. "And here's the remote control for the gate. Keep it with you."

"You can't imagine how much this means to me."

"Stop or I'll cry," Roberta protested as she left the cottage.

It was nearly ten o'clock when Cory filled the Jacuzzi and called Ben.

A sleepy voice answered, "Uh-hullo."

"Ben?"

He cleared his throat. "Yes, Cory. You okay?"

"Sorry I awakened you."

"It's fine." He yawned. "You interrupted my dream of you."

"Oh!" She felt flushed, imagining what he might have dreamed, and flashed on Morgan's response to her lewd call. Thank God, the phone didn't have a video monitor!

"Cory, are you still there?"

"Huh? Oh, yes." She told him about her evening, the worthless tire track photo, and her new digs.

"Your new crib sounds better than mine," he said, arousing her curiosity about his living style. "Listen. The credit report came. Where and when shall I bring it?"

"Great! Will tomorrow night at six be okay?"

"Now would be better, but I guess we're both too beat."

Certain that he was teasing her, she gave him Joe's office address in a business-like manner.

Cory awakened in an unfamiliar room. Momentarily confused, she lay in bed a few moments before she established she was at Joe and Roberta's cottage. She slid off the bed, wincing, and examined her deep purple wounds. She pulled on a pair of baggy sweats for a short walk before breakfast.

Outside the cottage door, Otto greeted her with his tail wagging and a lick on her hand. They had bonded. He joined her on a trek around the compound, and like a gentleman, waited outside the cottage while she showered and dressed.

He walked by her side to the main house. When Siggie ran toward them, the dogs chased each other across the lawn and through the trees.

The scent of coffee greeted Cory at the breakfast table where Joe and Roberta had their heads buried in newspapers. Roberta looked up. "You look well-rested. How do you feel?"

"Much better, thanks to you. I hope I haven't kept you waiting for breakfast." Roberta had said between eight and nine and it was now ten minutes after eight. "I'd love to take you out."

"Thanks anyway, pal," Joe said. "Look in the oven."

Cory flipped open the oven door and saw a big platter of pancakes oozing with cherries and walnuts. "Should I take it out?"

Roberta nodded.

"This looks like a lot of work. When did you whip this up, Ro?"

"I was up early and *potchked* around the kitchen a little."

"A little, huh?" Cory gave her a grateful smile, passed the platter, and poured coffee. "Sure beats my usual boring breakfast," she said after a few bites. "Mmm. Luscious."

"Regard this as a vacation, Cory. Indulging a bit won't hurt you. You've been through a lot. Give in to temptation once in a while," Joe advised.

"Has anyone told you, you're an excellent shrink?" Cory took another helping of pancakes. "My first session is at noon, so we're in sync."

"Let's leave here around ten, so I'll have time to show you around the office and you can get settled."

Despite Roberta's objections, Cory insisted on cleaning up the breakfast preparations. She scrubbed the fry pan until it shone, which was the least she could do. They hung out in the kitchen over coffee and newspapers until it was time to leave.

Cory followed Joe onto the freeway and relaxed her frequent checks of the car's mirrors. She shoved in a Cal Tjader disc and hummed along to "For All We Know", emphasizing "we will never meet again", wishing it would apply to the Saab.

Joe's office was located in Hillcrest, a neighborhood where many Victorian houses had been converted into doctor's offices, hence the Pill Hill designation.

The interior of the restored building looked as though Roberta had duplicated Sigmund Freud's quarters. She slid her shoed feet over the silky Persian carpets, and noticed the glistening hardwood floors and the warm glow from the stained glass windows. A paisley velvet couch invited her to sink into it. How would her patients respond to the old-world ambiance appropriate to Joe's psychoanalytic practice, but different from her own contemporary office setting?

"You know analysts don't have receptionists," Joe explained. "At appointed hours, patients press the doorbell and are buzzed in. When no one is expected, a timer disables the bell." He handed her the key and a card with the security system code and instructions. "Old buildings like this have thick walls," he said.

"Good sound barrier," she added.

"Patients help themselves." He pointed to an ornate silver urn, a selection of tea bags and porcelain china neatly arranged on a mahogany serving table. Classical music wafted at a low volume through a speaker. Viennese waltzes would have been too much.

"I'll leave you to settle in your office," he told her, sliding open a wood-paneled door to a cozy room. "When you aren't here, I'll use the space for my paperwork."

The two velvet armchairs with tapestry covered footstools, a love seat, and a small coffee table would do nicely. In the corner was a massive antique chestnut desk that held several incongruities to the Victorian period: a computer, printer, copier, halogen lamp, and a small telephone—a reminder to check her phone messages. And so she did.

"This is Liz Heller," said an agitated, but familiar voice of Morgan's sister. "Sorry to bother you, but I've left messages for Morgan and haven't heard from her. I'm worried sick. Please call me."

Her words chilled Cory. She slipped her arms into her black wool cardigan and collapsed in the chair to call Ben and relate the message. He said he'd be right over.

Cory reached into her briefcase and pulled out Morgan's questionnaire and the letter from Greece. She compared the two handwriting samples and chided herself for not being suspicious. The salutation read "Dear Dr. Cohen," but Morgan had always called her Cory. Although she wasn't a graphologist, Cory now saw obvious differences between Morgan's earlier writing and the letter.

"How could I be so stupid!" she shouted. Waving the two documents, she rushed through Joe's open door.

He looked up from his writing pad. "What's wrong?"

She explained.

"Don't get bent out of shape, Cory." He wrapped his arm around her shoulder. "Leave it to your private detective. I'm glad you've hired him."

"Me, too." In more ways than he imagined.

The bell rang and Joe opened the door. Two people stood outside: Ben and a middle-age woman. Joe escorted the patient to his office, while Cory ushered Ben into hers.

"Fancy digs," he said, looking around. "So, let's see what you've got."

She motioned him to sit at the desk. Flicking on the lamp, she slid the two handwriting samples to him. Ben whipped out a magnifying glass and compared them. "An obvious forgery. Now it's time to notify the authorities."

"Can this be kept from the media, Ben?"

"We could ask Lewis to keep it quiet, but I doubt he can. Once a report is made, it's open season for reporters and this is a headliner."

"Morgan could be dead."

"Don't jump to conclusions."

"The only reason I see for someone wanting her out of the way is the election," she decided. "But murder?"

"Once the police find out about this, they'll check out the two guys she's running against, assuming they haven't already done so. You can be sure they'll be very thorough. This is a high profile case."

"Yes. It'd be nice if we were all treated equally."

"Dream on, Cory. Listen. Someone wants you to think Morgan is in Athens with her father so you won't be suspicious of her absence and blow a whistle. I doubt they'd do that if they'd killed her. I bet she'll be returned after the election." Was Ben trying to mollify her?

"You think they'd take a chance and release her when she could identify her captors?"

"Hired hands can vanish. Listen, everyone with whom she's had contact will be investigated. This means you, too."

"I'll have to give the police the microphone."

"Not much good to them. They'll recognize it as a government issue. The FBI knows it's connected to a case I'm working, and the partial prints are yours and George's."

"I have to call Morgan's sister, but I can't locate her. When she phoned me, she was so alarmed that she forgot to leave a phone number."

"Write down pertinent information on her and I'll call you later with her number."

"How will you get it?"

"When we have time, I'll show you on the computer."

Leafing through her appointment book, Cory found the notation she had made of Liz's old address and phone number taken from her old file. She jotted it on a slip of paper. "She had been a professor at Columbia, the English Department. She's also a published author."

"And I'll need info on Morgan."

Cory photocopied the top sheet of her confidential questionnaire and handed it to Ben.

"Here is the credit report." He handed her an envelope. "I'll call you later." He dashed out.

She paced the small office. Where was Morgan? Was she alive?

The police would connect Morgan's disappearance to the microphone and Cory wouldn't be able to protect her patients from an investigation. None of her other patients mentioned any threats apart from Jolene, and Carlos admitted he'd rigged the blackmail scheme on her.

Last year, Cory had fingered managed care for leaks that endangered lives. Now psychotherapists considered her the confidentiality watchdog and she expected them to inform her of threats to patients, but so far, no one had come forward. She concluded the microphone must have been targeted specifically for Morgan.

Cory had a graver problem: how long would she remain safe from the stalker? She couldn't remain Joe and Roberta's guest indefinitely.

The bell signaled her patient was at the door and Cory eagerly went for it, grateful to work. Other people's problems saved her from fretting about her own.

While waiting for Joe to finish his fifty-minute hour, she documented her sessions. A few minutes before six, he strolled in. "So how'd you like it here?"

"I found myself probing deeper and adding more uh-huh's."

"Is that good?"

"It's different. It's what you analysts do."

"How did your patients take the change?"

"Most said they liked this place. I'm not sure how they felt about my technique."

"It's an interesting experiment, Cory. Change can be beneficial. Was that your detective who came in with my patient?"

"Yes."

"I picked up the vibes between you two."

"Ah-hah."

"Well, Cory?"

She shrugged. "I'm scared of getting hurt."

"When you have feelings for someone, it renders you vulnerable. It's the price of admission to pleasure." He stuffed a thick folder into his briefcase. "Roberta's expecting us for dinner at eight or so. Would you like to invite him?"

"I don't know how he'll feel about a date."

"Ask him, then you'll know."

"Okay. I will. She phoned and left a message, inviting Ben to dinner at the Klein's.

After arriving at the compound, she showered, wrapped herself with a towel, and plopped on the couch. She ripped open the envelope containing the credit report.

Kevin Jason Holloway had one Visa card issued two years ago with a credit limit of two thousand dollars. She figured some rich folks chose low limits to protect against card loss or temptation. The report stated he was delinquent in payments and had an outstanding balance of six hundred dollars since last year, including late charges. Now that was odd.

A ninety-five hundred-dollar auto loan with several late payments last year was listed, but now current. Amazing what the threat of repossession will do to the automobile dependent. The absence of a mortgage loan sparked her suspicion and she wondered if the report was for the same Kevin Holloway who had a large trust and owned his own home. Perhaps he had recently paid off the mortgage. He had told her it was his only debt. And what about his auto loan and his Visa balance? She thumbed through the files in her briefcase and checked the social security number. It matched the one on the credit report.

Cory would not be able to find the name on the deed to Kevin's house until next week because the County Recorder was closed for a long weekend. She opened her appointment book. Noticing Kevin's name in his usual time slot, she rested her head in her hands. She couldn't confront him with information gleaned from her unorthodox method, even though she suspected him of using a false ID and of stalking her. Better cancel his appointment until she had more information.

Cory phoned Ann.

"How are you holding up?" Ann asked.

"Not bad. And you?"

"All is well, but I do worry about you, Cory. You've got a spooky situation."

"I have lots of support. Don't worry. Keep plugging away at school and let's hope it pays off. I have a favor to ask, Ann."

"Sure."

"Please call Kevin. Tell him we must cancel his appointment because of office repairs and we'll let him know when we're back in service."

"You think he's the stalker?"

Cory sighed. "I hope not. It's strange, Ann, but I kind of like him."

"I can't imagine why. He's a cold fish, but then again, I don't know him like you do."

"I'm not sure I do know him, Ann." They chatted a few more minutes and then Cory had to dress for dinner. Just as she stepped into her shoes, the phone rang.

"Hi, Cory. I have Liz Heller's phone number. Ready?"

"Yes."

Ben recited the number.

"Are you coming to dinner?"

"I'm on the way."

It was nearly eleven o'clock in New York, but she had to call Liz even if she awakened her. A man answered.

"I'm sorry to disturb you, but I'm returning Liz's call about her sister."

"Oh, sure. She's expecting you." He sounded wide-awake.

"Cory?" Liz asked.

"Yes," she began and spared few details.

"I'm leaving as soon as I can for San Diego," Liz replied.

"I can imagine how you feel, but right now, it won't do any good—unless you think it would make you feel better."

"Maybe I can figure out a way to help."

"You already have helped. If you hadn't called me, I'd have believed she was in Greece taking care of your father. The detectives just got the case, Liz. Let's give them a little time." Cory regretted she was a stickler for rules and had tried to preserve Morgan's privacy at the expense of her safety. What they said about hindsight was true.

"I can't wait, Cory. I'll tie up some loose ends here and leave when I have a reservation. I'll call you when I get there."

Cory gave Liz the numbers where she could be reached.

Attacked by a compulsion to find Morgan, Cory didn't know where to begin. She'd be sailing in darkness, with no moon or stars, no compass to guide her.

She sighed. She did a lot of sighing these days. There was one saving grace to her situation—Ben. Standing in front of the mirror, she noticed her face was flushed just thinking about him. She smiled at her reflection, spritzed on a lavender scent, and off she went to the main house.

Roberta and Joe were splendid hosts and Ben fit right in. After dinner, they played scrabble and nibbled on popcorn until midnight.

Cory offered to show Ben the cottage, but he said he was tired. She wondered why he avoided being alone with her. Couldn't he notice her desire for him? She forced herself to think about something else as she prepared for bed.

Kevin's credit report gnawed at her. Confident that it was possible to solve a problem by sleeping on it, Cory closed her eyes.

⩽38⩾

At seven the next morning, the answering service had Detective Kipinski on the line. Cory caught her breath, recalling his name from the card under Morgan's door. He was the man assigned to check on Morgan, when she hadn't shown up for Rothenberg's arraignment.

They made an appointment for nine o'clock at Joe and Roberta's. Now that it was clear Morgan was not with her father, would the police find her?

Cory scrambled through her morning ritual and strolled to the main house with Otto, her new buddy.

The scent of freshly baked bread and coffee permeated the kitchen. Her friends sat at the table, reading *The New York Times* and munching from a large platter of cheese and fruit. They looked up at her. "Well, good morning," Roberta said.

"Same to you." Cory refilled their cups. "That was fun last night. What do you think of Ben?"

"Seems like your type, Cory, but I'm surprised he didn't go back with you to the cottage." Roberta's eyebrows raised.

"Probably afraid he couldn't keep up with you," Joe observed.

She blushed over the rim of the coffee cup. "I hope you don't mind, but I expect a police detective here at nine. He'll interview me in the cottage. When we're done, I'll go pick up my mail at the Del Mar post office. Is it okay to take Otto along? He can run loose on Dog Beach."

"Of course," Roberta said.

"Anyone wants to join us?"

"I have to go the gallery this morning and won't be back until evening. How about you, Joe?" Roberta asked, yawning.

"No. I have to get some papers ready for the accountant."

"Rejection. That's all I get lately," Cory kidded.

"I bet not for long," Joe said.

"I hope not."

After breakfast, Cory cleared the table and put the dishes in the dishwasher. The bell chimed and on the security video, she saw a pale car at the gate. "Sergeant Kipinski," the driver identified himself and Joe pressed a button.

Cory scooted out to meet the detective, reaching the curve of the circular driveway just as he parked his beige-colored Chevrolet. "Good morning," he said, stepping out of his car. "I'm Sergeant Stanley Kipinski." He flashed a badge. "I'm here to see Doctor Cohen." The man's resemblance to Kevin Holloway startled her. He too, appeared to be in his late thirties with similar sandy-colored hair, light eyes, and complexion and had a medium build.

"Hi. I'm Cory Cohen. Mind taking a stroll? I'm staying at the little house up ahead until this case is settled."

"That's fine."

He traipsed alongside her with Otto chaperoning.

"The dog looks well-trained," the detective remarked.

Cory nodded. When they entered the cottage, Otto ran off. The detective parked himself on the leather couch.

"Care for coffee or a cold drink?" she asked.

"No thanks."

Cory seated herself on the Eames chair with Morgan's folder on her lap. She explained about patient confidentiality and told him she was afraid of the consequences to her practice should her patients learn of the microphone. She told him about the threatening call she'd had and the vandalism. Kipiniski's expression was that of non-committal as he wrote it all down.

At the end of the twenty-minute meeting, he handed Cory his card and urged her to call if anything turned up. She walked him to his car and as he drove off, Otto raced toward her.

Cory strapped on her fanny pack and tossed Otto's leash on the backseat of the Buick. "Let's go for a ride, my man."

In he jumped.

On Saturday, the post office closed at noon. Keeping to the speed limit, Cory made it in ample time to collect a carton of mail. She tossed the box in the trunk, planning to go through the letters in the evening. What a way to spend Saturday night when there was a guy she ached to be with.

Otto and Cory started to gallop to the shore, but her leg was too sore to keep up the pace. At Dog Beach, she unleashed her new friend and watched him leap into the surf to catch a ball thrown to another dog. The dog chased him and they ran around in circles. People laughed at the spectacle. Finally, Otto released the ball at Cory's feet.

"Sit," she said sternly as she threw the ball to the other dog. Otto remained still.

"That's my dog," a woman said, pointing to Otto's playmate. "His name's Shnook. Befitting, yes?"

"Got the name, play the game." Cory smiled. "My dog's Otto Rank."

"Otto. Hmm. Perfect for a German Shepherd," the woman replied. "But why Rank?"

"His master is a psychoanalyst like Doctor Otto Rank."

The woman gave Cory a puzzled look.

After Otto frolicked for a quarter of an hour, they left Dog Beach and walked the deserted shore. Sun warmed her back and the ocean breeze fanned her face. Filling her lungs with salt air, she felt at peace. Safe.

Approaching footsteps slapping the wet sand startled her. Otto growled. She froze and gripped his leash. The footsteps came closer. Otto barked and tugged at the leash. Cory turned to see a huge figure of a man a few feet from her. He wore a hooded oversized blue sweat suit and dark wraparound sunglasses. The hood was tightly fastened, concealing much of his face. His appearance on the isolated portion of the beach sent a chilling ripple down her spine.

"Oh, my God!" she cried, as the man came closer. Afraid he was about to attack her, she dropped Otto's leash, turned around ready to spring in a well-rehearsed karate move. The dog ran toward the man. The man turned in the opposite direction and sprinted toward the beach exit. Otto chased him. Cory started to run after them, but her knee hurt and she couldn't continue. She listened for barking, but heard nothing. Otto had disappeared, leaving her with an icy chill and that familiar emptiness.

Cory dragged herself to the lifeguard station and explained her predicament.

"Are you sure the guy was after you?"

She kneeled down and held her head in her hands. "I don't know. I'm not sure. But after all that's happening... and now my friend's dog!"

"What are you talking about? What's happened?"

"This is how I repay their hospitality, by losing their pet!" Cory sniffled.

"Lady, that dog sensed your fear. He was trying to save you. He'll come back. He's probably done a number on the poor guy. Why don't you sit here and wait. Lighten up. The dog will return."

Cory closed her eyes, held back the tears and waited.

Soon she felt a wet tongue on her hand. She opened her eyes and there was Otto!

She hugged him, examined his mouth for blood or fabric, but found neither. The huge runner had probably scaled a fence and ran off the beach. Cory was about to limp away with Otto, when another lifeguard approached.

"That's your dog?" he asked gruffly.

"Yes."

"Please don't bring him here, again. He just chased my buddy. Scared the hell out of him."

"Well, your friend scared me. Looked like he was after me. And the way he was dressed? Why cover up his face like that?"

"Didn't it occur to you that maybe he's allergic to the sun, or just had plastic surgery?"

"Or needs plastic surgery," the other lifeguard said, laughing.

"Or doesn't want to be recognized," Cory objected. "Listen, maybe I overreacted. I've had a lot of scares lately."

"Do you want to talk about it?" His question surprised her. Maybe he was a psychology student or a therapy patient.

"The other day, I was nearly killed by a hit and run. My house was vandalized, and someone's stalking me."

The lifeguards stared at each other. Cory figured they thought she was paranoid. She had to redeem herself. "Look. I know this sounds incredible, but please believe me. I'm a psychologist." She hoped her profession would cloak her in normalcy. "My office is in this neighborhood. When I saw this guy behind me... well, he looked ominous. I figured he was going to attack me. I tensed. Just as you've suggested, Otto must have sensed my fear. This dog is gentle. Please tell your friend, I'm sorry."

"Sure. You know, lady, the dog can't protect you everywhere."

"I know. And thanks for your concern. I've taken precautions. Only those I trust know where I am."

The lifeguard frowned. "Maybe you're trusting the wrong people."

⤠39⤠

The lifeguard's words of caution haunted Cory on her drive to the cottage. She began to doubt her judgment. She ticked off the names of all the current patients she had rejected as suspects and found no reason to change her mind. When she thought of her friends and associates, she came up empty.

She fumbled with the stubborn door lock of the cottage. "Oh, man, I'm really in trouble," she muttered, realizing she had tried her own house key. "Force of habit," she told Otto. Finally, she opened the door and found a sheet of pink notepaper on the floor.

Rachel called. Ben called. See you later. R.

A pang of guilt struck her. "A *shanda*, a shame on you! A parent too self-involved to call your kids. You haven't spoken to Rachel since her party, or to Noah," It was Grandma's haunting voice, the voice of Cory's conscience scolding her. She imagined Grandma shaking her finger at her.

Noah couldn't be reached because he was on a photo retreat. But Rachel? "Okay, Grandma, here goes." She called Rachel's number and waited for her sweet voice.

"Mom, what's going on? I called home and was transferred to Roberta."

"I'm sorry, Rachel. I should have phoned you. I'm involved in a big problem here that I couldn't tell you about before."

"What? Don't tell me you're playing detective again."

"Not quite. Listen, are you busy this weekend? I'd like to visit."

"I'm sure I can get tickets for the ballet on Sunday. Want to go?" Rachel asked.

"Of course. I'll leave here in about an hour."

"Cool." She imagined the look of delight in her daughter's eyes.

Cory packed a change of her tired but laundered clothes and left a message for Joe and Roberta on their voice mail. She was halfway out the door when the phone rang.

"Hi, Cory. Ben here. Tried to reach you this morning. You okay?"

"Not exactly." She related the beach incident.

"Listen. You had reasons to be scared—nothing to be ashamed of."

"You don't know what went through my mind. I began to doubt everyone. Too much has happened and I hate having to look over my shoulder. I need a rest from it. I'm going away for the weekend."

"I'd hoped you'd go sailing with me today."

"I wish you had called me earlier."

"Maybe I'm afraid of getting involved with you, Cory."

"Why? Damn! You know I'm attracted to you."

"I'm not interested in just a roll in the hay."

"Neither am I. Look, I appreciate your honesty. Let's talk about this in person. I'll call when I get back."

"I'm not even going to ask where you're going."

"You just did. To Rachel's. My daughter."

"That's a relief."

This was a guy worth getting to know, she hoped.

⇐40⇒

Cory smiled, thinking of Rachel and how independent she had become living away from home. Not long ago, she had been a child and now she was a young woman. Rachel's ability to make good decisions comforted Cory.

She exited the freeway at Dana Point and headed up the Coast Highway. The salty ocean breeze brought back memories of carefree childhood summers at Brighton Beach, where she built sandcastles and played in the waves. She could almost taste Grandma's chicken salad sandwiches and Mrs. Stahl's potato knishes with a hint of onion, crisp on the outside and delectably moist inside. Sunday summers under stripped beach umbrellas where women clicked Mah Jong tiles and men played pinochle and kibitzed. A safe place. A safe time.

Suddenly the wind picked up and howled through the car windows. Palm trees swooned and particles of debris sprinkled the windshield. Cory gripped the steering wheel tightly to steady the rented Buick which didn't handle the road as well as her old BMW. She held her breath. How she longed for the old car and for her own house. She missed Ann and the office, too. "Damn!" she cursed her pursuer.

In a few minutes, the wind had died down. Cory exhaled and began to enjoy the view of the ocean dotted with pleasure craft. Getting away from stalking Saabs was the ticket to lift her mood.

She arrived at her daughter's off-campus apartment and a table set for lunch.

"It's pay-back time," Rachel said. "My turn to make a meal for you."

"Marinated tofu and veggies on pita bread, fresh fruit, and mineral water? You know how to whet my appetite, sweetie."

"Most people would scrunch up their faces at this," Rachel said. "But you compliment me. I'm ready for more."

"Okay. You have a knack for solving difficult problems. You'd make a good psychologist."

"No, Mom. Like you, I cry easily. I'm afraid other people's pain will become mine."

"That's empathy, Rachel."

"But I'm too sensitive."

"True," Cory nodded. "Could be you'd prefer a career that defines you as separate from me."

"Stop being my psychologist, Mom."

"Okay. I have confidence in you, Rachel. You'll find your own path."

"Now, tell me why you're staying at the Kleins'."

Cory wanted to shield her daughter from worry, but Rachel persisted.

"Come on, Mom. You've preached that a load is lighter when shared."

"I was wrong, sweetie. An emotional load can't be divided."

"I should know what's going on with my own mother."

Cory took a deep breath and told all. Even about Ben.

"Cool! You're ready for romance. And I'm glad you're staying at the Kleins. They live in a veritable fortress."

"The microphone..."

"It must be tied to the woman's disappearance. Now I understand why you didn't want my friend, the electronics maven, to know what you do for a living. You showed him the microphone. Now that it's gone, why would that patient you suspect continue in therapy?"

"To avert suspicion."

"Hmm. He may have no use for the bug now, doesn't know it's gone. Maybe he's decided to stay in therapy because you're a good shrink."

Cory rolled her eyes. "Or he knows the bug isn't transmitting. Maybe he's playing sick games with me."

"What does the detective think?"

"About my therapy skills?"

"Quit joking, Mom."

"I haven't told him."

Rachel scowled. "You've hired a private investigator, but won't use his skill because of this almighty confidentiality privilege. Give it a rest, Mom. He should investigate all your suspects. What would other psychologists in your situation do?"

"A good question for an ethics committee."

"Well?" Rachel asked.

"I don't want to draw attention to my predicament."

"Frame it as hypothetical."

"It could create suspicion."

"Stubborn people are difficult, Mom." She shook her head. "Do me a favor. Discuss it with Joe, or Betty or Harold. You trust them."

"I have. Now let's have some fun."

"Fine. We'll take the ferry over to Balboa Island." Rachel locked her apartment door behind them.

Cory welcomed the change of scene—the quaint waterfront cottages, art galleries, and boutiques reminiscent of Cape Cod. Away from office problems, she felt like her old self. "Any idea about a gift for the Kleins?" she asked Rachel.

"Let's try this art gallery." Rachel pointed across the street.

They selected a small statue of Aphrodite signed by a local sculptor. The gallery gift-wrapped it in a stunning mosaic paper tied with a lilac bow. On a purple card, Rachel wrote in gold ink:

> To Roberta and Joe,
> We are grateful for your wonderful hospitality and friendship.
> Love and Kisses,
> Cory, Rachel, and Noah.

Cory felt blessed to have a daughter who had become her dearest friend.

On Sunday afternoon, Rachel and Cory decked themselves out for the ballet.

Cory drove them to the Orange County Performing Arts Center and pulled into a space near the entrance. They strolled into the bright hall and stopped for a beverage before the performance.

"To preserve the carpet, only mineral water or white wine is sold here," Rachel said, as several stunningly-clad patrons came into view. "Kinetic sculpture." She grinned.

After the performance, they hurried toward the Buick. "I can't believe it," Cory shrieked, approaching the car.

"Mom, what's wrong?"

Cory's finger shook as she pointed to a dark blue Saab parked next to the Buick. "That's the car that's been tailing me."

"How can it be? Let's check the license tag."

"WBW three-nine-two-five," Cory recited as Rachel jotted it down.

"Let's tell security," Rachel said. They rushed inside and located the manager.

"There's an All Points Bulletin for a car that tried to run me down in San Diego. I think it's here," Cory shouted. "Please hurry and call security and the cops before that car leaves."

"Calm yourself, Madam. I'll find security." He staggered away.

Rachel picked up the phone, hit 911, and explained the situation.

Fifteen minutes later, the Orange County officers arrived, but when they looked for the Saab, it was gone. "I'll need the license number of the car that tried to run you over," the deputy said.

Cory squeezed her eyes shut for a moment. "I have it at home."

"It may not be the same car," he said.

"You're right, officer, but blue Saabs in southern California are rare."

"Here's the license number of the car that was parked next to us." Rachel handed him the slip of paper.

"Please tell me who owns that car," Cory requested.

"Sorry, ma'am. I can't."

"I need to know if he's the stalker," she muttered.

"Come on, Mom. Let's go. I'll drive. You're too upset."

Trembling, Cory handed Rachel the keys.

"Mom, it's unlikely that someone followed you to my house, hung around all weekend, and then tailed us to the ballet. We'd have noticed. You're so freaked out that you suspected that Saab to be the same one that hit you. You wished it was the same car so the problem would end."

"Maybe so."

"I made a copy of the license number. Let's call the San Diego police and give them the number of that car. Okay, Mom? And please stay here with me."

"Thanks, sweetie, but I'm safe at the Kleins'. I don't want to run away. I need to settle this. It's getting late now and I've got to go back," Cory said as they reached the apartment.

Rachel slid out of the car and repeated her plea for Cory to stay with her. Cory was appreciative, but adamant.

"Okay, Mom. Don't play detective. Promise you'll call me daily."

"I promise. Don't worry. I'll handle this okay."

During the traffic snarl on the freeway toward San Diego, Cory had time to tidy her thoughts.

She figured Sergeant Stanley Kipinski, investigating her patient's disappearance, would know Morgan's license number, or Ben would get it. She'd ask tomorrow. She was annoyed at herself for forgetting to tell Kipinski that she suspected someone driving Morgan's car was stalking her.

Within an hour, she had reached the cottage and found a message under the door:

Ben called. Important. Call him immediately. We're at a recital.

Don't know when you'll read this, so we'll call later about dinner.

R

Cory dropped her gear on the bed, kicked off her shoes, and picked up the phone. Ben answered on the first ring. "What's up?" she asked.

"Plenty. There was a break-in at your office today."

Her stomach felt like it had dropped to the floor. "Oh my God! Did they arrest anyone?"

"No. I caught it on the surveillance tape. If you have a VCR, I'll play it for you. See if you recognize the intruder."

"How soon can you get here?"

"I'm on my way. Have you had dinner?"

"No. I can hardly wait for this. I'll have to meet you outside the gate."

"Can I bring over a pizza?"

"You bet," she said.

"Okay. I'll call when I arrive. Probably within the hour."

Cory undressed, tossed her clothes into the washing machine, and hopped into the shower, all the while expecting to see Kevin on Ben's tape. She toweled off, pulled on a pair of freshly laundered dark green sweats, tied her hair in a ponytail, and nervously applied lipstick.

She tugged out the carton of mail she'd retrieved from the post office yesterday. It needed sorting and the task would help her feel in control. She tossed advertisements and hurried through bills and conference notices, hoping to be finished in time to meet Ben at the gate.

Just as she completed the job, he rang. Cory dashed outside, whistling for Otto. The dog raced over, tail wagging, and walked beside her. She grabbed the gate opener and was about to walk away when she noticed Otto sitting in the backseat of the Buick. She had forgotten to roll up the window. It made her wonder what else she may have missed. "No, Otto. Sorry. We're staying here. Come on. Let's go for a walk."

Cory could swear she saw a look of disappointment in his eyes. Otto jumped out and didn't make the fuss she had expected. "Dogs. Perfect friends," she said, happily.

Ben waited, motor running, while she opened the gate. Cory and the dog hopped into Ben's car. "Hope you don't mind Otto."

"The dog? No. He's not a serious rival, is he?"

"He may well be." The garlic scent invaded the car and Otto sniffed at the box.

"Pizza smells great, but I can't wait to see the tape."

Ben pulled into her driveway, grabbed the pizza box, and handed Cory a video. She clutched it to her bosom and watched Otto run off.

"Listen. Don't leave that opener in your car. Someone could steal it."

"Thanks. I didn't even think of that, Ben."

"This must be cold by now." He pointed to the box.

"I'm too excited to eat, anyway." While Ben fiddled with the VCR, she slid the pizza into the oven.

"I collected the tape today. There's no security staff at your building on Sunday, so they didn't detect the break-in, but your alarm went off and officers responded. By then, the intruder had split." Ben sat next to Cory on the couch. "Here we go."

The video started. Cory leaned forward, elbows on her knees, watching the door to her office swing open. A slim figure clad in Harley clothes—metal-studded black leather jacket, pants, boots, and cap entered, flipped the couch on its back, and ran gloved hands over the frame. Unable to see the face, Cory moved closer to the screen. The intruder looked up and Cory gasped in surprise.

⸏41⸏

After recovering from the shock, Cory shrieked, "Oh, my God! It's Sara, Morgan's secretary! When could she have planted the microphone? The first time I saw her in my office was after Morgan disappeared."

"Very interesting. When I checked your door earlier, there were no scratches on the dead bolt or the tumblers, but this afternoon, during my routine inspection, there were freshly made marks on the dead bolt. I played the tape, discovered the break-in, and phoned Coastal Security. Apparently the alarm went off at eleven this morning and the sheriff was immediately alerted, but Coastal's people should have also called us. I complained to the supervisor. Anyway, by the time the officers arrived, the intruder was gone. After we show the tape to the investigators and you identify her, she'll be arrested for breaking and entering."

"And maybe lead us to Morgan."

Suddenly there was loud buzz, a stream of smoke, and the stench of something burning. "It's the smoke alarm," Cory yelled. "The pizza!" She ran to the oven and pulled out a seared cardboard box. Inside was a bubbling, burnt-at-the-edges pizza.

"I like it crispy," Ben said, disconnecting the smoke detector.

Cory opened the door to fan out the smoke and heard the dogs barking. "It's okay, boys," she yelled as they raced toward the cottage. They stood outside while she petted them. "You can go home now, guys." And off they went.

"I'll call the Sheriff's dispatcher," Cory said.

"Don't bother. It's Sunday and Monday is a holiday. The detectives won't be in until Tuesday. They'll want us to bring the tape to Encinitas."

"Isn't the desk staffed by detectives seven days a week?"

"Contrary to what you see on TV, they don't work weekends unless they're on special assignment. Your break-in doesn't fit the category of a big deal to them."

"Damn! I wish we didn't have to wait so long. Sara could get away." Cory picked up the phone. "Maybe George can help."

"Sara must have known that the security crew was off Sunday," Ben said.

"It's not hard to find out. She could have pretended to be a prospective tenant and asked management about the security routine or staked out the building."

"Good detection, Cory. Sara probably was unaware of the burglar alarm in your office. The noise must have surprised her; makes a good case for silent alarms. She didn't know how soon the cops would arrive, so she quickly searched the couch and split. "Come on. Let's dig into that pizza."

Cory brought out a couple of chilled bottles of Pete's Wicked Ale and told Ben about her exciting weekend.

"Your daughter's a smart kid. I doubt you were followed there."

"I realize that, but I was unnerved. It's possible I misread the letters on the license number I gave you earlier."

"We'll see what the police come up with. They may find something close."

The phone rang and Cory leaped. The caller was Joe, asking if she'd like dinner.

"No thanks. Ben is here. He's brought a pizza and—listen to this—his surveillance camera caught a break-in at my office."

"No kidding! Who?"

"My missing patient's secretary."

"Wait 'till I tell Roberta. What's next?"

"I've paged my friend the lieutenant and we'll show the tape to detectives."

"Now aren't you glad you hired Ben?"

"Without a doubt."

"Fine. I'll let you continue whatever you were doing."

"You have a good imagination. See you in the morning."

Although very crispy, the pizza was delicious and they took their time munching and chatting.

"It's your job to figure out who was Sara's accomplice," Ben said.

"I know." After draining the bottle of beer, Cory soon became groggy. "I'm not from the drinkers," she explained.

"Neither am I. I'd better let you get some sleep." Ben went to tidy up the kitchen.

After he made everything spic and span, he kissed her forehead. "I'll call you tomorrow. Ciao."

She would have liked him to stay, but she was weary from all the excitement and needed a good night sleep.

Fifteen minutes after her head hit the pillow, she found that insomnia was her new companion. She slid off the bed, put on the stereo, and grabbed a notepad and pen. The last name she wrote on her list was Kevin's. His inability to keep his stories straight continued to gnaw at her.

⹀42⹀

By the time morning rolled around, Cory had made a plan. From the window, she saw the dense fog. She wrapped her cold hands around a cup of hot tea at the table, listened to Mozart's Jupiter Symphony, and studied a map of Kevin's neighborhood. She took particular notice that his street was near an elementary school.

It was eight o'clock, the time she was expected at the main house for breakfast. She phoned Roberta. "Remember that curly black wig and big hat that you wore at the costume party last year?"

"Yes."

"Do you still have them and your long black and white polka dot dress?"

There was a long pause. "Uh-oh. You need a disguise. What are you up to?"

"Don't worry, Ro. I'll be safe in daylight where I'm going, if this fog will lift."

"We thought Ben stayed over and you were too busy for us."

"I wish. After one beer, I was too tired for company."

"Joe said something about a break-in. Come on over and tell us over omelets."

"You're spoiling me, Ro. I'm on my way."

Cory pulled on tights, a sweatshirt, and sneakers. She opened the door and whistled for Otto. In a flash, her sweetheart was at her heels, leash in his mouth. Good thing, too, because she didn't think she could find her way. She hooked his collar to the leash and he led her to the main house. "You're the smartest, nicest dog and I love you," she said.

Otto responded by a wag of his tail lightly brushing against her shin. She opened the front door and placed the gift on the hall table. "Ro, is it okay for Otto to come in?" she called. "He deserves a treat for leading me here."

"Oh, sure."

Joe handed her a box of dog treats. Otto sat at Cory's feet with his face in her lap while she fed him.

After everyone finished breakfast, Roberta crooked her finger in Cory's direction and the two women darted into Roberta's dressing room. "It's all here," Roberta said, handing Cory the requested ensemble.

Cory slipped into the garment and Roberta helped her apply makeup, the wig, and the hat. They stared at Cory's reflection in the mirror and giggled like two schoolgirls.

"Here. Take my sunglasses. Let's see if Joe recognizes you."

Barefoot, Cory padded downstairs into the kitchen.

Joe looked up from the newspaper. "What the devil! Why a disguise? What are you up to, Cory?"

"If we met on the street, Joe, would you recognize me?"

"No. Because I wouldn't think you'd wear something so silly."

"Good."

He flung the newspaper down. "Why do you need a disguise? You have a detective. You're too damn infatuated with intrigue. That's what's wrong with you, Cory."

"I can't help it. I was pulled into this."

"Pulled, *shmulled*. It's not quicksand," Joe said. "But if you go that route, it may bury you."

"I'm going to butt in," Roberta said, frowning. "I must have been nuts to help you as if you were just dressing for a costume party! You came here seeking refuge, but you're running out in a disguise. Why?"

"As the fog lifts, the plot thickens." Cory motioned toward the window. The trees and the large gazebo had begun to take shape. "I really do appreciate your concern, but there's no need to worry. You'll see. I'll be back here in a few hours."

"If not, where should we tell the police to look?"

"I promise not to do anything dangerous." She laced up her sneakers, grabbed her clothes, and started for the door.

"Take Otto with you."

"Thanks." The dog walked by her side to the guest quarters. Cory remembered a TV series in which the private investigator used a variety of professional calling cards to disguise his identity. She fished in her purse for the card of a real estate agent she had met recently. She fingered the raised red lettering: Rita Flynn. Flynn Realty. Coastal Areas. She clipped the card to a writing pad, pulled off her sneakers, rolled on black pantyhose, and stepped into black pumps. Off to Pacific Beach, she went, joined by Otto in the backseat of the rented Buick. The fog had lifted and the day was beginning to look bright.

She located Kevin's frame and stucco house and circled the street several times. Most of the homes in the neighborhood were at least forty years old. Kevin's sported mature foliage, a beach location, and proximity to schools and shopping. The house should command a hefty sum.

His windows and garage door were open. From across the street, she saw two bicycles and gardening equipment in the otherwise empty garage. She was in luck. Kevin had probably taken off. A young man in his twenties, wearing a Tee shirt and jeans, was washing a blue Honda Civic in the driveway.

Cory parked the Buick, fetched her clipboard, and cranked down the window for Otto to jump out in case she needed him. She stepped briskly across the street.

"Good morning. It sure is a nice day." She extended her hand. "I'm Rita Flynn of Flynn Realty."

"Hey there," the young man said. He tucked the polishing cloth in the back pocket of his jeans, smiled, and shook her hand. "I'm Kevin Holloway."

⹀43⹀

When she heard his name, Cory nearly choked and pretended to have a coughing spell.

"Would you like some water?" he asked.

"No, thanks. I'm fine. It's nice to meet you, Kevin. I'm looking for the owner of this house. I've got a client who is very interested in buying property near the school." She held out Rita's card, but he didn't take it.

"My roommate owns it, but he never said nothing about selling it. That'd be a bummer. Hard to find such low rent in this neighborhood."

"Oh, don't worry. He hasn't told me he wants to sell. I'm just canvassing houses in the neighborhood in hope that I can find one for my client."

"I've seen a 'FOR SALE' sign around the corner. Try there."

"For sure, I will. Just for my records, what's the owner's name?"

"Seth Smith."

"Seth Smith? Really! I wonder if he's the same guy I met some time ago. Wavy hair, kind of sandy color? In his thirties and single?" Cory emphasized the last word.

"Yeah, that's him."

"Where does he hang out these days?"

"With his love, Sally Forth," he said, chuckling. "She's docked in Harbor Island."

"Oh, that's nice to know. Well, thanks."

The sky was cloudless and the sun shone brightly as she took off for the docks at Harbor Island.

Cory drove along the main thoroughfare lined with swaying palm trees and passed several yacht clubs and moorings. Sailboats decorated the bright blue water.

She squeezed the Buick into a parking space on the public street and jumped out of the car. The wind picked up and carried off her hat. She clutched the wig that was about to follow its partner, chased after the hat, and retrieved it.

Cory hurried back into the car, rummaged through her purse, and found a couple of clips to fasten the headgear. She dashed across the street to the boat dock.

Most of the slips were empty. This was a holiday weekend and perfect sailing weather. The Sally Forth had probably sailed off, but she continued her search, reading the cute names on the sterns in vain. She passed *TGIF*, *Molly's Folly*, and *My Fair Lady*, and then headed for the next yacht club.

After checking around, she entered the lobby and asked for someone who would know if a particular vessel was docked there. One of the members directed her to a short, stocky man wearing a visor cap embroidered with an anchor emblem. She felt queasy approaching the man.

"I'm sorry to trouble you, but I'm looking for the Sally Forth. Someone told me she was docked here."

"Ah, yes. But she set sail yesterday."

"Do you know when she's expected back?"

"Can't say for sure, but I think I overheard them talking about Coronado at dinner last night."

"Does that mean they could be gone for a few days?"

"They usually come back same day, mostly."

"Thanks a bunch."

Cory started to walk away. The man called after her, "Come here."

Her heart pounded like a kettledrum. "Yes?"

"Who shall I say asked?"

"Flora Dora. Looking for Seth Smith," she said, heading toward the car. She had to make a quick getaway before she burst out laughing for making up such a silly name.

It was late afternoon by the time Cory returned to the Klein's compound. She slipped out of Roberta's gear and ran water into the Jacuzzi, then phoned her answering service. One message. Lieutenant Lewis had left his home phone number. "Thank God for friends in high places," she greeted him when he picked up the phone. Then she told him of Sara's break-in.

"You know, I kinda thought that'd happen," George said.

"But the detectives aren't available now."

"I'll see what I can do, Doc. You'll need to bring the tape to them. They'll ask some questions and give you some advice. Better damn well listen to them. Okay?"

"Of course."

"Be safe and stay put. Don't play detective. That's why you have Ben, you know."

George's intelligence and friendship were a solace to her. She wondered if he picked up her interest in Ben. When it came right down to it, she was like everyone else who imagined detectives and psychologists were mind-readers.

"By the way, I have the info on the Orange County Saab. Does William B. Williams III, of Newport Beach, mean anything to you?"

"No," she answered.

"He's an elderly gentleman who bought the car new. Drives it once a week. Keeps it locked up in his garage. Swears he's the sole driver."

"I'm sorry you went through so much trouble. I must have made a mistake."

"When and where did you first notice you were being tailed?"

"I was on my way to my friend's house in La Jolla for dinner, a little before seven-thirty. It was the same day I'd found the microphone."

"You don't remember seeing the car before then?"

"The first time I noticed a dark blue Saab, it had belonged to Morgan Heller."

"The prosecutor? Why didn't you tell me?"

"Because I don't think she'd harm me," Cory said. "I think someone may have stolen her car and is tailing me."

"Hold on. I can get her license number in seconds, you know." It didn't take him long to get back on the line. "NIB 9876," he said.

"That's close to what I thought I saw. I must have mistaken the initials N and I for M, and figured the B as R."

"Happens a lot. Especially if there's dirt covering parts of the letters," George said.

Her mind whirled with the dots she needed to connect.

≈44≈

A sliver of moon in an overcast evening sky could help camouflage her appearance. Cory fastened her hair into a tight bun, pulled on a pair of blue jeans, a sweatshirt, and a black, bulky knit hooded sweater. With her height and slim hips, she could easily be mistaken for a guy. She examined her reflection on the mirrored closet door and decided she had found an outlet for her creativity: disguises R-Us. She emptied the canvas sack of CDs she had first packed for her stay at the Kleins' and slipped her cell phone and Maglite inside it.

Her friends were right about her; she loved intrigue. Under the guise of protecting patient privacy, she chose to investigate when she could leave it to a professional. Still, She hated to admit she did it for the adrenaline rush.

Heading toward Harbor Island, Cory stopped at a supermarket for a six pack of Budweiser and a bag of chips. She parked the Buick across from the Harbor Island Marina, grabbed the provisions, and jogged to the pier, leaving Otto in the backseat.

Many of the boats were anchored and appeared unattended. She started combing the area for the *Sally Forth* until a man stopped her.

"May I help you?" he asked.

"Suppose so. I was invited to a party and am looking for the Sally—uh Sally—something. Can't remember her complete name. *Silly Sally* or..."

"*Sally Forth?*"

"Could be."

"A Beneteau? Forty-two feet?"

"Gee, I don't know. Some guy named Seth owns her."

"Yeah. That's the one. Took off this morning. Our members usually tell the dock master where they're sailing and when they expect to return. For safety, you see." He removed his cap to scratch his baldhead. "But this one keeps to hisself. Hmm. A party, you say? Maybe it isn't the Sally Forth. Maybe there's another Seth and you got the wrong club. Maybe you want the San Diego Yacht Club."

"My friend said Harbor Island Marina. Isn't this it?"

"Well, it sure is. Maybe she'll be back soon. Wanna have a drink with me?" He pointed to the six-pack.

"Thanks, but I better hang around here. I promised to meet my friends this evening. Here, have one on me." She offered him a beer.

"Better keep it for your party." He sauntered into the parking lot. She watched him drive off in a dark, late model Mercedes.

Cory jogged back to the car to wait and watch. Disappointed that there was no action on the dock, she grew bored and hungry. An hour later, she ate the chips and closed her eyes.

A tapping on the window startled her. "Are you okay?" a uniformed officer asked as she rolled down the window.

"Oh, yes. Thanks. I'm waiting for a friend." She glanced at her Timex. It was ten-thirty-two.

"Sorry, you can't park here."

"Okay." Cory started the car and pulled into the nearly vacant parking lot of Harbor Island Marina. She lugged the six pack, slung the sack over her shoulder, and poked around for a sign of life around the sailboats anchored at the dock, but the sound of water sloshing against the hulls was all she heard. No sign of anyone. And no Sally Forth.

The night air was nippy and despite the warm sweater, she felt chilled and too tired to hang around. Her mission thwarted, she returned to the car and headed to the cottage with Otto, her quiet companion.

When she arrived, she checked her answering service. One call from Rachel. Too late to phone her tonight. She undressed, slipped under the bedcovers, and imagined Ben's arms around her.

≈45≈

Last night must have been more stressful than Cory had realized. She awoke with a pounding headache, probably because she'd missed some meals. A hearty breakfast and a bag of chips weren't enough for someone on the go all day. She dragged herself out of bed, did her morning ablutions, and whistled for Otto, but he didn't turn up. He was probably angry because she hadn't fed him yesterday. And he hadn't let on. Smart dog to keep away from her and her single mindedness.

She trudged to the main house, expecting to find Joe and Roberta at the breakfast table, but they weren't there. The sparkling kitchen showed no signs of recent use. What was going on? Her ears grew hot. She felt dizzy. Edgy. Her nerves as raw as her flesh wounds. When the clock chimed seven times, she realized it was too early for their breakfast.

The throbbing in her head increased. She found a bottle of Advil in the kitchen cabinet, checked the expiration date, and downed a capsule with water. Making herself at home, she brewed coffee, whipped up seven-grain flour, milk, and eggs for a large batch of pancakes, and heated a pan. As it warmed, she ate a banana and began to feel better. She juiced some oranges and put the beverage in the wood-paneled refrigerator to cool. While she was busy frying the batter, Joe and Roberta arrived.

"Thanks for doing breakfast, Cory. It must have been a late night. You look awful."

"That's the nicest thing anyone's said to me, today, Ro."

"Sure. The only thing." she replied.

"Don't rub it in, Ro."

"Sorry. Guess I'm a little sore at you about the disguise. You finagled me to be your conspirator."

It came as a blow to Cory that she had taken advantage of a friend without giving it a thought. "I'm glad you told me and I apologize."

"Accepted. How did it work out?"

"It turned out well. There was nothing to worry about."

"Have you discussed your action with your private eye? Or maybe your analyst?" Joe asked.

"I know you mean well, but I've got a splitting headache."

"I'm not surprised," Joe said.

"Forgot to eat yesterday and forgot to feed Otto. That's the end of our love affair."

"He's forgiving. Don't worry. He eats twice a day. He ate yesterday morning, and there's always some dry food in his bowl."

"I still feel bad about it, Ro."

"I wish you'd feel bad about the risks you take, Cory," Joe said. "You're safe here, but when you go off… "

"I am careful. And I appreciate you both for everything. I don't know how to show you how much."

"That's easy," Joe said. "Don't flirt with danger. By the way, thanks for the beautiful gift. Very appropriate. Aphrodite the Goddess of Love."

"It's perfect on top of the piano." Roberta squeezed Cory's shoulder.

After breakfast, her headache subsided. She tidied the kitchen, and then took a brisk walk, pleased that her knee no longer hurt.

She called Rachel and told her about the surveillance tape.

"Cool! Now, they'll find out what happened to your missing patient."

"I hope so."

"Promise you'll let me know. And you'll stay out of it. That's what you've got the P.I. for. Right? I've got to run to class now, Mom."

"Love you, sweetie." Cory smiled at how easily Rachel slipped into a role-reversal.

"Me, too. Bye."

As soon as she put the phone down, Ben called. "Hello, Cory. Listen. I'm sorry I didn't get back to you yesterday. I had an unexpected visit from my kids and we went sailing all day. George called me. He's set up a meeting for us with the detectives. How soon can you leave for Encinitas?"

"I'm ready and a little nervous. Hope it won't take too long. I've got a busy schedule today."

"I'll meet you there in fifteen minutes or so. Okay?"

The San Diego County Sheriff station was located a few miles from her office and her home. Heading in that direction Cory felt nostalgic for her own turf and her old car. She longed to resume a normal life

177

with Morgan alive and Sara in prison. In exchange for those conditions, she'd willingly give up on figuring out Kevin. "Quit this magical thinking," she mumbled. Fate doesn't make deals.

She pulled the Buick into the steep driveway and parked between a Sheriff's black-and-white vehicle and Ben's Mustang. Taking a deep breath, she strode into the station.

In the sparsely furnished, utilitarian reception room behind a low gate, several men pored over paper work. She gave her name to the middle-aged uniformed officer at the front desk. He held the gate open and escorted Cory into a small inner office where Ben was seated at a table opposite two men.

The taller man stood and introduced himself as Detective Lee and the other as Detective Levi. Cory stifled a nervous chuckle, wondering whether there was another detective named Strauss or Jordache. *Grow up, Cory*, she told herself, clearing her throat.

Detective Levi pulled out a straight back metal chair for her and centered a cassette recorder on the table. A stocky deputy rolled a TV and VCR combo into the room and plugged it into the wall socket. The house lights dimmed and the show was on.

"Doctor Cohen, can you identify this woman?" Detective Lee asked.

"Yes. I know her as Sara Jaspers, secretary to Morgan Heller of the District Attorney's office. Ms. Heller has vanished."

Lee and Levi nodded to each other.

"Did you give Ms. Jaspers permission to enter your office in your absence?" Levi asked.

"Absolutely not."

"Did you give her permission to search your office?" asked Lee.

"No."

"Does she have a key to your office?"

"Not to my knowledge."

"Excuse me, Detective, but I've explained this already." Ben interjected. "When I checked the lock on Sunday after the break-in, I found freshly made scratches that weren't there earlier."

"Yes, I know, but we need Doctor Cohen's statement for the record. Is Ben Fortuna in your employ," he asked.

"Yes."

"Why do you require the services of a private investigator?"

"Unless it's essential, I'd rather not discuss it."

"Have you any idea what Ms. Jaspers was looking for?"

Cory took a deep breath before offering her explanation.

"Now we understand why you've employed Mr. Fortuna. We'll submit information about the break-in to the Intelligence Division downtown. I am advising you not to discuss this case with anyone at all. Do not say anything about the video or break-in. Do not speak with any member of any law enforcement agency or the D.A. This is highly sensitive," Lee warned.

"A political bombshell," added Levi.

Cory shook her head. "The break-in occurred on Sunday and because of the holiday, you weren't available for this interview until today, Detective."

"Yes. That is unfortunate," Lee said.

"I'm sorry, but I've already told my two close friends and my daughter, but I'll ask them to keep quiet about it."

"We can't expect more."

"What will happen now?" Cory asked.

"A complaint will be issued and we'll get a warrant for Ms. Jaspers' arrest. Is there anything else you can tell us about her?" Lee asked.

"When you get your arrest warrant, can you look for drugs, too?"

"Only if they are in plain view."

"I see. Please let me know what happens. I'd like to return to a normal life instead of being hounded by this woman."

"You say she's hounding you. What else has she done?"

"I suspect she's vandalized my house and is responsible for a threatening call to me. You have reports of these incidents."

"How do you know she's the culprit?"

"I don't know for certain, but I strongly suspect her."

"What does she have against you?"

"In my opinion, she is a disturbed woman with anti-social behavior. I refused to treat her and offered to refer her to another psychologist. Ms. Jaspers has serious problems and doesn't accept rejection."

Lee and Levi rose from their chairs. "We appreciate the information. We'll be in touch. If anything comes up, please call." Lee handed Cory his card.

Ben and Cory walked to the parking lot.

"You did very well, Cory."

She felt patronized. "Did you expect something different, Ben?"

"No, but you seem touchy today."

Cory shrugged. She was tired of this mess and disappointed that Ben didn't show more interest in her. She was worried because Sara was on the loose and capable of continued damage. And Kevin's deception alarmed her.

"I've got a busy schedule, Ben, and a lot on my mind. Call me later, please."

"Ciao, Cory."

"Ciao, back," she said.

She plugged in her cell phone to recharge the battery and placed her trusty Maglite on the passenger car seat. Joe had no morning appointments, so she headed to his office, expecting to be alone.

Zipping downtown, she had a strange feeling in the pit of her stomach—the kind you get when you're expecting the unexpected.

≈46≈

Despite Joe's high tech security, Cory had a strange sense of unease in the lonely office. She missed Ann and decided to phone her.

"How goes it, Sherlock?" the woman answered.

Cory resisted the urge to tell her about Sara. "It's okay, but I miss you. Were you able to reach Kevin?"

"No problem."

Oh, sure. That's what she thought. They chatted until the bell rang and Cory buzzed Alan in.

"Wow, Doc. This place is great," he said, appraising the reception room. "It must be at least a hundred years old and kept up nice. It fits your line of work. Say, if you have a construction problem at your regular office, I'm the guy for you!"

Sure. He wanted to be every woman's guy! "Thanks, Alan. My regular office is a rental and the building management will take care of it."

"What's wrong there?"

"I appreciate your concern, but I'd rather not take time away from your session. Let's talk about you."

"Well, my old girlfriend dumped me. I don't care. She was too demanding sexually. Even for me!"

"What attracted you to her?"

"She's female."

"Come, come Alan."

"Oops, you did it again, Doc."

Cory held back a smile. "Be serious. Was there something special about her?"

"Mr. Rogers says everyone is special."

"I'm not asking him. This isn't his neighborhood."

"Well... I could tell she had a problem with sex. I'm different from other guys that way. You see, such women challenge me. But if her pan's ready to fry, that's fine, too."

So Alan liked challenges. Morgan would sure be one for him. Her middle name was Westinghouse or maybe Frigidaire. For a moment, Cory toyed with the idea that he could be Sara's accomplice. After all, they each saw themselves as hot stuff. *No. That's too absurd*, she said to herself.

Her work with Alan threw her off balance and her headache returned. Stuck between two roles, she had to nudge herself to play the one for which Alan paid her.

"I'm going to try to lay off women," Alan declared.

Cory laughed. "Listen to your verb choice."

"I'm doing your thing, Doc."

"Well, let's eliminate the word *try*, Alan. When temptation strikes, tell yourself you won't succumb." Shades of Morgan, to whom she had given the same mantra.

As she walked him to the front door, Alan said, "I prefer this office. I feel like I'm in therapy with Freud. Except you don't have facial hair."

"I'm glad of that." She rubbed her chin.

There were patients who made the day seem gray and heavy. And then there was Alan. Cory would miss him when his therapy ended.

She leaned back in the chair wondering why no one except Rachel had called her. She wanted to hear from Betty. When Betty was involved with a guy, her friendship with Cory took a back seat. Cory figured Betty was "busier than a chigger at a picnic"—to use Jolene's words. Even Otto had rejected her. A damn dog.

No use standing on ceremonies, she thought as she called Betty. Much to her surprise, her friend answered.

"Hey Cory. Nice to hear from you. What's up?"

Cory told her where she was living and working.

"I'm glad you're not taking chances. It sounds like you've got a dynamite safe house. You're lucky to have Joe and Roberta for friends."

"I'm fortunate you're my friend too, Betty."

"But I can't put you up in luxury."

"So what?"

"I admit I'm jealous of their comforts."

"It's their relationship that I envy, Betty."

"That too. Oh! I must tell you something. I've managed to keep my rotten attitude toward the police under control, and now one of them is interested in me. He's kind of cute, a bit younger than I'd like, but anyway, I managed to wangle information from him about Terry's case."

"For heaven's sake, tell me, already," Cory said.

"Do you know that detectives trained in computer technology are able to take a computer apart to find data?"

"Yes."

"Terry was an expert. Unfortunately, she'd successfully deleted everything personal. Nothing there about Sara."

"That's a shame. Does this mean they've closed the investigation?"

"All I know is they're sticking with suicide."

"I wish we could do something about that, Betty."

"Stay away from it, Cory. The next thing I know, you'll be investigating your Sara. Haven't you been told about playing with matches?"

"I just can't sit still while a suspected murderer goes free."

"You can and you will! Stop this melodrama. You hear?" Cory heard Betty's exasperated sigh. "Boundaries, Cory. Remember yours. Please! Now tell me. Anything new with your detective?"

"He hasn't made a pass and it's driving me nuts."

"Does he know you're interested?"

"I've made it obvious."

"I'll give you lessons on the art of seduction."

"How soon?"

"Are you serious?"

"Yes and no. When I'm ready, I'll call. Ciao."

"Ciao? Probably what he says. Charming."

"Oh, yes."

"Hey! Let's double date with our two detectives."

Cory smiled. The prospect made her feel young again. "That'd be fun. Let's talk more, later."

Detectives. Ah, yes. She phoned Detective Lee and was connected immediately.

"Cory Cohen, here. There's something else," she said. "I have reason to believe that Sara Jaspers murdered Terry Salmonica. The woman whose body washed up on Coronado Shores."

"I don't understand," he said. "What's your connection?"

"Please take my word for it. I can't betray a confidence. I'm certain Terry did not commit suicide. Prior to her death, she had received blackmail threats from her lover, a woman named Sara. The woman's description in behavior and appearance matches Sara Jaspers."

"Oh?"

"Terry had met Sara in a chat room on the Internet. Perhaps you could find information on this and more from Sara's computer."

"The Coronado Police investigated this."

"Terry deleted any reference to Sara on her computer."

"Based upon your information, we'll ask the judge to allow us to confiscate Sara Jasper's computer."

"Thank you, Detective."

*　*　*

"It's good to see you looking so well, Barney," Cory said, welcoming Blum into her office.

"I'm feeling great. Therapy has helped tremendously."

"You had the tools to fix your problems. All you needed was the repair shop."

He grinned. "I'm glad Morgan recommended you. I hope she'll have time to get back into the race. A fine woman—putting her father over her career."

Cory longed to tell Barney the truth, but she couldn't blow it. He'd find out soon enough. It gave her pause that the media hadn't gotten wind of Morgan's disappearance. She wondered who had forged the letter. Sending it from Greece would have been easy enough. Someone had known of the psychiatric conference her father had attended.

"Morgan will be glad when she finds out that guy Rothenberg she was after now has more troubles," Barney said. His chit-chat wasn't part of therapy, but Cory wasn't about to stop him. "Remember that guy Horace? The one I felt guilty about adding to the group?"

"Yes," she said, happily back on track.

"Well, seems Rothenberg hired him to threaten witnesses." Cory wasn't surprised. She remembered Morgan's suspicion.

"Not only that, he wanted Horace to kidnap Rothenberg's wife and son from the shelter. With a guy like Rothenberg, who knows? He may have wanted to kill them."

Cory shivered. "Sometimes a mistake such as the one you worried about turns out to be good luck in disguise."

"If that were always true..."

"We'd live in a perfect world."

"I'm more than merely content about the way my life is going now. I'm really in great spirits."

Cory believed him. "Then it's time to sum up what you've learned here and we'll tie up any loose threads."

At the close of the session, Barney thanked her and they shook hands.

"Therapy is never completely finished," he said. "We'll probably meet again."

～47～

After Barney drove away, Cory figured she'd make good use of a three-hour break in her therapy schedule. From the trunk of the rented Buick, she snagged her red baseball cap, a pair of old sweats and sneakers, and rushed to the office to change clothes.

She secured the office and climbed into the car, stashing the cell phone and Maglite into the canvas sack. She drove the short distance to Harbor Island. Since she had learned about Kevin's sailboat, she suspected him of holding Morgan on board, but she had no evidence to interest the police—nothing strong enough for them to obtain a search warrant. She had to find proof—anything that could point them in that direction.

The air was still this Tuesday afternoon. The day was a poor one for sailing and boats crowded the dock. No one was in sight. With the canvas sack slung over her shoulder, Cory strolled around the marina in search of the Sally Forth.

At the far end of the pier, she approached a large sailboat that she hadn't seen yesterday. The dark lettering painted on her stern read "Sally IVth". Cory's heart slammed against her chest. She scanned the deserted area, leapt onto the deck, knocked on the hatch, and shouted, "You hoo! Friend on board."

Cory listened for a sign of life, but only heard the splash of waves lapping against the hull. She called again. There was no answer. To her surprise, the hatch was unlocked. An unattended boat with the hatch open suggested someone could be nearby—perhaps on the way from getting provisions. She'd have to act fast.

Ignoring the nagging voice inside her head, telling her to go back, she scampered down the narrow ladder and found herself in a corridor with two cabin doors on either side and a well-appointed galley up front. "Anyone here?" she called. No answer. She pulled open a cabin door.

Assaulted by the stench of body odor, urine, and diesel fuel, Cory's stomach lurched. She held her breath and stepped over the threshold. The door closed behind her.

A woman lay face down on the floor. Gasping in horror, Cory raced to her. She knelt down to see the woman's face. Morgan! Her eyes were open and glazed and she appeared to be dead. She must have been through hell. She wore the same clothes she had worn the last time Cory had seen her. Now, they were rumpled, torn, and dirty. Her complexion was pale, ghost-like, and her hair, dull, knotted. The corners of her mouth were smudged with particles that resembled dried-up food.

Cory said a prayer as she checked Morgan's wrist. Finally, she felt a weak pulse. Morgan stirred. Cory moved closer and listened to Morgan's shallow breathing. Then Morgan's eyes rolled back and she seemed to slip into a coma.

Cory fumbled for her cell phone. She pressed 911 and gave the information to the dispatcher who assured her an ambulance and the Harbor Patrol were on the way. Cory prayed they would come before Morgan's captor did. She thought about moving her, but decided it could do more harm. Instead, she covered her with a blanket from the closet. She took the pillow from the bunk and put it under Morgan's head.

The minutes she waited seemed like hours as she sat beside the young woman, stroking the pale face, trying to rouse her. She heard a faint whistle, but couldn't identify the tune. Flashlight in hand, she left the cabin and stood outside the door.

Suddenly the boat swayed. The whistler had jumped aboard. The deck creaked under his feet. The sound grew clearer and louder as he approached the open hatch. She recognized the tune as "Happy Days." *Not for me*, she thought. She could see his large deck shoes cautiously descend each step. Her heart banged like a kettledrum. If he was armed, she couldn't chance a karate move in the close quarters of the galley. She must hide.

She fled back into the cabin and stood behind the door. Her knuckles whitened as she gripped the heavy flashlight, ready to strike the moment he stepped into the room.

His feet made a shuffling noise as he approached the cabin. Cory's pulse raced. She covered her mouth with her hand to still the panting noise of her own breath. He was coming closer. Her heart, ready to burst, pumped louder and louder. The shuffling stopped. He was just outside the cabin door. Would he open it now? She was ready to pounce when the shriek of an ambulance wailed in the distance. The siren grew louder and louder and then slowly whined down as Morgan's rescuers reached their destination.

Footfalls sounded on the deck. Cory heard the squeak of the ladder as the whistler clambered topside. "Hold it. Don't move," someone yelled. Cory stood still and held her breath until she heard a thud and the sound of men's voices. She opened the cabin door and climbed up the ladder.

A Harbor Patrol officer held on to Kevin. "Is this the man you reported?" he asked her.

Cory nodded as another officer handcuffed the startled man.

Kevin turned to face her. "My God, what are you doing here?" he asked, as they pulled him aside to make way for the paramedics and their paraphernalia.

"The woman..." she said, pointing to the cabin.

"What woman? What's going on?" Kevin asked.

Cory followed the paramedics as they scrambled toward Morgan.

"She's heavily sedated," a dark-haired paramedic said to his partner. "Blood pressure very low. Breathing shallow. Let's keep her airway clear and get her to the E.R." He inserted a plastic tube in Morgan's mouth.

"They'll have to run a tox screen and contact poison control," the light-haired man replied.

Within seconds, they gently lifted Morgan onto the gurney and gingerly hoisted her up the ladder.

"What's her name?" the dark-haired paramedic asked.

"Morgan Heller. She's the Deputy D.A. A kidnapping victim," Cory said. "Where are you taking her?"

"The nearest hospital, U C Med Center."

"No. Take her to Thornton Hospital," Kevin said. "She's less likely to be recognized there."

"Why should you care? You nearly killed her. Who the devil are you, anyway?" Cory asked.

"Seth Smith. A private investigator."

The officer took the wallet from the man Cory had known as Kevin and was scrutinizing the ID. "That's true. He has a license."

"What?" she yelled. "What kind of detective abducts someone and drugs her?"

"May I see your identification, ma'am?" the officer asked.

With trembling hands, Cory fumbled through her wallet and handed over her license. She shook her head at her bogus patient.

"I had nothing to do with this," he said.

"Who hired you?" she asked angrily.

"That's enough, ma'am," the officer cautioned, leading him away.

"Why did you pretend to want therapy?" Cory called after him.

"It wasn't a pretense."

"You used a false identity."

"For security."

"Security? What are you saying?"

"Sorry, ma'am. There'll be no further questions here. We have to take him in. You stay on board with an officer and a detective will be along soon to take your statement."

"I'm sorry, but I have to leave. My patients are waiting for me." She fished out her card, scribbled Joe's address on the back, and handed it to the policeman. "I'll be there for the next few hours."

He was about to restrain Cory when Kevin said, "Let her go. She'll cooperate."

The policeman nodded to Cory. "Are you the one who called this in?"

"Yes, officer, I am. You have everything you need from me."

"Okay. Someone will be in touch with you later, ma'am."

She joined the parade to the parking lot, jumped into the Buick, called Ben, and gave him a rundown.

"What? Seth Smith? I know him well. We worked together at the Bureau. Why didn't you ask me to investigate, or at least go with you? Never mind. It's obvious. You had to take a risk to show what a gutsy lady you are, huh?"

"Maybe now that you know the real me, you won't be interested."

"I can't be more interested. Listen, what time are you finished working?" he asked.

She didn't know how she would make it through the day. "Three o'clock. Look, Ben. About Sara. I haven't heard from the police yet. I'd like to know if she was arrested, but I have to go to work now."

"I'll find out. Want me to meet you at your office?"

"No. Make it five at my place at Joe and Roberta's."

"Let's celebrate. How's dinner downtown at the Gaslamp?" he asked.

"I hope it will be a celebration."

Heading back to Joe's office, Cory tried to sort her spinning thoughts and steady herself for work.

Comforted at the sight of Joe's Lexus, she rolled the Buick next to it.

The door to his consulting room was ajar. Barging in, she flung herself across his couch.

"You ready for a session, Cory? Or wiped out?"

After she told him what had happened, he pulled out a bottle of brandy and poured a drink for her. "It's medicinal. Take it."

She sat up and slowly sipped.

"I won't reprimand you, Cory, because you're big on self-castigation. However, you do need a reminder not to go off half-cocked and put yourself in danger just because you once earned a black belt. You don't keep up with it and are out of practice."

"I had my Maglite. It weighs a ton and can crush bones."

"Since when do you feature weapons? You've always found them repulsive."

"Since all this mess started. Don't worry. I'm going back to karate. Do you think because I'm a woman, I'm weak?"

"Don't pull that feminist rhetoric on me, Cory. You know me better than that. Figure out why you play the hero role. This isn't the first time."

"You've just explained it, Joe. I'm trying to overcome the stereotypical female image."

"Not so quick, Cory. There's more to it."

"Maybe you've got something there; we haven't time now, but I will examine it."

"Don't put it off, Cory. It bothers me. And Ro, too."

Her eyes welled with tears and she tugged a tissue from the box next to the couch. Demonstrations of tenderness and caring always made her weep. "I don't want to sound maudlin, but you've no idea how much I value your friendship. Sheltering me. Feeding me."

"We enjoy having you with us."

She threw her arms around Joe. Tears rolled down her cheeks on to his shoulder. She wiped them with her fingertips.

"Go wash your face and change your clothes before your next patient arrives," he said.

After freshening up, she again passed Joe's open door.

"Have they arrested your patient's secretary yet?" he asked.

"I haven't heard. And look how late it is."

The bell buzzed and they both started for the reception room. "Here's my schedule, Cory." Joe handed her a printout. "Can you change your appointment times so our patients won't collide?"

"Of course. How thoughtless of me! I forgot you're traditional. Your way is better."

Jolene and Joe's patient, an attractive man, stood together, smiling.

"This is quite embarrassing," Jolene said, following Cory into the consulting room.

"I'm sorry, Jolene. Do you know that guy?"

"Know him?" She smiled and twisted the wedding ring on her finger. "He's a competitor."

"Well, it isn't as if you ran into each other when you were with your respective lovers."

She laughed. "We were lovers."

"Oh?"

"It was long ago, before I met Carlos."

Serendipity. Jolene's running into this man today led to an exploration of her past relationships. Cory's work with her had only just begun. She titled the session: "Needy meets Randy." A narcissistic, self-involved woman, Jolene considered little else in her relationships with men apart from being adored. She wasn't after sex, but adulation. Therapy would help her find other sources of satisfaction. Although she had complained that Carlos spent much time investigating stories for his work, he wasn't her problem. She was the one who had to control the misdirected engine inside her psyche.

When the session ended, they made another appointment for a time that wouldn't bring her into contact with other patients.

As Cory opened the front door to let Jolene out, a man darted in.

She froze. He pulled out his badge. He was the detective assigned to take her statement. She showed him into her office. The interview was brief and he was out the door before her next patient arrived.

Cory struggled through the few remaining sessions.

She yearned to soak in the Jacuzzi, freshen up, and dine with Ben, but she feared she would conk out early.

Joe planned to work late so Cory drove to the Kleins' manse without an escort, humming "I Don't Know Why" while trying to figure out why Kevin did what he did. And where the heck was Sara?

When she arrived, she called the hospital for an update on Morgan's condition, but the operator wouldn't reveal any information or verify that Morgan was a patient. Cory asked for a nurse she knew on staff. Through her, she learned the unidentified comatose woman brought in this afternoon was stable and would be allowed restricted visitors the next day.

Cory phoned Liz and gave her the news.

"Thank the Lord. I'll catch the next available flight," she said breathlessly.

Cory's mind whirled. Every part of her body felt tense or spent. She slid into the Jacuzzi, closed her eyes, and began to relax. She would miss the wonderful tub, but it would be worth it to get her life back in order. After a few minutes, her ideas took shape.

Kevin aka Seth had seemed genuinely concerned about Morgan. Was it because he wanted her to stay alive to save his own skin and to protect himself from worse charges? He had to deny that he abducted her, but she was drugged and held on his boat.

Ben said Seth Smith was a former FBI agent. Now, he was a private investigator. Who was Seth's client? And what was Sara's role?

⸝48⸜

"Dinner at the Gaslamp. A celebration," Ben had said. Her feelings for him hadn't cooled, but she felt drained from her rescue efforts. She tried to doll herself up, but her reflection in the mirror showed weariness.

Chilling images of Morgan's ordeal haunted her. The poor woman could have died from an overdose. Soon, Sara, still on the loose, would hear about Morgan's release. Kevin—rather, Seth—knew where Morgan was. Hospitals were open to the public and security was lax.

Cory paged the sergeant. "Come on, come on, please answer," she begged. While waiting, she put on the pearl stud earrings she had worn the day she moved to the cottage. They helped dress up her all-occasion black dress.

Finally, Kipinski returned her call. "Cory Cohen, here," she said, breathlessly. "Have you heard the news about Morgan?"

"Yes. You took a big chance, Doctor Cohen. We should have been there."

"I need you now. Her abductor knows where she is and I'm afraid she may be in danger at the hospital. Can you provide her with police protection right away, please?"

"I don't know how quickly, or even if we can spare..."

"Listen. She's a prosecutor and deserves... damn... everyone deserves protection. She's in danger. Either get a couple of uniforms or recommend private security. Her sister is arriving tomorrow from New York and if anything happens..."

"I'll get on it now."

"Please, let's talk right after you take care of this."

"Okay. Hang in there and call me in fifteen minutes."

After Cory poked through several issues of Smithsonian, she glanced at the wall clock. She had waited twelve minutes. Time to call the detective. "Sergeant Kipinski, Cory Cohen, again. How did you make out?"

"They're sending a couple of uniforms as we speak."

"Thank you. Now I'd like Seth Smith charged for hit and run, in addition to abduction. He has stalked me and vandalized my house." Cory knew none of it would be easy to prove, but clapping her thunder gave her a temporary power fix. "He's held a woman captive. Is he in jail, now?"

"He's been arrested."

"You haven't answered my question. Is he in jail?"

"He may have posted bond. I'll have to get back to you."

She had wanted to ask if Sara had been arrested, but remembered having been advised against speaking about that matter. "Listen, I'm sorry to be snippy, but I'm scared. For Morgan and for myself."

"I understand."

"Thanks, sergeant."

Cory called the hospital, spoke to the charge nurse, and asked her to provide safety measures for Morgan until the police arrived. The nurse was about to page hospital security when Cory warned her against it. "I know I sound paranoid, but please indulge me. Let's not take any chances with Morgan's life. I'd appreciate your cooperation."

"I understand, Doctor Cohen. Her chart is in front of me. She's here under observation, at least until tomorrow. We've run a toxicology screen on her. She's come out of sedation." The nurse paused. "Tell you what. I'm off at midnight, but I promise to assign someone trustworthy for the graveyard shift."

"Thank you."

Hoping it wasn't too late to reach someone on duty, Cory grabbed the phone and Detective Lee picked up. "Has Sara Jaspers been arrested?" she asked.

"We got the warrant, searched her house, and found drugs in her bedroom. Thanks for the tip."

"Glad to help. Have you located her?"

"There's an APB out for her and she's considered dangerous. Her vehicle and the Heller woman's were located at the airport in the long term parking area. We suspect Sara Jaspers may have fled the country."

"Damn! You may be able to find her travel arrangements from her home or office computer."

"We're aware of that Doctor Cohen."

"Sorry. I'm only trying to help."

Cory fidgeted while waiting for Ben. Although tired, she couldn't sit still. She kicked off her shoes and paced. Too much excitement for one day. And romance, too? Could her little old ticker take it?

She met Ben at the gate. He was all spiffed up in a dark blue suit, white shirt, and stripped necktie. His dark hair and eyes gleamed. She wanted to wrap herself around him, but she restrained herself.

"You're ravishing, Cory." He smiled.

"Thank you. You ain't bad, yourself."

"I've made a reservation at the Horton Grand. They have great food. Is that okay?"

"Sure."

"Afterwards, if you like, we can catch a jazz combo at Croce's."

"I'd love it. My percussion teacher usually plays there."

He shook his head. "There's more to learn about you, everyday. I didn't know you're a musician."

"I hope you'll like what you find out, and that my energy holds."

"Listen. I want to spend time with you, but you've had an ordeal today. We'll just have dinner, and I'll take you back."

"Let's see how it goes. Maybe I'll get a second wind."

Ben drove downtown to the Gaslamp Quarter, an area her son Noah called "ersatz San Francisco". The upscale neighborhood swarmed with pedestrians and featured outdoor cafes, art galleries, theaters, fine restaurants, and brightly-painted, refurbished Victorian buildings. The Horton Grand, a small, quaint hotel with lace curtains and antique furnishings, was the picture of period charm. The area's popularity made parking difficult. Ben drove once around the block before giving his car to the valet.

They sauntered through the tiny lobby to reach the intimate restaurant where the host seated them at a softly lighted, lace-covered table. Ben ordered half a bottle of zinfandel and filled their glasses.

Cory had no appetite. After a few forkfuls of arugula drizzled with raspberry vinaigrette, she shoved her salad bowl aside. When Ben passed the bread tray to her, she shook her head. She watched him dole a thin layer of butter onto the warm bread. The spread melted, as did her heart.

Although she couldn't remember her last meal, when the well-presented platters of food arrived, Cory had no appetite. To be courteous and appreciative, she sliced the juicy stuffed tomato in half, poked at it, and forced herself to bite into the moist halibut.

"Aren't you hungry, Cory?"

She sipped the wine. "I'm too excited to eat."

"From your heroic effort with Morgan. How did you know where she was?"

Cory explained how the credit report led her to the sailboat.

"I'm beginning to think you don't need me."

"Not true. You put me on to credit reports. I just connected the dots. And it was your idea to install the camera. Without that, we wouldn't have learned of Sara's involvement."

"We make a good team." He touched her hand across the table.

"I'll drink to that," she said, lifting her glass.

When the server brought the dessert tray, Cory gave a cursory glance, smiled, and shook her head. "Suddenly, I feel dizzy," she admitted to Ben.

"You're tired and have barely eaten. I shouldn't have ordered wine. I'll take you home."

Cory leaned on him, while they waited for the car. "My head is spinning. I'm so sorry to ruin the evening, Ben," she mumbled.

She awoke with a start. Apart from her shoes, she knew she was fully dressed under the bedcovers. Ben was seated on a chair at her bedside in the cottage.

"What happened?"

"You fell asleep in the car."

"How long ago?"

"About twenty minutes."

"I'm sorry. I must be your worst date."

He chuckled. "Not really. Someday I'll tell you about that one."

"I really wanted tonight to be special," Cory said.

"Listen. I'd love to crawl under the covers with you, but it's not fair to take advantage of your weak condition."

"Even if you're invited?"

≈49≈

At the sound of the ringing phone, Cory bolted up in bed and grabbed the receiver. "It's Liz," an agitated voice exploded. "I took the red-eye and taxied to the hospital. When I arrived, Morgan was gone!"

"Oh my God! Have you notified the police?"

"They were already there."

"Posted outside her door all night?"

"Almost. There was an emergency and they were called away for a while. A skeleton staff took turns monitoring Morgan. When one of them returned from the restroom, he found her bed empty. He reported it to hospital security. The police came immediately."

"Do you have a key to Morgan's place?"

"No, but I know where there is one," Liz told Cory.

"Good. Take a cab to her house and I'll meet you there."

"Do you think…"

"Listen to me, Liz. Morgan might not have felt safe in the hospital. She may have escaped and gone home."

"But she didn't have her purse. She'd have no money to pay for a cab. And no clothes. Oh, wait. The nurse said a uniform is missing. A pair of white slacks and a flowered top. Morgan's filthy clothes are here. And her shoes are gone."

"I bet she took a cab and paid the cabby when she got home. I'll see you shortly."

Cory called 911, left a message for Sergeant Kipinski, then phoned Ben.

"How do you feel, sweetheart?" he asked in a Humphrey Bogart voice.

"Okay, but I don't remember last night, Ben."

"It wasn't memorable. You fell asleep in my arms. I tucked you in and went home. We'll make it up, Cory."

Her embarrassment had to take a back seat. "Look, Ben. The nurse reported that Morgan is gone. I told Liz to meet me at her sister's house."

"What! Give me the address. I'll leave now."

She gave him directions, then called Roberta with the news, before racing off.

Morgan's street brimmed with black and white police cars and local media vans, forcing Cory to park around the corner. She threaded her way through a throng of people, tripped on the wires strewn across the driveway, and collided with a cameraman from a local TV studio. "You've ruined a great shot," he muttered.

She glared at him as she started to barge into Morgan's house, but a uniformed officer stopped her.

"No one's allowed in," he said.

"I'm Doctor Cohen. Sergeant Kipinski's expecting me," she whispered to prevent the cameraman from hearing.

"Identification, please."

She pulled out her licenses.

"Okay. Go ahead."

Inside the living room, the sisters huddled on the couch. An afghan wool blanket was wrapped around Morgan. She looked positively haggard. Kipinski sat on a chair opposite them. When Morgan and Liz spied Cory, they rose for a group hug. "Thank the Lord, you're here. This has been such an ordeal. To think I trusted Sara and wanted her friendship," Morgan exclaimed. "And she conned me," she whispered.

"We'll talk about it later. What happened when you left my office, Morgan?"

"The beginning of a torturous nightmare. I found Sara pacing around my car and was very surprised to see her. I asked what she was doing there. She told me she'd come from an appointment with her therapist and was in a hurry to get to work, but her car wouldn't start. She asked to ride with me. Last I remember, I opened the car door and felt a prick in my arm. The needle must have been a shot of something because the next thing I knew I was stretched out on a bunk in a boat cabin, where Sara was pouring some liquid down my throat. The drink tasted sweet and had the texture of a milkshake."

"Maybe a spiked nutrition beverage," Cory suggested.

"All I remember is drinking and sleeping, and Sara always there when I awoke, ready to pour more stuff down my throat."

"Was anyone else there, ma'am?" Sergeant Kipinski asked.

"I don't know. I kept slipping in and out of consciousness. I remember Sara taking me to the toilet a few times...and yes, once I heard a terrific argument. A man and Sara. He called her names and said he'd have her arrested."

"Did you see him?" the detective questioned.

"No, but I heard him."

"Did you recognize his voice or hear his name?"

"I'm not sure. I was so out of it. Oh, wait! I do remember something. She said he'd be blamed because it was his sailboat. There must have been a windstorm because the boat started to pitch. The rolling made me dizzy and I fell asleep, again."

"How do you feel, now?" Cory wanted to know.

"Weak, but absolutely better."

"Why did you run away from the hospital?" Sergeant Kipinski inquired.

"All kinds of people were coming and going into my room. Perhaps they were just checking on me, but I was frightened. As soon as I felt stronger and the floor was quiet, I slipped out of bed. I found a uniform in a linen closet and changed into it. I called a cab from the nurse's station and nonchalantly headed out the hospital doors."

"Poor baby! You'll need to build up your strength," Liz said, her arm around her sister's shoulders. "I'll stay here with you for as long as it takes."

"And if you'd like, I'll make house calls," Cory offered.

"You've put yourself out enough, Cory. I can drive her to your office," Liz suggested. "Where is your car, Morgan?"

"I... I don't know."

"It was collected at the long-term parking area at the airport," Kipinski explained. "We're checking it for evidence. You'll have it back tomorrow."

After making arrangements to see Morgan again, Cory said goodbye and left in search of Ben. His Mustang was parked on the street at the fringe of the drama. "Everything okay?" he asked. "This case has made a big splash all over the news now. Your name was mentioned."

"Damn! I'm not keen on publicity. Let's get breakfast and I'll fill you in."

Cory followed him to an outdoor cafe on the coast. Over coffee, scrambled eggs, and toast, she told him what had happened.

"Let me tell you about Seth Smith," Ben said. "He was a good agent, but had personal problems. He resigned soon after a woman beat him out of a promotion, though he was more qualified. He taunted her with his constant jabs and got in trouble for it. He's got a bad thing for women with power."

"Was his sister a judge?" Cory asked.

"Yes. Rebecca. His family liked Biblical names."

"Hmm. Then some of what he'd told me was the truth. Apart from his identity."

"Listen. I don't think he'd harm Morgan." Ben sprinkled salsa on the eggs. "Physical violence with women isn't his style, but annoyance is. Big time. He's like a spiteful brat."

"Do you think he stalked me in Morgan's car?"

"I doubt it. Listen, why would Seth have anything against you, Cory? You tried to help him. You never crossed him."

"Okay. I agree, but he may have used his know-how to cause prominent women trouble. To him, they represented Rebecca."

Ben shook his head from side to side. "He's neurotic, but not that far out."

"We need to know who hired him and if Seth is in jail now."

"Listen. When he tries to make a deal, he'll squeal on his client. Go home. Relax. Tonight, let's have some fun."

"I'd like to, Ben, but I can't relax until I have some answers."

"Then I'll get them for you. Where and when should we meet?"

"Seven at the cottage."

In the parking lot, in bright sunlight, they stood and stared at each other. The weight of her problems dissolving, Cory wrapped her arms around Ben, kissed him on the lips, and held him tightly. He responded with warmth and a desire that matched hers.

An elderly woman passerby shouted, "How shocking! That sort of thing belongs indoors." If she could read Cory's mind, she'd have fainted.

They kissed and hugged again as though they couldn't get enough of each other. Finally, they parted. Cory was certain the glow she felt could light up the dark.

Heading for the guest cottage, she grinned. "Wow-oh-wow-oh-wow!" she repeated.

With no time to relax, she showered, dressed in her tired gray pantsuit, and drove to Joe's office. On the way, she thought about the man she had known as Kevin. Ben knew him well and didn't think he'd harm Morgan, but he was on the boat. Why?

She rolled the Buick between Joe's Lexus and another car, probably his patient's.

Cory settled in the office, waiting for Alan. This time, she was determined to find out if he was Jolene's lover. Apart from satisfying her curiosity, she was convinced he hadn't identified his women for another reason.

"It's odd you don't mention the names of your lovers," Cory remarked, after Alan sat down.

"Hmm. I see where you're going. I don't distinguish one from another. That's probably why I've called them all, Babe. Except for the last woman. She resented it."

Cory smiled, pleased with his insight and the launch of a productive session—at the end of which, she could no longer hide her curiosity. "By the way, what did you call your last lover?"

"Jolene. During sex, she insisted I say her name over and over again."

For a few moments after he left, Cory basked in the satisfaction that her hunch had proven correct. Jolene and Alan had been lovers. Jolene's need for attention translated into her demand for Alan to say her name repeatedly.

Cory's mind drifted to Jolene's husband, Carlos Sanchez, the investigative reporter Cory had suspected of breaking the stories about the judge and the mayor. Her suspicion dissolved when she realized she had no evidence and the source of the stories had not been acknowledged. The prospect of him interviewing her about her role in Morgan's rescue made her uncomfortable—after all, he was her patient.

≈50≈

At seven on the dot, Ben arrived. Cory liked his punctuality. She liked everything about him; the neat way he looked in his pressed khaki pants and stripped shirt. She liked his soap-scent, his smile, his eyes. She nearly forgot why he was there. Cory handed him a frosty bottle of Pete's Wicked Ale. He took a swig and parked himself in a corner of the couch. Determined to gain information, she resisted her desire for him, seating herself on the opposite end. It would be best that they cool off and behave like a pair of bookends for a while.

"I promised news and I'm true to my word," he said.

"Go ahead, please."

"You won't like it."

"Tell me already," she said impatiently.

"Seth Smith made a deal with the D.A. In return for revealing the name of the man who hired him to plant the microphone, the charges will be reduced."

"That is so unfair." Cory's jaw clenched. "It's strange calling him Seth when I knew him as Kevin. Imagine! He used his roommate's identity as a cover so I wouldn't suspect he was a detective. But he was a really bad actor and couldn't pull it off. He didn't remember his lines." She stood and paced the room. "When he became confused between reality and his fabrication, he aroused my suspicion. Ultimately it led me to his sailboat where Morgan was held prisoner."

"Yes, but Seth claims he didn't kidnap her and he's not the sole owner of the Sally Forth. He has papers to prove that he, his client Dale Rothenberg, and Jim Solas are all partners in the vessel. They take turns sailing."

Goose bumps erupted on Cory's arms. "What? Which one hired Seth to spy on Morgan?"

"Jim Solas. When he was picked up for questioning, he admitted he wanted to hurt Morgan politically, but he denied any responsibility for Sara's role. He insists she acted on her own."

Cory stopped pacing and sat down. "What a bunch of bull! That snake knows it's illegal to hold someone captive and he knew where Morgan was. Why didn't he free her?"

"Think about it, Cory."

She curled her legs under her and began to peel off the bottle label. "Sure. She'd have reported it to the authorities."

"Of course, but he was confident that if she was released after he'd won the election, no one would believe her outrageous tale."

"He actually said that?"

"Yes. Solas was confident he'd get away with it because Morgan wouldn't realize she was held captive on his sailboat."

"Give me a moment to digest this." Cory closed her eyes, reviewed the scenario, and then looked up at Ben. "Okay, I'm ready."

"No doubt Morgan will testify that she was abducted by Sara in the garage outside your office. She'll state Sara drugged her and held her captive until you rescued her."

"True. If Morgan's release had come after the election and she figured out Jim's involvement, he would have denied it and insisted she made up the absurd scenario."

"Or had taken drugs of her own volition," Ben said.

"She couldn't prove otherwise." Cory scowled. "Unless the police found Morgan's fingerprints and DNA samples on his boat."

"Good thinking, Cory. But he could claim she was once a guest on his boat. Such an explanation would be reasonable and easier than trying to sanitize the vessel."

Cory uncurled her legs and jumped off the couch. She walked to the window and peered out at the full moon in a night sky dotted with stars. She glimpsed a large furry creature, head thrown back as if ready to howl. Blinking, she looked again. The animal was Otto guarding the cottage. Unlike people, dogs are uncomplicated and faithful, she thought, turning away.

"That rat, Jim Solas thought he had it all figured out. Who would believe Morgan when her own secretary would support his story," she said.

Ben patted the seat next to him, motioning her to sit. "But he didn't consider the possibility of Morgan's rescue. Man, was he shocked!"

Cory walked back to the couch and jabbed her hands on her hips. "What a schmuck! Drugs must have warped his mind."

"You know drugs aren't the only thing that warps minds. Ironic. The prosecutor will be prosecuted."

Clutching the bottle of ale, Cory sat down again.

"Now about the microphone," Ben continued. "No doubt Sara overheard Seth and Jim talking about it when she stayed with Jim at his house."

"Sara and Jim Solas were lovers?" Cory choked, ale spluttering on her chin. She grabbed a napkin from the coffee table and dried herself. "I shouldn't be surprised. Sara probably has many lovers. I bet she manipulated one of them to make the calls to Morgan and me. That's her style."

"More than likely," Ben agreed.

"Just before she was abducted, Morgan had an earlier-than-usual session with me. How did Sara find out about it?"

"Easy. She must have staked out Morgan's house and tailed her to your office."

"Of course! If Sara took Morgan captive in the Saab, she'd have left her own car near my office and returned by taxi to collect it."

"Or had one of her entourage ferry her back."

"Sara, not Seth, stalked me with Morgan's car. And vandalized my house, too!"

"What's her motive?"

"Curiosity at first, then when I refused to treat her, she became angry and vengeful."

"But you must have had a reason—and for her to go to such lengths, she's one very sick chick."

"Because of professional ethics, I'm supposed to have my patient's approval before I can treat anyone close to her."

"And you couldn't ask her because she was unavailable."

Cory nodded.

"Even before you showed me her handwriting samples, I suspected Morgan was your patient. I knew you were trying to protect her privacy."

"The word is out now, and she and I will deal with that. I'm glad to hear I couldn't fool the detective," she smiled. "It gives me greater confidence in you."

"That's encouraging." He winked.

"Getting back to Sara. She was jealous of Morgan. She wanted to experience the intimacy Morgan shared with a therapist—not any therapist—only Morgan's would do. I referred her to my friend, Betty Pepper. She's a psychologist with a fine reputation, but Sara insisted on me."

"That's not so weird. I would prefer you, too," Ben said.

"You don't know Betty."

"I don't have to. I know what I like." He cocked his head to one side.

"I'd like you to prove it after we finish this discussion," Cory said, flushing. "Remember the drowned naval officer who was reported as a suicide victim?"

"Yes. I read about it in the paper."

"Her name was Terry Salmonica. I'm almost positive that Sara was involved with her for a time. When Terry rejected her, Sara threatened to expose her as a lesbian to the military."

"How do you know this, Cory?"

"My friend knew the victim very well. She knew that Terry told Sara the threat didn't matter to her because she was leaving the Navy. I think Sara became enraged and murdered her. I'm lucky she didn't kill me, too." Cory swept up shreds of the bottle label with her hands.

"Lucky for me she didn't hurt you. Listen, Sara drove Morgan's car to make you think Morgan was after you."

"Isn't that something!"

"Am I right in assuming she wanted to destroy the relationship between you and Morgan because she was jealous? Did she have a crush on Morgan?"

"Damn good thinking for an amateur psychologist," Cory said.

Ben smiled. "You're damn good for an amateur detective."

Looking into his eyes, Cory was certain they'd soon learn how good they were with each other, but she must wait. "When someone with a borderline personality has a crush, it's a potentially explosive situation. And I'm convinced Sara had the condition."

"What do you mean?"

"The hallmark of a borderline personality is an undeveloped or absent ego. Feeling a void in herself, Sara fixates on competent, powerful women. She wanted to be Morgan—to connect with the missing piece. She couldn't inhabit Morgan, so she drove around in her car. That's as close as she could get to identify with Morgan—to feel as one with her."

Ben smiled. "I see. A personal car is an intimate object. We spend a lot of time confined in it. Often in solitude. We caress the steering wheel, adjust the mirrors, live in it."

"That's right. Like the inside of a purse—full of personal belongings—an extension of ourselves. We're often judged by the cars we drive. Sara may have taken pleasure in seating her tush on the very seat Morgan had used. Much like some men feel when they wear their girlfriend's clothes."

"That's an interesting take on it, Cory."

"Haven't you heard men say, 'I'd like to get in her skirt'? The operative words: get-in-her."

"She really does need therapy."

"Yes. Therapy may help such patients grow an ego when they attach themselves to the therapist, emulate her, and hopefully mature."

"Sounds complicated."

"Therapy with such people is difficult, frustrating, and time-consuming; and often fails. I don't know if Betty could have helped her." Cory shrugged. "Anyway, Sara didn't have a therapist."

Ben smiled. "You brought me on board to teach you, but you're giving me a course in psychopathology. Maybe you haven't gotten your money's worth."

"Oh, yes I have!" In more ways than he imagined. "I've only provided theories. Don't underestimate your value to me," Cory objected. "I hadn't a clue about background checks and surveillance work."

She rose from the couch and paced. "Look, Ben. Sara knew personal things about me. She'd admitted finding out about people who interested her. Now I understand why she worked as a secretary in the D.A.'s office. It wasn't for the money. She made a helluva lot more as a prostitute. At first, I figured her civil service job was a cover to make her appear legitimate. Now I realize she positioned herself to gain information about people under investigation by her office. To blackmail or expose them."

"Listen, Cory. Apart from her job in that office, she had other ways to gather dirt on people."

"I know. This may sound far-fetched, but from her network of bed partners, or from her work, she could have learned about Mayor Evans's past and snitched it to the media. And that conspiracy between the judge and lawyer—the gifts for favors—that's her kind of shtick," Cory said. "I think Sara was envious of the woman's power and blew the whistle on her, too." She paused. "Isn't it curious that Seth and Sara shared a dislike of powerful women?"

"That's their hang-up, not mine." He smiled, sending a sweet shiver down her spine. "I'm no shrink, Cory, but Seth is not as cracked as Sara. That nympho broke into your office to steal the microphone for her own evil purposes. She knew that device is hard to come by."

"What about Sara and Jim?"

"Sara drugged Morgan to keep her out of the race so Jim would win. He's bad, but not bad enough to tolerate Sara murdering a woman simply because she was his political opponent," Ben guessed. "Sara enjoyed Jim's important connections. She knew just how far she could go before destroying her relationship with him. Now, with him out of the race, Morgan's a shoo-in. Everything will all work out," he said. "Now, come sit by me."

"Something is bothering me, Ben" Cory seated herself on the couch. "Why was Seth on the boat when I rescued Morgan?"

"Oh, that's a good one! The dock master called him at home about a tall, attractive woman named Flora Dora who was looking for him. Seth became suspicious and decided to check out the boat. Where did you dig up that name?"

"Don't ask. A moment of frivolity. I think my Grandma mentioned an old movie by that name and it stuck with me." She smiled.

"You took a chance going on board. Why didn't you ask me to go with you?"

She grinned sheepishly.

"I get it. You didn't want to share the excitement, huh?"

"I thought you'd talk me out of it. We couldn't involve the police. I suspected Morgan was held on the boat, but I had no evidence. That Kevin… uh… Seth had lied about his identity wouldn't be sufficient for the police to act. The falsehood was a private matter, between patient and therapist. When I got to the boat and saw the hatch unlocked, I figured someone would be returning soon. I had to check out my suspicion. After I found Morgan on board, I assumed Kevin was the one who had left the hatch open. But Sara must have been the one."

"Right. When she came back and saw the commotion, she fled." Ben's cell phone rang. The instrument seemed dwarfed in his large hand. He listened for several minutes, interjecting a few "Uh- huhs", and smiled. "Thanks," he said, before disconnecting.

"Good news! They've matched Terry Salmonica's hair samples and fingerprints with those taken from Sara's car. They've also located a computer record of Sara Jasper's current travel plans. When she steps off the plane, she'll be arrested."

""That's great!" Cory cried out, breathlessly. "There's only one problem left—Dale Rothenberg."

"Seth is gathering information as to his likely whereabouts. I'm going to help, too. I hate to see bad guys get away."

"A happy accident that I found the microphone, hired you, and your camera caught Sara on video tape."

"We make a good team, Cory. How would you like to help me with a case now and then?"

"Sounds intriguing, and I'm big on intrigue." Her eyes gleamed as they reached for each other.

About the Author

Sandra L. Ceren, Ph.D. a native New Yorker resides on the California coast. A clinical psychologist for over forty years she is a Diplomate from the American Board of Family Psychology, and Fellow of the Academy of Family Psychology.

She has appeared on *Oprah*, *Good Morning America* and BBC and has has reported on mental health research and answered queries in a weekly health column "Ask Dr. Ceren". This popular column was published in newspapers over many years.

A premarital counseling specialist, her books *Essentials Of Premarital Counseling*, addressed to mental health professionals, and *Look Before You Leap-A Premarital Guide For Couples* were published by Loving Healing Press.

Ceren has a passion for writing fiction. *Prescription For Terror*, the first in her series of psychological thrillers featuring a spunky psychologist/sleuth was published in 1999.

Stolen Secrets, book #2 in the Dr. Cory Cohen Mysteries will be followed by *Imposter For Hire* in 2011.

Over a dozen of her short mystery stories have been published in anthologies and magazines including: *Mystery Magazine*, *Detective Mystery Stories*, and *Criminal Kabbalah*.